i n n o v a t i o n s

Edited by Robert L. McLaughlin

AN ANTHOLOGY OF MODERN & CONTEMPORARY FICTION

DALKEY ARCHIVE PRESS

Library of Congress Cataloging-in-Publication Data:

Innovations : an anthology of modern and contemporary fiction / edited by Robert L. McLaughlin. 1st ed.
    p.   cm.
Contents: A character / Felipe Alfau — Ladies almanack: July / Djuna Barnes — Menelaiad / John Barth — The balloon / Donald Barthelme — You must remember this / Robert Coover — Szryk v. Village of Tatamount et al., U.S. District Court, Southern District of Virginia no. 105-87 / William Gaddis — Is it sexual harassment yet? / Cris Mazza — Lady the Brach / Gilbert Sorrentino — A little novel / Gertrude Stein — Little expressionless animals / David Foster Wallace — Bonanza / Curtis White — Surfiction / John Edgar Wideman.
    ISBN 1-56478-185-2 (alk. paper)
    1. American fiction—20th century. 2. United States—Social life and customs—20th century—Fiction I. McLaughlin, Robert L.
PS659.I56   1998
813'.508—dc21   97-51436
                                                      CIP

This publication is partially supported by a grant from the Illinois Arts Council, a state agency.

Dalkey Archive Press
Illinois State University
Campus Box 4241
Normal, IL 61790-4241

Printed on permanent/durable acid-free paper and bound in the United States of America.

contents

Acknowledgments

The editor thanks the many people who contributed at various times and in various ways to the imagining, the production, and the publication of this book.

John O'Brien was the inspiration for this project as well as guide and companion through the process of accomplishing it. This book would not exist without him.

Many people at various stages of this project generously offered suggestions, advice, and guidance. The following were kind enough to answer a call for suggestions for what should be included in this anthology: Mark Axelrod, Frederick Busch, George Elliott Clarke, Nicole Cooley, Simone Davis, Raymond Federman, Miriam Fuchs, Elizabeth Grubgeld, A. Waller Hastings, Barbara Henning, Allen Hibbard, Robert Lima, David Lloyd, Jane Marcus, Mary Mathis, Thomas McGonigle, Byron Nelson, Ben Rollins, Art Saltzman, Juliana Spahr, Jan Susina, James G. Turner, Carol Weir, and Stephen Yenser. I wish I had been able to include *all* the suggestions. I also received valuable advice and support from Ron Fortune, Charles Harris, and Steven Moore.

Assisting me in practical matters of putting the book together were Angela Weaser, Todd Michael Bushman, Melissa Demkowicz, Kent D. Wolf, Rebecca Kaiser, Christopher Paddock, and Kristin Schar, all of Dalkey Archive Press. I also received invaluable help from two "mentees," one-time students, now friends, Madeline Ostrander and Krista Hutley. I thank Ira Cohen and the Honors Program of Illinois State University for funding their mentorships.

Finally and most important, the unreasonably generous support and infinite patience of my wife, Sally E. Parry, make this book and everything I do possible.

Preface

Over three years ago, I asked Robert McLaughlin to put together an anthology of fiction that would demonstrate that
fiction, from its origins, is defined by innovation, parody, out-
landish comedy, self-indulgence, and imaginative ingenuity
that has little to do with what the *New York Times*, as well as
almost all other mainstream media, champion as the best of
what is being written and published today, namely conven-
tional fiction that starts at point A and painstakingly guides
the reader through a few hundred pages to point Z, with
characters and plots that one has seen hundreds of times before and in a style that almost anyone familiar with the English language can easily grasp; reviewers applaud this
fiction because, they argue, it is so much like life and because
it teaches us something. One wishes that these people would
once again begin attending Sunday school classes for instruc-
tion and get out of the business of writing about literature.

The "other" kind of fiction, that which is truly representative of fiction from its inception, is characterized by invention, newness, idiosyncracy, and a kind of playfulness, even
when the subject is serious. You usually do not know what
will come next, and part of the pleasure of such fiction is that
the reader is a player in the game rather than a passive observer. And this is precisely the kind of fiction—without A-Z
plots and typed characters—that the *Times* and its reviewers
get bewildered by and feel that they must warn their readers
about, as though they had uncovered an insidious disease
which, once unleashed upon the unknowing public, could
cause havoc in the streets of America. National Public Radio
also seems as intent upon serving the role of Surgeon General for Fiction, carefully warning readers that there isn't a
plot or that the language is confusing or that the reader must

be well-read. Amazingly, one knows that these same reviewers, if given the chance, would be assailing James Joyce, Marcel Proust, and William Faulkner for the same reasons, which is precisely what James Atlas of the *New York Times* did not too long ago, as Robert McLaughlin points out in his introduction to this anthology.

Despite the title of this book, *Innovations,* the selections here are not so much innovative as they are, in fact, *traditional,* if one seriously looks at the history of fiction and its major practitioners. As McLaughlin explains, the *traditional* story *is* innovative, playing off other works of fiction, playing off what the readers have already read, and playing with and creating variations upon the conventions of story and character. Rather than numbingly reminding us of everything we have already read and know, this fiction is an invitation to play in the field of the imagination. That the mainstream reviewer has difficulty with this fiction speaks to, one must assume, how profoundly ill-read most reviewers are and how dull they are. The assumption that appears to be at work among these critics is that literature should be easily accessible to anyone and everyone, and that literature directed to a higher level of reading than that possessed by the average high-school student is a threat to the Republic, an insult to the common man, and an insidious attack on one's right to be stupid. James Atlas might as well have entitled his *Times* article, "I'm Dumb and Proud of It!" Rather than saying that he does not like the game or is unable to play it, Atlas & Co. concludes the game is, in the words of many students encountering Henry James for the first time (or Fellini or Pollock or Bach), "bor-r-r-ing."

What follows is a collection that presents examples of this "other kind of fiction." The anthology makes no attempt at being inclusive. Realizing, at one point, that it was approaching nearly six hundred pages—ranging from the Romans to the present—and was becoming unwieldy, we decided to choose ten pieces that we thought were both representative and self-contained. And after hitting on that number, we then violated our own rule and added two others.

We also encountered a similar problem in making up a list of suggested reading, and so we decided to limit ourselves to 101 works, but this too could have been much, much longer.

Finally, we will not warn the reader that there are no plots, that the characters are not real people, that there are few if any lessons to be learned (except perhaps about fiction), and that these aren't for everyone.

JOHN O'BRIEN

Innovations
Robert L. McLaughlin

This anthology has been put together with two purposes in mind. The first is to present twelve pieces of innovative, avant-garde, experimental, postmodern (choose any of these words or one of your own), but—most important—readable fiction.

This kind of writing can be and has been called many things, and there seems to be no happy consensus on a term. *Experimental* sounds like something written in a laboratory. *Postmodern* ties this kind of writing to a specific historical time period (more on this later). *Avant-garde* is more satisfactory but suggests a place for this kind of writing at the forward margin rather than at the center of literature (more on this later too). So for our purposes, let's use the adjective *innovative* to describe the stories included here, stories that seek to expand our notions of what fiction can be, of how narratives can be organized (or whether there can be fiction without narrative), of how characters can be presented (or whether they're needed at all), of what language can do, of how fiction can mean. My goal is that the twelve pieces here from modern and contemporary American fiction represent a much longer tradition of literary innovation.

This leads to the second purpose for which this anthology has been published, and it starts with a question: How *postmodern* is postmodern fiction? When I teach my favorite course here at Illinois State University, "American Literature: 1945 to the Present," I teach it as a course in postmodernism. We learn about the various characteristics that seem to mark a postmodern text, we read poststructural theory so as to have an intellectual context for the issues about which postmodern literature seems to be concerned, and we tie the production of postmodern literature to historical and social developments arising after the end of the Second World War. This approach to postmodernism is valid, I think, but it also faces a challenging question: If postmodernism is defined as a literary movement connected to the historical and social events of a particular time period, then how do we account for earlier literary texts—some of them written hundreds of years before this time period—that seem to do the same things postmodern texts do and to have the same concerns that postmodern texts have? The answer, I think, is that the defining of postmodernism as a literary period has given us a frame through which to look back at the history of fiction and to come to an understanding of it different from that afforded by the frame of realism.

It's not hard to see how the frame of realism has become the dominant critical view point from which to understand and evaluate fiction. In England, while T. S. Eliot conceived of an ideal canon of literary works, each work "really new" because of its timelessness and its universal meaning, F. R. Leavis was setting his sense of this canon in concrete or, as he styled it, the Great Tradition: Eliot (George, not T. S.) to James to Conrad. In defining this Great Tradition, Leavis stressed the representational—the true-to-lifeness of the work—at the expense of the work's formal elements. He explains in reference to Jane Austen's *Emma*,

when we examine the formal perfection of *Emma*, we find that it can be appreciated only in terms of the moral preoccupations that characterize the novel's peculiar interest in life. Those who suppose it to be an "aesthetic matter," a beauty of "composition" that is combined, miraculously, with "truth to life," can give no adequate reason for the view that *Emma* is a great novel, and no intelligent account of its perfection of form. It is in the same way true of the other great English novelists that their interest in their art gives them the opposite of an affinity with Pater and George Moore; it is, brought to an intense focus, an unusually developed interest in life. For, far from having anything of Flaubert's disgust or disdain or boredom, they are all distinguished by vital capacity for experience, a kind of reverent openness before life, and a marked moral intensity. (8-9)

If the canon was to be a sort of exclusive club, it would seem that only fiction that sought to be representational—that is, that sought to present the world in a way that most readers would recognize as being true to life, that sought, in short, to hold to a mirror up to the world—could apply for membership.

In America Mark Schorer applied the Eliot aesthetic to the novel, looking for organic unity and universal meaning. More significantly, Ian Watt in his influential *The Rise of the Novel* tied the development of the novel to social and intellectual conditions in eighteenth-century England and then declared realism to be one of the defining characteristics of the novel. He writes,

the novel is a full and authentic report of human experience, and is therefore under an obligation to satisfy its reader with such details of the story as the individuality of the actors concerned, the particulars of the times and the places of their actions, details which are presented through a more largely referential use of language than is common in other literary forms. (32)

Watt thus, quite self-consciously, excludes all the prose narratives written before the rise of the British middle class from the category of the novel and in his final chapter manages to demonstrate how such seeming counterexamples as *Tristram Shandy* and *Ulysses* are actually realistic and so can be counted as novels.

I've been hinting here that I find the Eliot aesthetic and its American offspring, the New Criticism, inappropriate for dealing with prose fiction; similarly, I find the insistence on representationalism as the defining mode of prose fiction very limiting. But why are these issues important now? The years of English department theory wars have beaten the New Criticism pretty much to death, and poststructural theory has made claims to the representational seem naive. On top of this, after years of canon busting by feminists, multiculturalists, and postcolonialists, it's hard to say there even *is* a canon, much less a Great Tradition. So what's the big deal?

The big deal for me is less what's going on in English departments and more what's happening in the culture at large. The New Criticism and the theories of realism of people like Leavis and Watt, through, I suppose, their forming of the theoretical assumptions with which literature was taught for so long, have had far-reaching influences in the popular aesthetic. This popular aesthetic of realism or the representational is evident throughout our culture. I offer anecdotal examples. In my undergraduate English classes my students—frequently unconsciously—hold realism as a touchstone by which to judge the fiction they read. They approve of stories and characters they can "relate to" or "identify with" and fiction that seems to present the world more or less as they know it. They frequently resist fiction that strikes them as unbelievable. Many of them agree with my hypothetically offered assertion that a novel written by someone who has actually experienced the events written about (say, a doctor writing about a hospital) would necessarily be a "better" novel than one written on the same subject by an author whose knowledge came only from research. I say that they frequently hold the realism touchstone unconsciously, because when I suggest that realism in fiction isn't real at all but a set of literary conventions designed to create the illusion of reality—like the technique of perspective in a John Constable landscape—most of them readily agree. And this is what really concerns me: many of them—even those who have mastered poststructural theory—aren't even aware of the aesthetics that influence their judgment. Another example: every week when I read *TV Guide* (for scholarly purposes only) I see ad after ad for made-for-television movies claiming to be "based on a true story." The assumption here is clear: a movie that claims to represent actual events that happened to real people who share the world with us viewers will be better, truer, more meaningful than one that's simply the product of some writer's imagination. And apparently this assumption sells; they wouldn't waste advertising space with the claim if it didn't.

A third place this aesthetic of the representational seems to be at work is among the book-reviewing media. Pick up and read most of the major book-reviewing forums and you'll see the same thing: prose fiction is praised for its presentation of psychologically deep characters acting in a recognizable environment in a style that does not draw attention to itself as style—in short, for holding a mirror up to the world—the very same qualities Watt used in defining the novel; prose fiction that deviates from these qualities is dismissed, if not attacked, for having unsympathetic or unmotivated characters, for being laid out in confusing plot structures, or (honest!) for being too well written. The code words to look for when reviewers are dealing with nonrepresentational fiction are "Not for everyone." This aesthetic and its limitations are wonderfully illustrated in an essay called " 'Literature' Bores Me," written by James Atlas. Atlas argues that while there are many books he can read and enjoy over and over, books by Balzac, Flaubert, and Forster—authors squarely in the tradition of realism—once he gets into the modern and postmodern periods, he sometimes is able to read the books, but he certainly can't enjoy them. He writes,

Try as I might, I can't get past the first few pages of *Absalom, Absalom!* Writer friends have maintained that it's one of the great literary experiences. One confessed to envy me for not having read it yet; never again would he know the joy of first encounter. So how come I get bogged down right from page 1 by those mellifluous sentences unfurling for hundreds of words at a time? "There would be the dim coffin-smelling gloom sweet and oversweet with the twice-bloomed wisteria against the outer wall by the savage quiet September sun impacted distilled and hyperdistilled. . . ." Yeah, yeah. (41)

Yeah, yeah? Is the absurd difficulty—the unenjoyability—of the language supposed to be self-evident? It's not that Atlas doesn't understand why fiction might be written this way. He calls modernism,

that moment when literature retreated from the accessible style that had made it such a popular form and turned inward, to the exploration of consciousness. In the hands of James, Joyce, Proust and Virginia Woolf, literature became a means of registering states of mind rather than telling a story. In Woolf's *The Waves*, the style of interior reflection is an effort to mime the very process of thought— it's six characters in search of another character who never appears on the scene. If it was hard to read, that was the point. So is the human mind. (41)

Rejecting the argument that the modernist movement was an aesthetic reaction to historical and social events, Atlas claims that modern and postmodern literature is a sort of sour-grapes reaction by authors to the dwindling audience for "serious" literature, an audience distracted by an increasing number of popular outlets for entertainment. He writes, "Now we're stuck with the notion that literature is beyond the reach of the ordinary reader—in other words, the property of an elite. By making their work inaccessible, the writers in the vanguard of modernism resorted to a defeatist ploy: You can't fire me. I quit" (41).

Setting aside the issue of how much attention we should pay to the ideas of a man who's proud he hasn't read *Absalom, Absalom!*, we can see two assumptions behind Atlas's argument, assumptions common to much of the reviewing media. The first is that fiction should be enjoyable— and who can argue with that?—but that when fiction is presented in unfamiliar ways, when it asks us to work too hard to understand it, when it asks us to think too much, it's no longer enjoyable. And if I were to respond to Atlas's question about *Ulysses*, "how many of you have actually read the whole thing—or read it with pleasure?" (41), "I have!" or his later question, "*Gravity's Rainbow, The Sot-Weed Factor* and David Foster Wallace's recent *Infinite Jest* are cult classics that have their fans, but do they have readers?" (41), "I've read them!" I'd be dismissed as one of the elite (me?) for whom these books are supposedly written, not an ordinary reader.

That book reviewers would take such a position disturbs me. To say that unfamiliar fiction, fiction that seeks to challenge its readers to think or to see the world in new ways, alienates the so-called ordinary reader is to privilege on behalf of the ordinary reader formula fiction or fiction that shows us the world as we already know it. Granted, there will always be plenty of readers of formula fiction—in the forms of name-brand authors' best-sellers, romances, mysteries, Westerns, etc.—and I refuse to put down anyone who's reading *anything* in a culture full of so many other ways to fill our time. But for the reader of serious fiction—not necessarily serious in tone but fiction that seeks the status of the literary—is the familiar, the formulaic, the predictable really to be preferred? Viktor Shklovsky argues that the whole point of serious literature is to defamiliarize the world through language; the purpose of literature is to shake us out of the overly habitual perceptions that keep us from seeing the world around us. Ron Strickland, one of my colleagues at Illinois State, likes to tell his students that confusion is a positive thing: if you read something and you're not confused by it, you're not reading anything you don't already know or can't easily assimilate to what you already know; if you read something that confuses you, you're probably encountering something you don't know. In working your way through the confusion, in making sense of it, you have the opportunity to learn something new or to look at the world in a new way. One might think of the purpose of art as being to sow confusion. I like this idea of art, and I resist the idea that some undefined elite readers are the only ones up to the challenge of serious literature. I think the stories in this book support my belief: they are readable, enjoyable, and accessible to the reader of serious fiction. Are they for everyone? Probably not, but what fiction is? I don't like Westerns.

The second assumption behind the reviewing media's privileging of the representational—as we can see in Atlas's argument about the origins of modernism—is that the move away from realism is a fairly recent aberration from an otherwise clearly demarcated tradition of accessible, representational fiction. This assumption seems to me to be patently false. As theorists beyond Leavis and Watt have argued—

theorists like M. M. Bakhtin in his eccentric but enlightening history of the novel as a genre and Margaret Anne Doody in her exhaustive and encyclopedic *The True Story of the Novel*—the novel as a genre exists long before the rise of the British middle class, and its defining trait has only occasionally been realism. I would argue that if there is a Great Tradition of fiction, it is a tradition of the nonrepresentational, of self-conscious attention to form, of the comic and parodic—in short, of innovation.

To support this claim, I'll begin with what, to me, seems a commonsense observation that Watt, in his argument that the novel presents its realistic elements "through a more largely referential use of language than is common in other literary forms" (32), has missed: fiction is always about its form. What, after all, makes fiction different from other literary genres? Generally, you know that a poem is a poem without even reading it, just from seeing the way its form is laid out on the page. The same is generally true of drama. But you can't identify prose fiction by its form because its form is usually borrowed from some *other* form. This seems clear simply from looking at the books Watt focuses on, books that he claims mark the beginning of the novel. Both *Robinson Crusoe* (1719) and *Moll Flanders* (1722), by Daniel Defoe, are novels that take the form of memoirs. Most famously, the former is narrated by its title character, telling us the story of his life, from going to sea, to being shipwrecked on a deserted island, through his years of survival there, to his rescue and eventual safe return to England. The title character of the latter writes in her old age about growing up in an orphanage, being seduced by the older son of the family for whom she worked, trying to become financially secure by marrying a series of husbands (including her own brother—oops!), becoming too old to attract a husband and thus turning to thievery, being arrested and sentenced to hang, repenting and having a religious conversion, and then being transported to America. Defoe's novel not only takes the form of an autobiography but slyly comments on the issue of treating a life in the form of a narrative. The narrating Moll, writing from her postconversion position, shows us her younger, preconversion self so that we readers might learn from her mistakes. But her commentary on her past reveals that the older Moll still holds the mercenary amorality of her younger self and suggests that her religious conversion was a timely sham designed to save her life. Here's a wonderful example of Moll's rhetoric failing to maintain the pious persona she wants to create—note how the final clause undercuts the moral lesson of the main clause: "I kept true to this Notion, that a Woman should never be kept for a Mistress, that had Money to keep her self" (40).

This idea of fiction being about its own form is even clearer in the novels of Samuel Richardson, the author to whom Watt gives main credit as the founder of the novel. But far from being "more largely referential," Richardson's novels are written in the form of letters. *Pamela* (1740) is made up of the letters written by the title character to her parents about her experiences as a maid in the manor of the wealthy Mr. B. We are given, amid many tears and much hand-wringing, a blow-by-blow description of Mr. B.'s attempts to seduce the virtuous Pamela, her narrow escapes, and her eventual marriage to the reformed rake. For *Clarissa* (1747-48), at over a million words surely the longest novel ever written, Richardson upped the ante by presenting letters from multiple correspondents to multiple addressees. We are thus given a variety of points of view on the action: Clarissa Harlowe runs away from home to be with the man she loves but of whom her parents don't approve, Mr. Lovelace; her parents are apparently correct, because Lovelace keeps her prisoner in a bordello and, after failing to seduce her, rapes her, after which, she spends several hundred pages dying, even having brought to her room her coffin, on which she writes her last several letters. As much as these novels are about their characters, they are also about letters and letter writing: what letters can and can't be used for, what kinds of information and feelings can be expressed in letters, the necessary gap in time between the writing of the letter and its being received and read. Again, we see the novel using already-exisiting forms to create a fictive world.

Prose fiction's adaptation or parodying of other written forms is, as Bakhtin argues, one of its defining characteristics. Even the third-person narration, perhaps the most obviously "fictional" of the forms of fiction, is an adaptation of the history, in which a narrator, at some time after the events described are over, attempts to reconstruct them in the form of a story. Think of James Fenimore Cooper's narrators in the *Leatherstocking* novels (1823-41): they very clearly tie themselves to the reader's time period (the time of the original publication) as they look into a long-ago past. Think of the trouble Nathaniel Hawthorne takes to set up *The Scarlet Letter* (1850) as a historical document his narrator has discovered in the contemporary customs house of Salem, Massachusetts. In these cases the text's ability to recover the past completely and accurately becomes one of the text's concerns; in other words, once again the fiction becomes about the form it has adapted. Other examples are even more obvious. Herman Melville's *Typee* (1846) adapts and Jonathan Swift's *Gulliver's Travels* (1726) parodies travel writing. Vladimir Nabokov's *Pale Fire* (1962) is written in the form of a poem and a scholarly commentary on the poem. What written forms *can't* be adapted into fiction? Gerte Jonke's *Regional Geometric Novel* (1969) has a chapter of complex bureaucratic instructions. Donald Barthelme interrupts his novel *Snow White* (1967) to present the reader a survey. In this anthology you will find Djuna Barnes's "Ladies Almanack: July," a fiction in the form of an almanac, and William Gaddis's "Skzyrk v. Village of Tatamount et al., U.S. District Court, Southern District of Virginia No. 105-87," a fiction in the form of a court ruling.

If we accept this notion that prose fiction has no form of its own but instead borrows other written forms, then we can pursue two connected ideas that further challenge the representational tradition of fiction.

First, instead of being "more largely referential," prose fiction is self-referential; that is, prose fiction tends, sometimes more, sometimes less obviously, to pay attention to its own form, to make—as we have seen in the examples above—its own form one of the things it is about. In other words, rather than simply holding a mirror up to the real world (the representational argument), prose fiction is fascinated with the mirror, the means by which the representation is attempted. To support this, we can turn again to one of the focuses of Watt's study, Henry Fielding's *Tom Jones* (1749). This picaresque novel traces the multiple journeys its title character makes: from the country to London; from instinctive goodness to mature morality; from poverty to wealth. But the narrator never expects us to forget that we're reading a fiction. Each book begins with a chapter in which the narrator discusses the problems of writing such a novel—how to structure the plot, how to present the characters, how to keep the reader's interest. Moreover, the narrator presents his story in the epic form, and thus many of the episodes are self-consciously parodic. Indeed, for Watt, this is one of the weaknesses of the novel. It fails to adhere to "the dictates of formal realism" because events "are narrated in such a way as to deflect our attention from the events themselves to the way that Fielding is handling them and to the epic parallel involved" (253). I think this self-consciousness is not a weakness but rather a common if not defining trait of prose fiction. Look at Miguel de Cervantes's *Don Quixote* (1605, 1615): this is about a man who reads so many romances that he comes to think that he's living in one. Confusing the boundary between reality and fiction, he becomes a fictional character and expects the conventions of fiction to hold in real life. To complicate things further, in the second part, published ten years after the first, Don Quixote keeps meeting people who know about him because they've read the first part. In essence the novel is about the conflation of reality and fiction and the impossibility of drawing a firm line between them. Look at Laurence Sterne's *Tristram Shandy* (1760-1767): this is a fictional autobiography in which the narrator insists on explaining every detail of his life from conception on. The result is a series of digressions as readers are filled in on all necessary (and unnecessary) background information; these digressions overwhelm the slowly moving life story and frustrate the narrator, who fears he may die before his life story gets past his childhood. In this anthology Felipe Alfau's "A Character," John Barth's "Menelaiad," and Donald Barthelme's "A Balloon" are good examples of extremely self-referential fiction.

The second idea that follows from the novel borrowing its form from other forms is that the novel, far from being, as Watt would have it, "a full and authentic report of human experience" (32), is intertextual, or built on, adapted from, or made up of previously existing texts. This idea can be hard to accept, because we are so steeped in the romantic tradition that insists that art arises from the individual's unique experience of the world. From this tradition comes the fascination with authors' biographies, as readers search for clues in the life that will account for and explain the fiction. But this seemingly commonsense connection between an author's life and his or her fiction, which stresses the uniqueness of the human experience and the originality of art, was essentially unheard of in the centuries of literature before the middle of the eighteenth century. In the oral tradition the bards were expected not to create original stories but to perform stories that they had learned. For example, in *The Arabian Nights* Shahrazad earns the right to tell the stories that keep her alive not by having experienced the things she talks about but by having heard other storytellers speak of them: she begins her tales each night by saying "I heard, O happy King. . . ." This repetition of and transformation of previously heard stories—the practice of texts speaking through other texts— occurs throughout the history of literature. Think of Chaucer's retelling of well-known stories in *The Canterbury Tales*, some of them from the apparent model for his work, Boccaccio's *The Decameron*. Think of Shakespeare's reworkings of other plays and his mining of Holinshed's *Chronicles of England, Scotland and Ireland* for his plays. Think of Milton's reimagining of the Book of Genesis for *Paradise Lost*. This intertextuality is obvious even among the novels Watt focuses on. The success of Richardson's *Pamela* inspired Henry

Fielding to write a parody, *Shamela* (1741), and then to re-write Richardson's novel with the genders reversed: in *Joseph Andrews* (1742) Pamela's brother Joseph, virtuous like her, tries to escape the seductions of Mr. B.'s sister, Lady Booby. Good illustrations in this anthology of this notion of texts writing through other texts are John Barth's "Menelaiad," a revision of Greek myth, Robert Coover's "You Must Remember This," a rewriting of the classic film *Casablanca*, Curtis White's "Bonanza" written through the popular television Western, and John Edgar Wideman's "Surfiction," a commentary on a Charles Chesnutt novel.

I have two final points connected to prose fiction's self-conscious attention to its own form. The first has to do with its tendency to parody other forms of writing. Bakhtin argues that this tendency comes from prose fiction's origins in the marketplace, carnival, the feast of fools. As a mode of expression that comes from the masses of so-called common people, prose fiction will frequently parody the more highly respected or official discourses of society as a way of critiquing and at least metaphorically overturning the social order. This kind of parody and the marketplace origins of prose fiction help account for the tradition of, to put it delicately, the treatment of nonliterary subjects in nonliterary language or, to put it less delicately, the treatment of "vulgar" subjects—sex, bodily functions, disease—in earthy language or the language of the streets. And this is a *long* tradition. Among ancient texts, *The Arabian Nights*, Petronius' *Satyricon*, and Apuleius' *The Golden Ass* all treat serious subjects irreverently, this irreverence manifested through their sexual and scatalogical subject matters and language. Then think of Boccaccio's *The Decameron* (1353), Rabelais's *Gargantua and Pantagruel* (1534), and almost anything by Swift; among Watt's objects of study, *Moll Flanders*, *Pamela*, *Clarissa*, *Joseph Andrews*, and *Tom Jones* all owe their success at least partly to their more or less foregrounded appeals to prurient interests. Even in the heyday of literary realism and naturalism such books as Stephen Crane's *Maggie: A Girl of the Streets* (1893), Theodore Dreiser's *Sister Carrie*

(1900), and D. H. Lawrence's *Women in Love* (1920) were attacked for their sensational subject matter. Several of the stories in this anthology participate in this tradition.

The very last point that comes from prose fiction's concern with its own form is its attention to language. Watt, you'll remember, claimed that the novel uses "a more largely referential" language "than is common in other literary forms" (32), language that communicates information without drawing attention to the *way* that it's communicating, to itself as a medium of communication. The opposite, I think, it true: prose fiction is constantly calling attention to its own language's attempts—sometimes failed attempts—to capture and represent something outside of itself. We have already seen how, among Watt's focuses, both *Moll Flanders* and *Tom Jones* are at least in part about their own rhetoric. Think, also, of Henry James's narrators and characters using language like a net to try ever more precisely to express something, a something that forever eludes them and so must remain unspoken. Any of the pieces in this book will illustrate this point, but I especially direct you to Djuna Barnes's "Ladies Almanack: July," Cris Mazza's "Is It Sexual Harrassment Yet?," Gertrude Stein's "A Little Novel," Gilbert Sorrentino's "Lady the Brach," and David Foster Wallace's "Little Expressionless Animals."

The case I've been trying to make here is that innovative fiction, far from being out of the mainstream of the Great Tradition of prose fiction is in fact the tradition that best explains what writers of prose fiction have been doing and how they've been doing it. But this argument might suggest to some that contemporary authors, the postmodern crowd, aren't doing anything new after all: if Rabelais and Sterne and a host of other writers have been there and done that, what's innovative about innovative fiction? But this isn't what I've meant by this historical survey of the tradition. Rather, I've wanted to show that the history of the prose fiction of Europe and America—though I don't think this tradition is limited to Europe and America—demonstrates a continuing concern with certain questions, questions about the form of fiction, the relation of fiction's form to other literary and nonliterary forms, the relation of fiction to previously existing texts, fiction's subject matter, the ability of language to represent and mean. What's innovative in the tradition of innovation is that authors have tried and continue to try to find new answers to and new ways to answer these questions. The pieces in this anthology represent more recent attempts to do this. They are interesting for what they have in common with each other and with the tradition; they are also interesting for what they do differently in attempting to expand our ideas of what fiction can do and can be.

Read on. You'll see what I mean.

WORKS CITED

Atlas, James. " 'Literature' Bores Me." *New York Times Magazine*, 16 March 1997: 40-41.

Bakhtin, M. M. *The Dialogic Imagination: Four Essays*. Ed. Michael Holquist. Trans. Caryl Emerson and Michael Holquist. Austin: U of Texas P, 1981.

Defoe, Daniel. *Moll Flanders*. 1722. Mineola: Dover, 1996.

Doody, Margaret Anne. *The True Story of the Novel*. New Brunswick: Rutgers UP, 1996.

Leavis, F. R. *The Great Tradition: George Eliot, Henry James, Joseph Conrad*. London: Chatto & Windus, 1948.

Watt, Ian. *The Rise of the Novel: Studies in Defoe, Richardson, and Fielding*. Berkeley: U of California P, 1957.

A Character

Felipe Alfau

I

The story I intend to write is a story which I have had in mind for some time. However, the rebellious qualities of my characters have prevented me from writing it. It seems that while I frame my characters and their actions in my mind, I have them quite well in hand, but it suffices to set a character on paper to lose control of him immediately. He goes off on his own track, evades me and does what he pleases with himself, leaving me absolutely helpless.

I have, moreover, been particularly averse to writing this story because I intend to use in it Gaston Bejarano, my principal character, who is especially rebellious and always wants to do things of his own accord. He is quite a bad influence among the crowd and on more than one occasion has completely demoralized the cast.

However, I am now at the house of my friend Don Laureano Baez. He is not at home and I am waiting for his arrival. Not having anything to amuse me in the meanwhile, I shall set aside all scruples and begin my story:

Gaston Bejarano was returning home one night, when he met a girl. . . .

The doorbell has rung. I believe it is my friend Don Laureano. If you will excuse me I shall proceed with my tale some other time.

Now that my author has set me on paper and given me a

1

body and a start, I shall proceed with the story and tell it in my own words. Now that I am free from his attention I am able to do as I please. He thinks that by forgetting about me I shall cease to exist, but I love reality too much and I intend to continue to move and think even after my author has shifted his attention from me.

Well, he is quite right. I was returning home one night and was walking along upper Alcala Street by El Retiro. I don't remember the exact time, but I know that it was quite late and that it was raining.

I walked rather fast and began to overtake a group that walked in front of me. When I was nearer I noticed that two men were following at a short distance a woman, who in the dim light appeared to be young. I regulated my pace by theirs and watched.

The two men approached the girl (for by now I was sure it was a girl). There was a short exchange of words between them which I could not hear well, and the two men crossed the street and continued to walk parallel to her.

For reasons which are tedious to explain, I felt an urgent desire to make the acquaintance of the girl but I wanted no witness to my actions. It was, after all, my first escape into reality and I felt a bit shy. Therefore I followed her at a respectable distance waiting for the moment when the two inopportune individuals should disappear.

But I am growing impatient of waiting and as the author is not present, I shall take the liberty of upsetting the laws of logic and simply eliminate these two men.

Immediately after their disappearance, I quickened my step and began to overtake the girl. It was now raining quite heavily and she walked swiftly alongside the iron fence of El Retiro without minding the puddles, turning her head now and then to look at me. With the night and rain her figure was blurred and there was something of a vision in it, beckoning and luring, and I was afraid.

I waved at her and she stopped.

It was strange. She stood at the end of her own shadow against the far diffused light of the corner lamp post and there was something ominous in that.

For a moment I doubted whether she stopped to face an enemy or to welcome a companion. I hesitated. Her shadow pointed the way to her and I walked over its dark lane.

"Where are you going at this time, in this weather?"

What she said was not as important as the way she said it. I do not think that I can describe it. I was so surprised by her voice. She was a sweet type with innocent eyes, but there was depravity in her mouth and her voice was coarse and low, her inflection cynical.

"I am going to the corner of Alcala and Velazquez, I must meet a man to get some money from him."

I don't remember saying anything at this moment. She went on:

"I am late now and he probably will not be there. I will go and look around the corner anyway."

We were two blocks from Velazquez Street now. We walked.

And mind you. It was raining all this time, but I did not seem to notice it. Everything had changed inside and outside of me. I felt no longer a character. I felt real, fearfully real, like any other human being who walks up Alcala Street on a rainy night and meets a real girl. I spoke, too, in a plain and ineloquent manner as if I truly were a human being.

"Who are those two men who spoke to you?"

"I don't know them. They just wanted to have a good time and I told them I was busy."

"Oh, are you busy?" I stopped. She also stopped.

"I told you I was going to meet a man at Velazquez." She smiled in a way that started us walking again.

"You seem rather young to be out at this time meeting a man to get money from him."

"Young? How old do you think I am?"

"Seventeen or eighteen, I suppose. . . ." I was sincere.

"You silly, only the other day I passed my twenty-third birthday."

She had no desire to appear young and for once I almost doubted her reality. I liked the way she said *silly*.

During all this, I noticed two things:

First: I was terribly aware of the fact that her voice was coarse and low and no one will ever imagine how I liked it.

Second: Our two shadows were shrinking and gaining on us and, as we passed the light they slipped under our feet and advanced ahead, blending into one, growing larger, immense.

Half a block from Velazquez Street:

"I think you had better go on and meet your friend. If he sees you arriving with someone he might get suspicious. I will wait for you here. If he is not there come back to me."

She agreed with such indifference that I felt that the rain, the world and I were about the same thing so far as she was concerned. For a moment I realized that in comparison with her strong reality, I had become once more a character and everything about was just the setting.

When I was alone I thought:

Why had I spoken to this girl? Was it because of the habits acquired as a character, which had left in me a strong tendency to speculate on girls who go out late at night? If she came back it was because she had not found the man. That is, she would come back without money. Now as the character I am and as you will discover by the things my author will tell you about me, I should not be interested in her, in such an eventuality. If she found the man, she would probably get the money. But in that case she would not come back. Undoubtedly she belonged, like me, to the profession. I thought of her coarse voice. But again; she was a real being and I was only a character. Had I stolen into her world of reality, or had she entered into my world of fancy? Perhaps we were only between these two worlds, and were walking together along the fascinating frontier. I knew one thing: that our destinies were bound together and that either she would have to drag me definitely into her realm or I take her into mine. Who would be the stronger: she as a real being or I as a character?

And of course she came back.

I grew effusive. I took her arm and talked, bending my face close to hers. I said many things but again I felt real and of course eloquence failed me. For once I regretted having stepped out of my character. As such I could always speak brilliantly and in a convincing way. My speech was fluent and well chosen. But now I was speaking in a flat manner like a vulgar man. I wanted to appeal to her imagination and arouse her interest, but instead I said that I specialized in girls who spoke in a coarse, low voice and went out late at night looking for men to give or pay them money. I asked her name, what she did and where she lived and then, to feel the ground, I said that I was broke. Was she beginning to prove the stronger, would I definitely be dragged into her world of reality?

Her name was Maria Luisa Baez, but they called her Lunarito. She lived far from there and did nothing. She had no money either. But everything she said seemed to lack life. It condensed in the mist and rain and fell to the wet ground. Indeed, she was reality.

Then came the realization of the rain. I felt her damp clothes. It was necessary to get out of it. However, the weather, the hour and the place did not seem to affect her in the least. But I was human for the first time and I was drenched. It was imperative to get better acquainted because there was also another latent desire in me. I suggested a doorway.

"All right," she said and we went in.

Until that moment I had been but a description and now I felt real. Beyond the door of that sordid hallway, beyond the clouded sky, I could sense the stars, life pushing me to her. I never thought that reality could be so intense and plastic, and when she looked at me, I kissed her.

What happened then is beyond me. It was so unexpected that I doubted if that reality was anything but a dream. Her dense cloak of indifference collapsed. She responded immensely. Indeed, she was a human being and human beings are sometimes wonderful. And then such a strong contrast, for what she said did not fall dead but flourished on her lips.

Yet what she said was in keeping with her style of talking. The word she said was *silly* and I drew it from her and it penetrated me, shaking the innermost fibers of the male. It passed from her tongue to mine, through our blended lips.

If there is such a thing as a long kiss, that kiss was long.

"Have you a cigarette?"

Again she was indifferent. We smoked in silence and then she said she was going.

I said:

"I want to see you again, I must be always with you. Give me your address."

"It is no use. You will never find it."

And even now I do not understand what kept me from insisting. I gave her my address and said:

"Will I see you again soon? Write to me, come to me, very soon."

"All right."

"Take good care of yourself. Your clothes are all wet. Take good care of yourself, you belong to me now."

"I will always belong to you."

"Good-by, Lunarito."

"Good-by."

When I arrived home I was thinking that this was the second woman I had loved without an interest. The other woman was there in my home, perhaps oblivious of the fact that for the first time I had really been untrue to her, that our future relations would be now more of a grotesque pantomime, intensifying our mutual absurdity.

And even so I felt that the tragedy of our life had somehow been robbed of its strength. Yes, that woman who awaited me, that woman who was my lover, was like me, nothing but a character. Had I not ceased to be a character? I entertained strong doubts as I entered my former house of unreality. Yes, that woman and I more than belonged to the world of puppets. Did I really belong? Had I sunk back into my world since I bade good-by to Lunarito?

But Carmen, my mistress, was awaiting me. How could I find anything in common with her after having had a test of reality? How could I cross the abyss which separated us now, unless I trusted to sheer romanticism? And after my fleeting escape into the human world I had no taste for that.

Had I truly been unfaithful to her? She could not deem my fault so great with a being that belonged to another plane, to another world and different standards. An actor on the stage cannot feel jealousy because his stage lover steps out between the acts and falls in love with a spectator. But was I coming back to go on with the next act of our eternal comedy? And a mere puppet does not allow himself to step out and live and love like a human being between the acts. No, he must sink back into nonentity.

Carmen was sleeping that profound sleep I knew so well. I remembered that stupor into which a character falls when he is not called upon to act, when his strings have been released. But I had been perhaps walking in my sleep and my actions thus committed, no matter how transcendental to my future life, did not concern her.

I thought all this and even more, but when I entered the chamber where Carmen lay asleep, I felt remorse.

And this is the end. I have not heard from Lunarito since that night and now I think that everything was but a vision. All that happened that night tends to prove that. Her supreme indifference, the fact that she did not mind the rain, the swift manner in which she walked over the puddles. Yes, the whole thing did not exist. It was a hallucination, and perhaps that is why there was no man waiting for her at the corner of Velazquez Street, for there could be no human being waiting on such a night for something that does not exist. Undoubtedly it was a vision. For that which is reality for humans is a hallucination for a character. Characters have visions of true life—they dream reality and then they are lost.

And this is my predicament. Here I am: a character who has stepped past the edge of the paper and plunged into the abyss of reality, who now cannot go back to his own world. My comedy has expanded beyond the footlights, I have fallen in love with a woman in the audience. Can she be brought onto the stage, or shall we the puppets invade the house and mix with the humans in a general drama?

What can I do? To go back into my world when my main

interest is in reality seems hardly possible. To enter reality
which I scarcely know is a tremendous ordeal, because I have
no real past. What can I do? I appeal to the author to destroy
me completely or make me all over. To make a character out
of Lunarito in order that she shall be within my reach. . . .
But no, I want her real. It was reality that I loved in her.
Then to give me a past and let me be human. But can an author give a past to a real being?

I appeal to the author to solve a problem which is beyond
me.

II

This Gaston Bejarano, my character, is in quite a difficult
situation. Of course, he is the only one to blame. I interrupted my story and he took advantage of my absence in order to develop it on his own hook, with the result that he has
made a mess of it. The whole thing has not come to a proper
ending; it has been dissolved rather than solved for lack of
adequate interference.

However, what has happened to Gaston is a good lesson
to my characters. Now he is coming in a submissive way to
ask me to help him.

In order to solve, or at least explain, the problem of
Gaston there are two fundamental propositions which I as
the author must present:

First, I must explain how I, the author, met Gaston, the
character, and second, how Gaston, the character, met a real
person like Lunarito, which after all is not at all unusual,
considering that I also met him. What is really almost extraordinary is for a character to take a real person so seriously, the general habit being for people to take characters
with a seriousness that verges on the tragic (this book is an
instance of that).

Then I might make a character out of Lunarito, but I
don't want any more characters for the time being, they are
too much trouble. Besides, Gaston himself has said that he

wanted her to remain real and this is very significant.

It must be borne in mind that Gaston as a character is quite romantic at times, although he does not suspect it. Now, if a romantic human being had fallen in love with a vision, which is not likely to happen, according to romantic regulations he would want that vision to remain a vision, never to take shape, never to become plastic and human, because that would demolish his ideal. Well, a character is entirely the opposite of a real being, although it is sometimes our business to try to convince the reader to the contrary, and for him a vision is reality. That is why Gaston, as a character, wants Lunarito to remain real, because if she became fiction, she would enter and form part of the world to which he is used and his ideal would be destroyed. Therefore nothing will be done along that line and Lunarito will be left alone for the moment.

Strengthening the fictional side of Gaston, which is already beginning to weaken, remains to be done. He must be shoved back into his world of characters.

After that, if Gaston insists on becoming a real being in order to attain his ideal beyond the boundaries of his own world, I regret to admit that I shall not be able to help him. It is not in my power as a writer to create real beings, but only characters and that quite badly. Only his will to be, plus the mysterious and strange ways of life can help him. But I would not advise him to do that even if he were able. It would be assuming tremendous responsibilities, it would be a character who, because in a dream or perhaps a state of somnambulism, met a real person, became a human being and took upon himself the responsibility of conscious willful life, and all the unconscious actions of his past; who by becoming real lent all his actions a profound, serious meaning. All the things that once were nothing but play would then be real and truly affect his life and that of others. It would be a puppet who, by falling in love with a person in the audience, brought real life onto the stage, broke loose from all the threads which moved him and made a tragedy out of a comedy.

III

But now let me see how it happened that I met Gaston the character.

At the time I met him, he was generally known by the name El Cogote and that is the name I shall give to him for the time being.

I met El Cogote through Dr. José de los Rios, but before I met him I had already heard of this more or less notorious person.

El Cogote was known in Madrid as a prosperous *chulo*. Even more, he had graduated from that position into that one more respectable and profitable: an *empresario*. He owned one of the best amusement places in Madrid and was a rather influential personality in the gay world.

How El Cogote began and developed his career is a thing which I don't know very well. From the contradictory opinions and comments of people who pride themselves on being his intimate friends, or who even ran an account at his place, I have confusedly gathered that he began as a protégé of a well-known café singer called La Pelos.

I remember seeing and hearing La Pelos in a café quite some time ago. She was a pompous-looking female with furiously black eyes, a very hoarse voice that smelled of *chinchon* a league away and a pronounced growth of hair upon her upper lip.

Even from the faint memory I have of her, La Pelos struck me as a woman of tempestuous passions and it is not strange that she should fall for El Cogote, at that time a thick-lipped languid-eyed youth (according to a picture of him I had seen in *La Gaceta*). I have been told how their first meeting took place, although, as I have said, it is not to be considered authentic.

It seems that El Cogote (at that time he had not yet achieved this glorious name) was sitting alone at a table in the café where La Pelos sang. As she passed his table she bent over and said quite loudly:

"You need company, *chiquillo*. Are you willing to spend ten duros?"

And El Cogote had answered still louder:

"Certainly, have you got them?"

This answer made her laugh and won her. She sat by him and encircled his neck in her fat arm.

At that moment a stout, middle-aged gentleman with a large diamond ring and a gold watch chain, approached the table slowly, ominously. He was toying with a knife of fair proportions.

He tilted his *cordobes* forward over his right eye and regarded El Cogote squarely:

"It seems that you are filling in your own certificate of defunction."

El Cogote swept the man with a sidelong glance. There was a cigarette hanging from his lips that shook beating time to his words as he said simply:

"I don't think so."

The two men looked at each other long and in silence. Then the gentleman with the diamond ring and the gold chain shook his shoulders, spat a wry smile and went away majestically. His bluff had been called, and incidentally, El Cogote had just introduced a new school.

After that day La Pelos belonged body and soul to El Cogote and for him she went to the dogs. According to the friend who told me the foregoing incident, El Cogote never cared for La Pelos and only used her as a good thing. She gave him an apartment, money, silk shirts, the most fashionable suits with short jackets and tight trousers, baggy at the bottom, and patent leather shoes with tan uppers. In her carriage she took him to all the *verbenas* and he always had at his disposal the best seats for every bullfight.

And even so he was always running after other women and treated La Pelos shamefully. She was a very jealous woman and their love affair was a stormy one. In many instances their fighting assumed such proportions and their behavior was so scandalous that the police had to interfere, but it is said that El Cogote had pull with the Prefect of Police and always got away without trouble.

However, his popularity had increased and with it his opportunities. He soon found more admirers and protectresses and his career progressed rapidly and brilliantly.

Then came a romantic incident in the life of El Cogote, which I have also gathered from various sources.

El Cogote had always been in love with a certain young lady in Madrid. A disgrace befell her family. Her father was accused of some crime and went to prison. Some people say that it was a frame-up. Others say that he was guilty. Just the same, the fact remains that he went to jail.

Some people in Spain take such disgraces entirely too seriously and often seek consolation in religion. However, whether that was the only reason, which does not seem likely, or whether there was some other motive, which the friend who told me suspects, Carmen—that was the young lady's name—was sent to a convent in North Spain to be a nun.

They say that there a priest from a nearby convent fell in love with her and later committed suicide. This, according to my friend, is a fictional touch added by people's imagination. But what he tells me as authentic is that El Cogote and Carmen, his sweetheart, could not console themselves for the separation imposed upon them by her family.

The result is that El Cogote visited the town where the convent was and one night the nun eloped with him. He took her back to Madrid with him as his mistress.

Apparently the reaction from her restricted past and the still more restricted environment of the convent, threw her to the other side of the balance. Under the demoralizing influence of her lover and a mad thirst for freedom, she led the most unbridled, licentious life. Soon after their arrival in Madrid, El Cogote, who during his trip to the North had accumulated a respectable amount of money from unknown sources, opened a luxurious amusement place in which the main attraction was the former nun.

News of the elopement from the convent and her romance with the priest ending in his suicide had spread through

Madrid and soon assumed the proportions of a real novel. Therefore their clientele was large and select, including many high government and church officials which ensured a great degree of safety and success for the business.

This is what I know of El Cogote previous to the time of our meeting. Consequently, I was quite curious to know him personally and when my friend, Dr. José de los Rios, told me that he was his friend and patient, that he was going to see him and that I might accompany him, I accepted immediately.

On our way to the house of El Cogote, I inquired from Dr. de los Rios what he meant by his patient; whether El Cogote was sick.

"Yes," said Dr. de los Rios. "Very sick. It is an old malady with him, too. He has always neglected the treatment and instead does in excess everything he should not do."

Dr. de los Rios went on:

"You know? El Cogote is quite an extraordinary person. He will interest you. He is not at all a vulgar *chulo,* he seldom speaks like one when he is not in their company. You know? A strange thing just happened to him and has upset him in a terrible way . . . of course, his nerves are in bad shape and I think that his malady has already affected his brain. . . ."

I reminded Dr. de los Rios that he was not telling me what he had started out to say.

"Well, he tells me that the other night he was walking home. . . . Here in the same direction we are walking now. And that it was raining heavily. You know? I have told him time and again that in his condition he must avoid exposure, but he never wants to listen. . . ."

"Yes, but what happened to him?"

"Well, he met a girl. . . . He says that up to that moment, he had been convinced that no woman could interest him for herself aside from his mistress, but the moment he met this girl that conviction abandoned him completely. He says that in a moment he realized that the girl in question embodied all the ideals of his life, that he knew he would love her always and would not be able to live without her. . . . Well, I have never heard El Cogote express himself so sentimentally before."

"Yes, that is unusual in a man of his type, but I don't see anything so astonishing in his meeting a girl."

"But listen . . . the next morning he opened a newspaper and he saw a picture of the girl and an account saying that Maria Luisa Baez, known as Lunarito, the same name she had given him, had been murdered the afternoon before by a jealous suitor. Mind you, the afternoon before the night when he met her. . . . Of course, this has had a terrible effect upon him. Things like this are dangerous in the condition in which his mind is."

"But of course you don't believe that."

"Of course not. I don't believe in ghosts, but the whole thing is strange. I made inquiries and found out that the autopsy of her body took place at three o'clock of that afternoon. . . . But, by the way, didn't you see the account in the papers?"

"No, you know I don't read papers much."

"Just the same. I then told El Cogote that in his weak condition he might have gone to sleep for two days in succession and that he may have met the girl the night before the day she was murdered. I wanted to give him some explanation."

"That is more logical at any rate."

"Yes, but it is not true, because Carmen has told me so and she ought to know, and besides El Cogote has ascertained the dates from the things he did and people he met."

"But do you believe or don't you?"

"No, I don't."

And then Dr. de los Rios and I arrived at the house of El Cogote.

As we ascended the stairs we heard a voice yelling.

"There he goes raving again," said Dr. de los Rios. "For two days he has been calling for Lunarito. He says that he cannot live without her, that he cannot take that vision from his mind."

A woman in a red kimono opened the door for us. She held a handkerchief in her hand and showed plainly that she had been crying.

"This is Carmen," Dr. de los Rios said to me.

A very old-looking woman with an apron, apparently a servant, advanced toward us and stopped in front of Dr. de los Rios. She looked at him blankly and almost recited:

"If poor Gil should lift his head . If poor Gil should lift his head."

Carmen pushed her away gently:

"Go back to your kitchen."

And the poor woman walked away obediently, always repeating:

"If poor Gil should lift his head . . . If poor Gil should lift his head."

We followed her with our eyes and I was aware of a respectful silence. Then Dr. de los Rios addressed Carmen:

"Do not take things so badly. I will see what I can do for him. Are you coming in with us?"

"Oh, no, I cannot bear to look at him. He has such an expression! Besides, he does not want to see me. . . . I am terribly afraid, Don José . . ." She closed the door behind us, submerging the small lobby in thick shadows. We were silent again and I heard her sobbing in the darkness.

Since Carmen had opened the door for us, I had been under the impression that I had lived this scene before. The presence of Dr. de los Rios, that sick man in the house, the old insane woman and this other woman who had shut the door in silence. Everything convinced me that I had formed part of the same circumstances some time before, and all that followed I knew and expected. It was the strangest sensation of advancing ahead of time.

I followed Dr. de los Rios through a short corridor and entered the bedroom.

El Cogote lay upon a bed, the covers thrown aside, the coat of his pajamas torn from the shoulder down. He was panting with fatigue from his recent attack.

Dr. de los Rios said:

"I have brought a friend to cheer you. How do you feel today?"

With an obscene word, El Cogote informed us that he was done for.

Dr. de los Rios motioned me to a chair and then sat on the edge of the bed and held the sick man's wrist. He produced a watch and remained still for a while.

"Aha," he finished. "And how did you sleep last night?"

"Very badly, Don José, worse than ever. I had a terrible nightmare."

"Well, tell us your nightmare," said Dr. de los Rios in a jesting manner. "My friend here can tell your past, your future and your fortune from a dream."

There came a slight flush into the face of El Cogote.

And then he told us his dream.[1]

In his dream he found himself again at the house where he had lived with his family as a young man.

At the end of the corridor there was a room that had formed a kind of superstition in the family. No one liked it, they were all afraid of it.

On that particular day, he had tried in a joking manner to convince them of the absurdity of their fear. He told them that in order to do away with ghosts one had to do nothing but approach them. He told them that it would suffice to enter the room and the fear would leave them. He was then the only man in the house. His father had died and his younger brother was still a child.

El Cogote speaks:

"In my dream I was playing with my sister. Not the younger one but the other . . . you know, Don José?"

And Dr. de los Rios nodded.

"But in my dream my sister had the face of Lunarito, you understand me? Perhaps in my dream Lunarito was my sister. . . . Lunarito has been in all my dreams. I have not been able to get her away from my mind since that night."

In his dream he began to joke and play with her and then

---

[1] I must confess that when I heard the narrative of his dream by El Cogote, which I transcribe freely, I realized that Dr. de los Rios was right in saying that this man was an extraordinary person.

dragged her along the corridor and, in spite of the almost savage resistance she opposed, he took her laughing in his arms and precipitated her inside the room.

"No . . . ! No . . . !" she cried and the door closed, silencing her voice like a tombstone. Then he heard her no more. Undoubtedly, in her panic, she feared to arouse the horror of the room with her voice.

He did not give importance to the matter. He returned to the others, they spoke and no one gave another thought to the incident. Some time passed, they all sat at dinner and through one of those things which are inexplicable in dreams, no one missed her at the table. They had forgotten her. But there was a heavy atmosphere and all seemed worried. All hung their heads over the dishes and no one spoke. I don't think they even ate, and if one could see better when one dreams, he might have seen tears in their eyes.

After a while, something was heard rubbing a door. The sound was infinitely faint but they all heard it.

El Cogote speaks:

"Someone said, and I remember the very words:

" 'Perhaps it is some friend of the children who is shy and does not dare to ring the bell, but as they are afraid of the lonely corridor and the room at the end, they do not dare to open the door.' "

The corridor was illuminated by such a dim and sad light that they all understood and there was a long silence.

Then he was the one who spoke with words of forced gaiety, which sounded strident:

"If that is the important reason that prevents you from going, I will go." And he rose calmly and his steps resounded loudly. But when he opened the door he saw nothing but the empty stairway. At that moment, he remembered and walked to the end of the corridor and stood a moment before the door.

El Cogote speaks:

"I placed my hands upon the cold knob and as if someone had been pushing against it, the door flew open and a body brushed past me and leaned on the wall.

"It was she . . . Don José . . . It was she . . . changed, like a corpse. Her hair was white. She did not even look at me."

Her frosted eyes were fixed in a vision of horror. They protruded out of their sockets, flying from the phantom which hypnotized her, which she bore within.

"You have killed me . . . You have killed me . . ." Such were her only words. Empty mechanical words, as if by a mental repetition she had exhausted all their meaning.

What he felt in that moment is impossible to explain. It was a brutal, tearing sorrow. In a moment he reconstructed all his life linked to hers. She was so good and sweet . . . ! And he had done that horrible thing. . . . All the well-known love he bore for her invaded him, it swept his whole being like a squall and he hated himself as no one has hated anyone in this world.

Then the scene changed. There was nothing but a corridor, long and enclosed without another door, and there was that sinister dusky light so typical of dreams.

In a moment he was on his knees, caressing her, begging forgiveness. But she did not see him, her eyes were fixed in space and he felt between his arms, her poor body flagellated by panic, shaking in all its fibers in agonizing gasps.

He said:

"My sister . . . my poor sister . . ."

She said:

"You have killed me. . . . You have killed me. . . ."

And at the end of the corridor, the door was still open.

At the end of his narrative, El Cogote was obviously agitated. There was a glowing flush of exaltation in his face. I don't know what Dr. de los Rios felt or thought, but I know that the account of the dream impressed me strongly. In fact, I was so impressed that I don't remember clearly what took place afterwards. The memories of that last and extraordinary scene rush through my mind in disorder. But from that confusion, I retain the intense feeling of a profound realization of truth which dawned in my brain like a blast in a fog, a feeling that I was living a moment of ultrarealism, emanating from Dr. José de los Rios toward me.

I remember Dr. de los Rios looking into space with his deep clear eyes. Then I can hear, without seeing anything, the coarse voice of El Cogote:

"Lunarito, come to me. Even if you were murdered before I even met you. Even if I killed you again in my dream. Do not leave me. Come even if it is a miracle. . . . Come before I die!"

And then the door behind us opened slowly and I heard a voice say:

"Here I am."

Dr. de los Rios did not move. I stood up and turned around.

In the doorway, with her red kimono, stood Lunarito, his mistress.

IV

And now we come to the second proposition: how El Cogote, or Gaston, the character met Lunarito the real person.

Gaston thinks that he met Lunarito at the street of Alcala on a rainy night, but he is mistaken. Gaston met Lunarito at the house of my friend Don Laureano Baez and he imagined the rest.

It came about in this way:

One day I went to call upon Don Laureano Baez.

Incidentally, Don Laureano Baez was one of those extraordinary persons who happen in Spain now and then. His profession was begging and he lived rather luxuriously on the proceeds. Moreover, he had founded a school for beggary in which he and other teachers appointed by him taught all imaginable tricks for arousing human sympathy, from the art of declamation to that of contortion.

However, Don Laureano was not a common beggar. He was an artist in his profession and loved it. Even after success had piled upon him, he had refused to retire and at the time of these happenings he was still an active member of the begging classes, holding a central corner in the business district of Madrid. Yet this is not the point.

Don Laureano Baez lived with a girl who was everything to him. This girl was one-fourth daughter, one-fourth wife, one-fourth maid and one-fourth secretary to Don Laureano. Her name was Maria Luisa and she really meant a great deal to Señor Baez. He, a past master in the art of speculating on human weakness, had thoroughly educated her in the ways of life and she was a promising pupil.

Being a girl, Don Laureano had impressed upon her that her activities were not to be directed toward begging for alms, as she in her innocent admiration for him had tried to do; but rather toward trading for gifts.

Don Laureano had directed and concentrated her attention upon a tantalizing beauty spot which nature had dropped on a corner of her body. That beauty spot, which, by the way, had gained her the surname of Lunarito, could very well accomplish great deeds, Don Laureano had thought, with his profound wisdom, and he had even made out these rates:

For one peseta, the beauty spot could be shown.

For two pesetas, it could be touched.

And so on. It would be unnecessary to go through the whole list that Don Laureano Baez had planned. It will suffice to say that he had not left unrated a single possible use of that spot and that, in his list, Don Laureano displayed an amazing sense of values and a deep knowledge of human nature.

Don Laureano was right. The beauty spot soon contributed largely to the common capital. Lunarito became one thing more: Don Laureano's partner, and as such helped him in many of his businesses in and out of his official role of beggar, until one day Don Laureano did something which compelled the law to offer him a choice between death penalty and life imprisonment. Don Laureano, being quite old at the time, chose life imprisonment, and Lunarito was left alone to mourn and honor the memory of her idol and look for some other master.

The day I arrived at the house of Don Laureano Baez he was not at home and I decided to wait for him.

I chatted a while with Lunarito who was pottering around putting the house in order and then, not having anything better to do and not being able to find a single peseta in my pockets, I decided to begin a story I had had in my mind for a few days.

I sat at my friend's desk, took some paper and pencil, and began to write thus:

"Gaston Bejarano was returning home one night when he met a girl. . . ."

Lunarito, who had very bad manners, came near and looked over my shoulder. At that moment the doorbell rang; as I suspected it to be my friend, I rose and went to open the door.

It was Don Laureano, indeed, and when I reentered his study with him, I saw Lunarito by the desk, holding the piece of paper, with a dreamy expression in her eyes.

Don Laureano called out:

"Lunarito, did anything happen during my absence?"

Lunarito made no answer, she had not heard him. She was not there. At that moment she was living in the future, walking with Gaston Bejarano along upper Alcala Street on a rainy night.

Ladies Almanack: July

Djuna Barnes

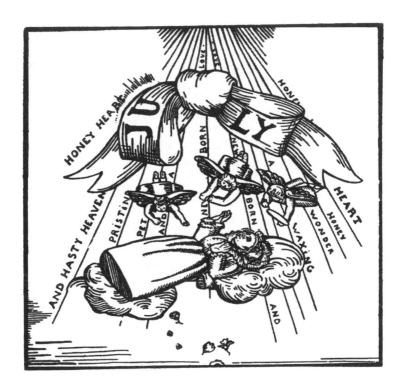

The Time has come, when, with unwilling Hand, I must set down what a woman says to a Woman and she be up to her Ears in Love's Acre. Should we not like to think it, at least if not of poetic Value, then strophed to a Romanesque Fortitude, as clipped of Foliage as a British Hedge, or at least as fitting to the thing it covers as an Infant's Cap, which even when frilled to the very frontal Bone, and taking into account the most pulsing Suture, is somewhat of a Head's proportion, nor flows and drips away and adown, as if it were no Covering for probability ?

Nay, nowhere, in all the fulsome data of most uncovered and naked backrunning of Nature, nor in the Columns of our most jaundiced Journals, can be gathered the vaguest Idea of the Means by which she puts her Heart from her Mouth to her Sleeve, and from her Sleeve into Rhetorick, and from that into the Ear of her beloved. To the Ancients, Love Letters and Love Hearsay (though how much Luck and how much Cunning this was on the part of the Outrunners in the Thickets of prehistoric proability, none can say, for doubt me not but from Fish to Man there has been much Back-mating and Front to Front, though only a Twitter of it comes out of the Past) were from like to unlike. Our own Journals teem with Maids and their Beards, whose very highest encomiums reach no more glorious Foothold than "Honey Lou", or "Snooky dear", or "my great big beautiful bedridden Doll," whose Turnabout it would seem, is only one side proper to the Lord. But hear how a Maid goes at a Maid: "And are you well my own ? But tell me hastily, are you well ? for I am well, oh most newly well, and well again. And if all's well, then ends well all ends up ! But if you be about to be nowise probable but tell me, and I will burst my Gussets with hereditary Weeping, that we be not dated to a Moon and are apart by dint of diddling Nature, and parting is such sweet Sorrow ! How all too oft are we but one in our Team ! So tell me if you but be well for well I be !"

Or such Words as this : "I may have trifled in my Day, or in Days to come, or today itself ; or even now be rifling Hours for the penning of this to you, but though I gather dear Daffodils abroad, plunge Head first into many a Parsley Field, tamper with high strung and low lying ; though I press to my Bosom the very Flower of Women, or tire myself to a prostrate Portion, without a Breath between me and her ; toss her over the off-leg to bring her to rights, say never that I do not adore you as my only and my best. To her I give but a Phoenix Hour, she is but the hone to my blunt, which shall Toledo to you. To you I give my Bays, my Laurels, my Ever-

lastings, my Peonies, my hardy Perennials and my early per-
cipient Posies, that bloom for such effulgence as shines alone
from your Countenance ! (Viz., to wit : were she haggard,
gray, toothless, torn, deformed, damned, evil, putrid and no
one's Pleasure ; or if on the other Hand she were lovely,
straight, marble browed, red in her bloom, bright in the Eye,
headed with Hair, and Venused to boot—'tis all one to a Girl
in Love !) For you alone I reserve that Gasp under Gasp, that
Sigh behind Sigh, that Attention back of feigned ; that
Cloud's Silver is yours—take it ! What care I on whom it
rains ! The real me is your real yours, I can spend myself in
Hedgerow and Counter-patch, 'tis only the Dust of my reality,
the Smoke that tells of the Fire, which my own Darling
Lamb, my most perfect and tirelessly different, is yours, I am
thine ! You compel me. !"

Compels her ! Yea, though the Recipient be as torpid as a
Mohammedan after his hundredth Ramadan, as temperate
as a Frost in Timgad, as stealthy as a Bishop without a Post,
still and yet, and how again it will command her ; so encore.
Were it of as good a quality and as sharp as Madagascar Pep-
per, Still it commands her, it can command her up-stairs and
down, right side and wrong, peek-a-boo, or all fronts-face, in
Mid-moon and Mad-night, in Dawn, in Day, yea, still it will
command her, so pricked is she with longing, and so primed
to a Breath, that should her Honey-heart hang mincemeat
Tartlets about her Waist for a Girdle, would she preen to the
Pie, and clap with Delight ; or should she be ordered to wear
a Wig backward, with its curl well over her Nose, still she
would do it, a Lamb both fore and aft and all at the one look,
saying : "You know my quick Step, my real Run, my true Bite.
My intake and withdraw are at your behest, I am but a Shade
of myself an I am not by your Side, and what I am is because
you are, and should you turn and not find me, it is because I
have taken that not worthy of you to another, who may blow
me bright again to shine toward your Lightning, a Sun to my
Beam !"

Nay——I cannot write it ! It is worse than this ! More
dripping, more lush, more lavender, more midmauve, more

honeyed, more Flower-casting, more Cherub-bound, more downpouring, more saccharine, more lamentable, more gruesomely unmindful of Reason or Sense, to say nothing of Humor. Nowhere, and in no Pocket, do such keep a Seed of the fit on which to sneeze themselves into the fitting, they be not happy unless writhing in Treacle, and like a trapped Fly, crawl through cardinal Morasses, all Legs tethered and dragging in the Gum of Love !

And just as some others are foul of Tongue, these are sweet to sickness. One sickens the Gorge, and the other the Heart. For what can you, an a woman thus leans upon the purple, and so strews Blandishments that the clear Nature of Facts are either so candied and frosted to a Mystery, or so bemired that they are no find. Surely it is admirable to have a Fancy and a Fancy when in Love, but why so witless about a witty Insanity ? It would loom the bigger if stripped of its Jangle, but no, drugged such must go. As foggy as a Mere, as drenched as a Pump ; twittering so loud upon the Wire that one cannot hear the Message. And yet !

Menelaiad

John Barth

I

Menelaus here, more or less. The fair-haired boy? Of the loud war cry! Leader of the people. Zeus's fosterling.

Eternal husband.

Got you, have I? No? Changed your shape, become waves of the sea, of the air? Anyone there? Anyone here?

No matter; this isn't the voice of Menelaus; this voice *is* Menelaus, all there is of him. When I'm switched on I tell my tale, the one I know, How Menelaus Became Immortal, but I don't know it.

Keep hold of yourself.

"Helen," I say: "Helen's responsible for this. From the day we lovers sacrificed the horse in Argos, pastureland of horses, and swore on its bloody joints to be her champions forever, whichever of us she chose, to the night we huddled in the horse in Troy while she took the part of all our wives—everything's Helen's fault. Cities built and burnt, a thousand bottoms on the sea's, every captain corpsed or cuckold—her doing. She's the death of me and my peculiar immortality, cause of every mask and change of state. On whose account did Odysseus become a madman, Achilles woman? Who turned the Argives into a horse, loyal Sinon into a traitor, yours truly from a mooncalf into a sea-calf, Proteus into everything that is? First cause and final magician: Mrs. M.

"One evening, embracing in our bed, I dreamed I was back in the wooden horse, waiting for midnight. Laocoön's spear still stuck in our flank, and Helen, with her Trojan pal in tow, called out to her Argive lovers in the voice of each's

26

wife. 'Come kiss me, Anticlus darling!' My heart was stabbed as my side was once by Pandarus's arrow. But in the horse, while smart Odysseus held shut our mouths, I dreamed I was home in bed before Paris and the war, our wedding night, when she crooned like that to *me*. Oh, Anticlus, it wasn't you who was deceived; your wife was leagues and years away, mine but an arms-length, yet less near. Now I wonder which dream dreamed which, which Menelaus never woke and now dreams both.

"And when I was on the beach at Pharos, seven years lost en route from Troy, clinging miserably to Proteus for direction, he prophesied a day when I'd sit in my house at last, drink wine with the sons of dead comrades, and tell their dads' tales; my good wife would knit by the fireside, things for our daughter's wedding, and dutifully pour the wine. That scene glowed so in my heart, its beat became the rhythm of her needles; Egypt's waves hissed on the foreshore like sapwood in the grate, and the Nile-murk on my tongue turned sweet. But then it seems to me I'm home in Sparta, talking to Nestor's boy or Odysseus's; Helen's put something in the wine again, I know why, one of those painkillers she picked up in Africa, and the tale I tell so grips me, I'm back in the cave once more with the Old Man of the Sea."

One thing's certain: somewhere Menelaus lost course and steersman, went off track, never got back on, lost hold of himself, became a record merely, the record of his loosening grasp. He's the story of his life, with which he ambushes the unwary unawares.

2

" 'Got you!' " I cry to myself, imagining Telemachus enthralled by the doctored wine. " 'You've feasted your bowels on my dinner, your hopes on my news of Odysseus, your eyes on my wife though she's your mother's age. Now I'll feast myself on your sotted attention, with the tale How Menelaus First Humped Helen in the Eighth Year After the War.

Pricked you up, that? Got your ear, have I? Like to know how it was, I suppose? Where in Hades are we? Where'd I go? Whom've I got hold of? Proteus? Helen?'

" 'Telemachus Odysseus'-son,' the lad replied, 'come from goat-girt Ithaca for news of my father, but willing to have his cloak clutched and listen all night to the tale How You Lost Your Navigator, Wandered Seven Years, Came Ashore at Pharos, Waylaid Eidothea, Tackled Proteus, Learned to Reach Greece by Sailing up the Nile, and Made Love to Your Wife, the most beautiful woman I've ever seen, After an Abstinence of Eighteen Years.'

" 'Seventeen.' "

I tell it as it is. " 'D'you hear that click?' " I tell myself I asked Telemachus.

" '*I* do,' said Peisistratus.

" 'Knitting! Helen of Troy's going to be a grandmother! An empire torched, a generation lost, a hundred kings undone on her account, and there she sits, proper as Penelope, not a scratch on her—and knits!'

" 'Not a scratch!' said Telemachus.

" 'Excuse me,' Helen said; 'if it's to be *that* tale I'm going on to bed, second chamber on one's left down the hall. A lady has her modesty. Till we meet again, Telemachus. Drink deep and sleep well, Menelaus my love.'

" 'Zeus in heaven!' " I say I cried. " 'Why didn't I do you in in Deiphobus' house, put you to the sword with Troy?'

"Helen smiled at us and murmured: 'Love.'

" 'Does she mean,' asked Peisistratus Nestor's-son, come with Telemachus that noon from sandy Pylos, 'that you love her for example more than honor, self-respect; more than every man and cause you've gone to war for; more than Menelaus?'

" 'Not impossibly.'

" 'Is it that her name's twin syllables fire you with contrary passions? That your heart does battle with your heart till you burn like ashèd Ilion?'

" 'Wise son of a wise father! Her smile sows my furrowed memory with Castalian serpent's teeth; I become a score of warriors, each battling the others; the survivors kneel as one before her; perhaps the slain were better men. If Aeneas Aphrodite's-son couldn't stick her, how should I, a mere near mortal?'

" 'This is gripping,' " I say to myself Telemachus said. " 'Weary as we are from traveling all day, I wish nothing further than to sit without moving in this total darkness while you hold me by the hem of my tunic and recount How Your Gorgeous Wife Wouldn't Have You for Seven Full Postwar Years but Did in the Eighth. If I fail to exclaim with wonder or otherwise respond, it will be that I'm speechless with sympathy.'

" 'So be it,' I said," I say. "Truth to tell," I tell me, "when we re-reached Sparta Helen took up her knitting with never a droppèd stitch, as if she'd been away eighteen days instead of ditto years, and visiting her sister instead of bearing bastards to her Trojan lovers. But it was the wine of doubt *I* took to, whether I was the world's chief fool and cuckold or its luckiest mortal. Especially when old comrades came to town, or their sons, to swap war stories, I'd booze it till I couldn't tell Helen from Hellespont. So it was the day Odysseus's boy and Nestor's rode into town. I was shipping off our daughter to wed Achilles' son and Alector's girl in to wed mine; the place was full of kinfolk, the wine ran free, I was swallowing my troubles; babies they were when I went to Troy, hardly married myself; by the time I get home they're men and women wanting spouses of their own; no wonder I felt old and low and thirsty; where'd my kids go? The prime of my life?

"When the boys dropped in I took for granted they were friends of the children's, come for the party; I saw to it they were washed and oiled, gave them clean clothes and poured them a drink. Better open your palace to every kid in the countryside than not know whose your own are in, Mother and I always thought. No man can say I'm inhospitable. But I won't deny I felt a twinge when I learned they were strangers; handsome boys they were, from good families, I could tell, and in the bloom of manhood, as I'd been twenty years before, and Paris when he came a-calling, and I gave him a drink and said 'What's mine is yours . . .' . . ." . . . .

Why don't they call her Helen of Sparta?

"I showed them the house, all our African stuff, it knocked their eyes out; then we had dinner and played the guessing game. Nestor's boy I recognized early on, his father's image, a good lad, but not hero-material, you know what I mean. The other was a troubler; something not straight about him; wouldn't look you in the eye; kept smiling at his plate; but a sharp one, and a good-looking, bound to make a stir in the world one day. I kept my eye on him through dinner and decided he was my nephew Orestes, still hiding out from killing his mother and her goat-boy-friend, or else Odysseus's Telemachus. Either way it was bad news: when Proteus told me how Clytemnestra and Aegisthus had axed my brother the minute he set foot in Mycenae, do you think Helen spared him a tear? 'No more than he deserved,' she said, 'playing around with that bitch Cassandra.' But when we stopped off there on our way home from Egypt and found her sister and Aegisthus being buried, didn't she raise a howl for young Orestes's head! Zeus help him if he'd come to see his Uncle Menelaus! On the other hand, if he was Odysseus's boy and took after his father, I'd have to keep eye on the wedding silver as well as on the bride.

"To make matters worse, as I fretted about this our old minstrel wandered in, looking for a handout, and started up that wrath-of-Achilles thing, just what I needed to hear; before I could turn him off I was weeping in my wine and wishing I'd died the morning after my wedding night. Hermione barged in too, almost as pretty as her mom, to see who the stranger-chaps were; for a minute it was 'Paris, meet Helen' all over again, till I got hold of myself and shooed her out of there. Even so, a dreadful notion struck me: what if Paris had a son we didn't know about, who'd slipped like slick Aeneas our Trojan clutch, grown up in hiding, and was come now to steal my daughter as his dad my wife! Another horse! Another Hector! Another drink.

"Even as I swallowed, hard and often, the fellow winked at the door I'd sent Hermione through and said, 'Quite a place, hey, Nestor's-son?' Which was to say, among other things, Peisistratus was tagged and out of the game. Nothing for it then but to play the thing out in the usual way. 'No getting around it, boys,' I declared: 'I'm not the poorest Greek in town. But I leave it to Zeus whether what you've seen is worth its cost. Eight years I knocked about the world, picking up what I could and wishing I were dead. The things you see come from Cyprus, Phoenicia, Egypt, Ethiopia, Sidonia, Erembi—even Libya, where the lambs are born with horns on.'

" 'Born with horns on!'

"I did my thing then, told a story with everyone in it who might be the mystery guest and looked to see which name brought tears. 'While I was pirating around,' I said, 'my wife's sister murdered my brother on the grounds that she'd committed adultery for ten years straight with my cousin Aegisthus. Her son Orestes killed them both, bless his heart, but when I think of Agamemnon and the rest done in for Helen's sake, I'd swap two-thirds of what I've got to bring them back to life.'

"I looked for the stranger's tears through mine, but he only declared: 'Lucky Achilles' son, to come by such a treasure!'

" 'Yet the man I miss most,' I continued, 'is shifty Odysseus.'

" 'Oh?'

" 'Yes indeed,' I went on," I go on: " 'Now and then I wonder what became of him and old faithful Penelope and the boy Telemachus.'

" 'You know Telemachus?' asked Telemachus.

" 'I knew him once,' said I. 'Twenty years ago, when he was one, I laid him in a furrow for his dad to plow under, and thus odysseused Odysseus. What's more, I'd made up my mind if he got home alive to give him a town here in Argos to lord it over and leave to his son when he died. Odysseus and I, wouldn't we have run through the grapes and whoppers! Pity he never made it.'

"The boy wet his mantle properly then, and I thought:

'Hold tight, son of Atreus, and keep a sharp lookout.' While I
wondered what he might be after and how to keep him from
it, as I had of another two decades past, Herself came in with
her maids and needles, worst possible moment as ever.

" 'Why is it, Menelaus, you never tell me when a prince
comes calling? Good afternoon, Telemachus.'

"Oh, my gods, but she was lovely! Cute Hermione drew
princelings to Sparta like piss-ants to a peony-bud, but her
mother was the full-blown blossom, the blooming bush! Far
side of forty but never a wrinkle, and any two cuts of her
great gray eyes told more about love and Troy than our bard
in a night's hexameters. Her figure, too—but curse her figure! She opened her eyes and theirs, I shut mine, there was
the usual pause; then Telemachus got his wind back and
hollered: 'Payee-*sis*tratus! What country have we come to,
where the mares outrun the fillies?'

"Nestor's-son's face was ashen as his spear; ashener than
either the old taste in my mouth. If only Telemachus had
been so abashed! But he looked her over like young Heracles
the house of Thespius and said, 'Not even many-masked
Odysseus could disguise himself from Zeus's daughter. How
is it you know me?'

" 'You're your father's son,' Helen said. 'Odysseus asked
me that very question one night in Troy. He'd got himself up
as a beggar and slipped into town for the evening . . .'

" 'What for?' wanted to know Peisistratus.

" 'To spy, to spy,' Telemachus said.

" 'What else?' asked Helen. 'None knew him but me,
who'd have known him anywhere, and I said to my Trojan
friends: "Look, a new beggar in town. Wonder who he is?" But
no matter how I tried, I couldn't trick Odysseus into saying:
"Odysseus." ' '

" 'Excuse me, ma'am,' begged Peisistratus, disbrothered
by the war; 'what I don't understand is why you tried at all,
since he was on a dangerous mission in enemy territory.'

" 'Nestor's-son,' said I, 'you're your father's son.' But
Telemachus scolded him, asking how he hoped to have his
questions answered if he interrupted the tale by asking

them. Helen flashed him a look worth epics and said, 'When I got him alone in my apartment and washed and oiled and dressed him, I promised not to tell anyone he was Odysseus until he went back to his camp. So he told me all the Greek military secrets. Toward morning he killed several Trojans while they slept, and then I showed him the safest way out of town. There was a fuss among the new widows, but who cared? I was bored with Troy by that time and wished I'd never left home. I had a nice palace, a daughter, and Menelaus: what more could a woman ask?'

"After a moment Telemachus cried: 'Noble heart in a nobler breast! To think that all the while our side cursed you, you were secretly helping us!'

"When I opened my eyes I saw Peisistratus rubbing his, image of Gerenian Nestor. 'It still isn't clear to me,' he said, 'why the wife of Prince Paris—begging your pardon, sir; I mean as it were, of course—would wash, oil, and dress a vagrant beggar in her apartment in the middle of the night. I don't grasp either why you couldn't have slipped back to Lord Menelaus along with Odysseus, if that's what you wanted.'

"He had other questions too, shrewd lad, but Helen's eyes turned dark, and before I could swallow my wine Telemachus had him answered: 'What good could she have done the Argives then? She'd as well have stayed here in Sparta!' As for himself, he told Helen, next to hearing that his father was alive no news could've more delighted him than that the whole purpose of her elopement with Paris, as he was now convinced, was to spy for the Greeks from the heart of Troy, without which espionage we'd surely have been defeated. Helen counted her stitches and said, 'You give me too much credit.' 'No, by Zeus!' Telemachus declared. 'To leave your home and family and live for ten years with another man, purely for the sake of your home and family . . .'

" 'Nine with Paris,' Helen murmured, 'one with Deiphobus. Deiphobus was the better man, no doubt about it, but not half as handsome.'

" 'So much the nobler!' cried Telemachus.

" 'Nobler than you think,' I said, and poured myself and

Peisistratus another drink. 'My wife's too modest to tell the noblest things of all. In the first place, when I fetched her out of Troy at last and set sail for home, she was so ashamed of what she'd had to do to win the war for us that it took me seven years more to convince her she was worthy of me . . .'

" 'I kiss the hem of your robe!' Telemachus exclaimed to her and did.

" 'In the second place,' I said, 'she did all these things for our sake without ever going to Troy in the first place.'

" 'Really,' Helen protested.

" 'Excuse me, sir . . .' said presently Peisistratus.

" 'Wine's at your elbow,' I declared. 'Drink deep, boys; I'll tell you the tale.'

" 'That's not what Prince Telemachus wants,' Helen said.

" 'I know what Prince Telemachus wants.'

" 'He wants word of his father,' said she. 'If you must tell a story at this late hour, tell the one about Proteus on the beach at Pharos, what he said of Odysseus.'

" 'Do,' Peisistratus said.

" 'Hold on,' I said," I say: " 'It's all one tale.'

" 'Then tell it all,' said Helen. 'But excuse yours truly.'

" 'Don't go!' cried Telemachus.

" 'A lady has her modesty,' Helen said. 'I'll fill your cups, gentlemen, bid you good night, and retire. To the second—'

" 'Who put out the light?' asked Peisistratus.

" 'Wait!' cried Telemachus.

" 'Got you!' cried I, clutching hold of his cloak-hem. After an exchange of pleasantries we settled down and drank deep in the dark while I told the tale of Menelaus and his wife at sea:

3

" 'Seven years,' " I say et cetera, " 'the woman kept her legs crossed and the north wind blew without let-up, holding us from home. In the eighth, on the beach at Pharos, with Eidothea's help I tackled her dad the Old Man of the Sea and followed his tough instructions: heavy-hearted it back to Egypt, made my hecatombs, vowed my vows. At once then, wow, the wind changed, no time at all till we re-raised Pharos! Not a Proteus in sight, no Eidothea, just the boat I'd moored my wife in, per orders. Already she was making sail; her crew were putting in their oars; my first thought was, they're running off with Helen; we overhauled them; why was everybody grinning? But it was only joy, not to lose another minute; there was Helen herself by the mast-step, holding out her arms to me! Zeus knows how I poop-to-pooped it, maybe I was dreaming on the beach at Pharos, maybe am still; there I was anyhow, clambering aboard: "Way, boys!" I hollered. "Put your arse in it!" Spang! went the mainsail, breeze-bellied for Sparta; those were Helen's arms around me; it was wedding night! We hustled to the sternsheets, never mind who saw what; when she undid every oar went up; still we tore along the highways of the fish. "Got you!" I cried, couldn't see for the beauty of her, feel her yet, what is she anyhow? I decked her; only think, those gold limbs hadn't wound me in twenty years . . .'

" 'Twenty?' 'Counting two before the war. Call it nineteen.'

" ' "Wait," she bade me. "First tell me what Proteus said, and how you followed his advice."

" 'Our oars went down; we strained the sail with sighs; my tears thinned the wine-dark sea. But there was nothing for it, I did as bid:

4

" ' "Nothing for it but to do as Eidothea'd bid me," ' " I say to myself I told Telemachus I sighed to Helen.

" ' "Eidothea?"

" ' "Old Man of the Sea's young daughter, so she said," said I. "With three of my crew I dug in on the beach at sunrise; she wrapped us in seal-calfskins. 'Hold tight to these,' she told us. 'Who can hug a stinking sea-beast?' I inquired.

She said, 'Father. Try ambrosia; he won't get here till noon.' She put it under our noses and dived off as usual; we were high in no time; 'These seals,' my men agreed: 'the longer you're out here the whiter they get.' They snuggled in and lost themselves in dreams; I would've too, but grateful as I was, when she passed the ambrosia I smelled a trick. Hang around Odysseus long enough, you trust nobody. I'd take a sniff and put the stuff away till the seal stink got to me, then sniff again. Even so I nearly lost my grip. Was I back in the horse? Was I dreaming of Helen on my bachelor throne?"

" ' "Hold on," said deckèd Helen; I came to myself, saw I was blubbering; "I came to myself, saw I was beached at Pharos. Come shadeless noon, unless I dreamed it, the sea-cow harem flipped from the deep to snooze on the foreshore, give me a woman anytime. Old Proteus came after, no accounting for tastes, counted them over, counting us in, old age is hard on the eyes too; then he outstretched in the cavemouth, one snore and I jumped him.

" ' " 'Got you!' I cried" I cried' I cried" I cry. " ' "My companions, when I hollered, grabbed hold too: one snatched his beard, one his hands, one his long, white hair; I tackled his legs and held fast. First he changed into a lion, ate the beard-man, what a mess; then snake, bit the hair-chap, who'd nothing to hold onto." ' '

" 'Neither did the hand-man,' observed Peisistratus, sleepless critic, to whom I explained for Telemachus's sake as well that while the erstwhile hand-man, latterly paw-man, had admittedly been vulnerably under both lion and snake, and the hair- then mane-man relatively safely on top, the former had escaped the former by reason of the quondam beard-man's fortunate, for the quondam paw-man, interposition; the latter fallen prey to the latter by reason of the latter's unfortunate, for the quondam mane-man, proclivity to strike whatever was before him—which would have been to say, before, the hand-paw-man, but was to say, now, which is to say, then, the beard-mane-man, thanks so to speak to the serpent's windings upon itself.

" 'Ah.'

" ' "To clutch the leopard Proteus turned into then, then, were only myself and the unhandled hand-man, paw- once more but shielded now by neither beard- nor mane- and so promptly chomped, what a mess. I'd have got mine too, leopards are flexible, but by the time he'd made lunch of my companions he'd become a boar . . ."

" ' "Ah."

" ' "Which bristle as he might couldn't tusk his own tail, whereto I clung."

" ' "Not his hindpaws? I thought you were the foot-paw—" '

" ' 'Just what I was about to—'

" ' "Proteus to lion, feet into hindpaws," I answered,' I answered. ' "Lion to snake, paws into tail. Snake to leopard, tail into tail and hindpaws both; my good luck I went tail to tail."

" ' "Leopard to boar?"

" ' "Long tail to short, too short to tusk. Then the trouble started." (?)

" ' "!"
" '!'
" '!'
}

"I replied to them: ' "A beast's a beast," I replied to her. "If you've got the right handle all you do's hang on . . ." ' "

. " ' "It was when the Old Man of the Sea turned into salt water I began to sweat. Try holding an armful of ocean! I did my best, hugged a puddle on the beach, but plenty soaked in, plenty more ran seaward, where I saw you bathing, worst possible moment, not that you knew . . ." '

" '?'
" '?' [?]
}

" 'It's Helen I'm telling, northing in our love-clutch on the poop. "I needed a bath," she said; "I a drink," said I; "for all I knew you might be Proteus all over, dirty Old Man of the Sea. Even when my puddle turned into a bigbole leafy tree I wasn't easy; who said he couldn't be two things at once? There I lay, philodendron, hour after hour, while up in the limbs a cuckoo sang . . ." ' "

My problem was, I'd too much imagination to be a hero.
" ' "My problem was, I'd leisure to think. My time was mortal,

Proteus's im-; what if he merely treed it a season or two till I let go? What was it anyhow I held? If Proteus once was Old Man of the Sea and now Proteus was a tree, then Proteus was neither, only Proteus; what I held were dreams. But if a real Old Man of the Sea had really been succeeded by real water and the rest, then the dream was Proteus. And Menelaus! For I changed too as the long day passed: changed my mind, replaced myself, grew older. How hold on until the 'old' (which is to say the young) Menelaus rebecame himself? Eidothea forgot to say! How could I anyhow know that that sea-nymph wasn't Proteus in yet another guise, her counsel a ruse to bind me forever while he sported with Helen?" '

" 'What *was* her counsel, exactly?'

" 'Peisistratus, is it? Helen's question, exactly: "What *was* her counsel, exactly?" And "How'd you persuade her to trick her own dad?" "Everything in its place," I said,' I said. ' "Your question was Proteus's, exactly; as I answered when he asked, I'll answer when he asks."

" ' "Hard tale to hold onto, this," declared my poopèd spouse.' Odysseus'- or Nestor's-son agreed." I agree. But what out-wandering hero ever journeyed a short straight line, arrived at his beginning till the end? " ' "Harder yet to hold onto Proteus. I must have dozed as I mused and fretted, thought myself yet again enhorsed or bridal-chambered, same old dream, woke up clutching nothing. It was late. I was rooted with fatigue. I held on." (' ') "To?" (' ') "Nothing. You were back on deck, the afternoon sank, I heard sailors guffawing, shorebirds cackled, the sun set grinning in the winish sea, still I held on, saying of and to me: 'Menelaus is a fool, mortal hugging immortality. Men laugh, the gods mock, he's chimaera, a hornèd gull. What is it he clutches? Why can't he let go? What trick have you played him, Eidothea, a stranger in your country?' I might've quit, but my cursèd fancy whispered: 'Proteus has turned into the air. Or else . . .' " " ' "

Hold onto yourself, Menelaus.

" ' "Long time my shingled arms made omicron. Tides lapped in and kelped me; fishlets kissed my heels; terns dunged me white; spatted and musseled, beflied, befleaed, I might have been what now in the last light I saw me to be holding, a marine old man, same's I'd seized only dimmer.

" ' " 'You've got me, son of Atreus,' he said, unless I said it myself."

"(((("Me too.")))')

" ' " 'And I'll keep you,' I said, 'till I have what I want.' He asked me what that was," as did Helen,' and Telemachus. ' " 'You know without my telling you,' " ' I told them. ' "Then he offered to tell all if I'd let him go, I to let him go when he'd told me all. 'Foolish mortal!' he said, they speak that way, 'What gives you to think you're Menelaus holding the Old Man of the Sea? Why shouldn't Proteus turn into Menelaus, and into Menelaus holding Proteus? But let that go . . .' " ' " Never. " ' " 'We seers see fore and aft, but not amidships. I know what you've been and will be; how is it you're here? What god teaches men to godsnatch?'

" ' " 'It's not a short story,' I warned him." '

" 'I don't see why it needed telling,' Peisistratus declared. 'If a seer sees past and future he sees everything, the present being without duration et cetera. Or if his clairvoyance is relative, shading into darkness as it nears the Now from the bright far Heretofore and far clear Hereafter, even so there's nothing he needn't know.' 'Oh?' 'Today, say, he knows tomorrow and yesterday; then yesterday he knew today, as he'll know it tomorrow. Now to know the past is to know too what one once knew, to know the future to know what one will know. But in the case of seers, what one once knew includes the then future which is now the present; what one will know, the then past which ditto. From all which it follows as the future from the present, the present from the past, that from him from whom neither past nor future can hide, the present cannot either. It wasn't you who deceived Proteus, but Proteus you.' "

I tell it as it was. "Long time we sat in the dark and sleepful hall: hem-holding Menelaus, drowseless Nestor's-son, Telemachus perhaps. When windy Orion raised his leg over Lacedemon I put by groan and goblet saying, 'I tell it as it is. Long time I wondered who was the fooler, who fool, how much of what was news to whom; still pinning Helen to the pitchy poop I said, "When shifty Proteus vowed he had all time to listen in, from a leaden heart I cried: 'When will I reach my goal through its cloaks of story? How many veils to naked Helen?'

" ' " 'I know how it is,' said Proteus. 'Yet tell me what I wish; then I'll tell you what you will.' Nothing for it but rehearse the tale of me and slippery Eidothea:

5

" ' " 'Troy was clinkered; Priam's stones were still too warm to touch; the loot was depoted on the beach for share-out; Trojan ladies keened and huddled, eyed us with shivers, waiting to be boarded and rode down the tear-salt sea. We were ten years out; ten days more would see our plunder portioned, our dead sent up, good-trip hecatombs laid on the immortal gods. But I was mad with shame and passion for my salvaged wife; though curses Greek and Trojan showered on us like spears on Scamander-plain or the ash of heroes on our decks, I fetched her to my ship unstuck, stowed her below, made straight for home.

" ' " ' "Hecatombs to Athena!" Odysseus cried after us.

" ' " ' "Cushion your thwarts with Troy-girls!" Agamemnon called, dragging pale Cassandra—' "

" ' "Bitch! Bitch!"

" ' " ' —by her long black hair. To forestall a mutiny I hollered back, they could keep half my loot for themselves if they'd ship the rest home for me to emprince my loyal crew with. As for me, all my concubines and treasure waited below, tapping her foot. Wise Nestor alone sailed with me, who as Supervisor of Spoils had loaded first; last thing I saw astern was shrewd Odysseus scratching his head, my brother crotch; then Troy sank in the purpled east; with a shake-plain shout, I'm good at those, I dived below to reclaim my wife.

" ' " 'Call it weakness if you dare: unlike the generality of men I take small joy in lording women. Helen's epic heat had charcoaled Troy and sent ten thousand down to Hades; I ought to've spitted her like a heifer on her Trojan hearth. But I hadn't, and the hour was gone to poll horns with the vengeful sword. I thought therefore to knock her about a bit and then take at last what had cost such a fearful price, perhaps vilifying her, within measure, the while. But when I beheld her—sitting cross-legged in the stern, cleaning long fingernails with a bodkin and pouting at the frames and strakes—I forebore, resolved to accept in lieu of her death a modest portion of heartfelt grovel. Further, once she'd flung herself at my knees and kissed my hem I would order her supine and mount more as one who loves than one who conquers; not impossibly, should she acquit herself well and often, I would even entertain a plea for her eventual forgiveness and restoration to the Atrean house. Accordingly I drew myself up to discharge her abjection—whereupon she gave over cleaning her nails and set to drumming them on one knee.

" ' " ' "Let your repentance salt my shoeleather," I said presently, "and then, as I lately sheathed my blade of anger, so sheathe you my blade of love."

" ' " ' "I only just came aboard," she replied. "I haven't unpacked yet."

" ' " 'With a roar I went up the companionway, dashed stern to stem, close-hauled the main, flogged the smile from my navigator, and clove us through the pastures of the squid. Leagues thereafter, when the moon changed phase, I overtook myself, determined shrewdly that her Troy-chests were secured, and vowing this time to grant the trull no quarter, at the second watch of night burst into her cubby and forgave her straight out. "Of the unspeakable we'll speak no further," I declared. "I here extend to you what no other in my position would: my outright pardon." To which, some moments after, I briskly appended: "Disrobe and receive it, for the sake of pity! This offer won't stand forever." There I had her; she yawned and responded: "It's late. I'm tired."

" ' " 'Up the mast half a dozen times I stormed and shinnied, took oar to my navigator, lost sight of Nestor, thundered

and lightninged through Poseidon's finny fief. When next I
came to season, I stood a night slyly by while she dusk-to-
dawned it, then saluted with this challenge her opening eyes:
"Man born of woman is imperfect. On the three thousand two
hundred eighty-seventh night of your Parisian affair, as I lay
in Simois-mud picking vermin off the wound I'd got that day
from cunning Pandarus, exhaustion closed my eyes. I
dreamed myself was pretty Paris, plucked by Aphrodite from
the field and dropped into Helen's naked lap. There we committed sweet adultery; I woke wet, wept . . ."

" ' " 'Here I paused in my fiction to shield my eyes and
stanch the arrow-straight tracks clawed down my cheek.
Then, as one who'd waited precisely for her maledict voice to
hoarsen, I outshouted her in these terms: "Therefore come to
bed my equal, uncursing, uncursed!"

" ' " 'The victory was mine, I still believe, but when I made
to take trophy, winded Helen shook her head, declaring: "I
have the curse."

" ' " 'My taffrail oaths shook Triton's stamp-ground; I fed
to the fish my navigator, knocked my head against the mast
and others; hollered up a gale that blew us from Laconic
Malea to Egypt. My crew grew restive; when the storm was
spent and I had done flogging me with halyards, I chose a
moment somewhere off snakèd Libya, slipped my cloak,
rapped at Helen's cabin, and in measured tones declared:
"Forgive me." Adding firmly: "Are you there?"

" ' " ' "Seasick," she admitted. "Throwing up." To my just
query, why she repaid in so close-kneed coin my failure to
butcher her in Troy, she answered—'

" ' " 'Let me guess,' requested Proteus."

" ' "What I said in Troy," said offshore Helen. "What I say
to you now." '

" 'Whatever was that?' pressed Peisistratus."

"Hold on, hold on yet awhile, Menelaus," I advise.
I'm not the man I used to be.

" ' " 'Thus inspired I went a-princing and a-pirate. Seven
years the north wind nailed us to Africa, while Helen held
fast the door of love. We sailed no plotted course, but supped

random in the courts of kings, sacked and sight-saw, ballasted our tender keel with bullion. The crew chose wives from among themselves, give me a woman anytime, had affairs with ewes, committed crimes of passion over fids and tholes. None of us grew younger. The eighth year fetched us here to Pharos, rich sea-quirks, mutinous, strange. How much does a man need? We commenced to starve. Yesterday I strolled up the beach to fish, my head full of north-wind; I squatted on a rushy dune, fetched out my knife, considered whether to slice my parchèd throat or ditto cod. Then before me in the surf, a sudden skinny-dipper! Cock and gullet paused on edge; Beauty stepped from the sea-foam; long time I regarded hairless limb, odd globy breast, uncalloused ham. Where was the fellow's sex? A fairer yeoman I'd not beheld; who'd untooled him? As as his king and skipper I decided to have at him before myself, it occurred to me he was a woman.

" ' " 'Memory, easy-weakened, dies hard. From its laxy clutch I fetched my bride's dim image. True, her hair was gold, the one before me's green, and this was finned where that was toed; but the equal number and like placement of their breasts, congruence of their shames' geometry—too miraculous for chance! She was Helen gone a-surfing, or Aphrodite in Helen's form. With a clench-tooth wrench I recollected what a man was for, vowed to take her without preamble or petition, then open my throat. Better, as I knew my wife no weakling, but accurate of foot and sharp of toe, I hit upon a ruse to have her without loss of face or testicle, and cursed me I hadn't dreamed it up years past: as Zeus is wont to take mortal women in semblance of their husbands, I would feign Zeus in Menelaus' guise! Up tunic, down I sprang, aflop with recommissioned maleship. "Is it Helen's spouse about to prince me," my victim inquired, "or some god in his fair-haired form? A lady wants to know her undoer. My own name," she went on, and I couldn't.

" ' " ' "Eidothea's the name," she went on: "daughter of Proteus, he whose salt hands hold the key to wind and wife. You won't reach your goals till you've mastered Dad. My role in your suspended tale is merely to offer seven pieces of ad-

vice. Don't ask why. Let go of my sleeve, please. Don't mistake the key for the treasure. But before I go on," she went on,' " " "
and I can't.

    " ' " ' "But before I go on," she went on, "say first how it was at the last in Troy, what passed between you and Helen as the city fell. . . ." ' " '

"Come on. 'Come on. "Come on. 'Come on. "Come on," Eidothea urged: *In the horse's woody bowel we groaned and grunt* . . . Why do you weep?" ' " ' "

6

Respite.

    " ' " ' "In the horse's bowel," ' " ' " I groan, " ' " ' "we grunt till midnight, Laocoön's spear still stuck in our gut . . ." ' "
"Hold up," said Helen; " 'Off,' said Proteus; "On," said his web-foot daughter.' " You see what my spot was, boys! Caught between blunt Beauty's, fishy Form's, and dark-mouth Truth's imperatives, arms trembling, knees raw from rugless poop and rugged cave, I tried to hold fast to layered sense by listening as it were to Helen hearing Proteus hearing Eidothea hearing me; critic within critic, nestled in my slipping grip . . .'

    " 'May be,' Peisistratus suggested, 'you can trick the tale out against all odds by the following device: to Eidothea, let us say, you said: "Show me how to trap the old boy into prophecy!"; to Proteus, perhaps, for reasons of strategy, you declare: "I begged then of your daughter as Odysseus Nausicaa: 'Teach me, lady, how best to honor windshift aid from your noble sire' "; to Helen-on-the-poop, perhaps, you tell it: "I then declared to Proteus: 'I then besought your daughter: "Help me to learn from your immortal dad how to replease my heartslove Helen." ' " But to us you may say with fearless truth: "I said to Eidothea: 'Show me how to fool your father!' " '

    "But I asked myself," I remind me: " 'Who is Peisistratus to trust with unrefracted fact?' 'Did Odysseus really speak those words to Nausicaa?' I asked him. 'Why doesn't Telemachus snatch that news? And how is it you know of fair Nausicaa, when Proteus on the beach at Pharos hasn't mentioned her to me yet? Doesn't it occur to you, faced with this and similar discrepancy, that it's you I might be yarning?' as I yarn myself," whoever that is. " 'Menelaus! Proteus! Helen! For all we know, we're but stranded figures in Penelope's web, wove up in light to be unwove in darkness.' So snarling him, I caught the clew of my raveled fabrication:

" ' "What's going on?" Helen demanded.

" ' " 'Son of Atreus!' Proteus cried. 'Don't imagine I didn't hear what your wife will demand of you some weeks hence, when you will have returned from Egypt, made sail for home, and floored her with the tale of snatching yours truly on the beach! Don't misbehave yesterday, I warn you! We seers—'

" ' " ' "My next advice," Eidothea advised me, "is to take nonhuman form. Seal yourself tight." How is it, by the way,' I demanded of Proteus, 'You demand what you demand of me in Menelaus's voice, and through my mouth, as though I demanded it of myself?' For so it was from that moment on; I speeched his speeches, even as you hear me speak them now." "Never mind that!" ' 'Who was it said "Never mind!"?' asked Peisistratus. 'Your wife? Eidothea? Tricky Proteus? The voice is yours; whose are the words?' 'Never mind.' 'Could it be, could it have been, that Proteus changed from a leafy tree not into air but into Menelaus on the beach at Pharos, thence into Menelaus holding the Old Man of the Sea? Could it even be that all these speakers you give voice to—' " "Never mind," I say.

No matter. " ' " ' "Disenhorsed at last," I declared to scalèd Eidothea, "we found ourselves in the sleep-soaked heart of Troy. Each set about his appointed task, some murdering sentries, others opening gates, others yet killing Trojans in their cups and lighting torches from the beacon-fire to burn the city. But I made straight for Helen's apartment with Odysseus, who'd shrewdly reminded me of her liking for lamplit love." ' " '

" 'How—'

" 'Did I know which room was hers? Because only two lights burned in Troy, one fired as a beacon on Achilles' tomb by Sinon the faithful traitor, the other flickering from an upper chamber in the house of Deiphobus. It was by ranging one above the other Agamemnon returned the fleet to Troy, but I steered me by the adulterous fire alone, kindling therefrom as I came the torch of vengeance.

" ' " ' "Why—"

" ' " ' "Did Odysseus come too? Thank Zeus he did! For so enraged was Deiphobus at being overhauled at passion's peak, he fought like ten." ' "

" ' "Not only fought—" " ' "But I matched him, I matched him," I pressed on, "all the while watching for my chance to sink sword in Helen, who rose up sheeted in her deadly beauty and cowered by the bedpost, dagger-handed. Long time we grappled—" '

" ' " 'I'm concerned about my daughter's what- and whereabouts,' Proteus said—" '

" 'Could it be,' wondered Peisistratus, in whose name I pledged an ox to the critic muse, 'Eidothea is Proteus in disguise, prearranging his own capture on the beach for purposes unfathomable to mortals? And how did those lovers lay hands on arms in bed? What I mean—'

" ' "Dagger I had," said Helen, "under my pillow; and Deiphobus always came to bed with a sword on. But I never cowered; it was the sheet kept slipping, my only cover—"

" ' " ' " 'Take it off!' cried subtle Odysseus. Long time his strategy escaped me, I fought Deiphobus to a bloody draw. At length with a whisk my loyal friend himself halfstaffed her. Our swords were up; for a moment we stood as if Medusa'd. Then, at the same instant, Deiphobus and I dived at our wife, Odysseus leaped up from where he knelt before her with the sheet, Helen's dagger came down, and the ghost of her latest lover squeaked off to join his likes." ' " '

" 'Her latest lover!' Peisistratus exclaimed. 'Do you mean to say—'

" ' "That's right," Helen said. "I killed him myself, a better man than most."

" ' " ' "Then Odysseus—" began Eidothea.

" ' " ' "Then Odysseus disappeared, and I was alone with topless Helen. My sword still stood to lop her as she bent over Deiphobus. When he was done dying she rose and with one hand (the other held her waisted sheet) cupped her breast for swording." ' "

" ' "I dare you!" Helen dared.'

" 'Which Helen?' cried Peisistratus.

"I hesitated . . . 'The moment passed . . . " 'My wife smiled shyly . . . "My sword went down. I closed my eyes, not to see that fountain beauty; clutched at it, not to let her flee. 'You've lost weight, Menelaus,' she said. 'Prepare to die,' I advised her. She softly hung her head . . ." ' " '

" 'How could you tell, sir, if your eyes—'

" ' " ' "My next advice," said Eidothea,' " ' interrupting once again Peisistratus . . ."

Respite.

" ' " ' "I touched my blade to the goddess breast I grasped, and sailed before my flagging ire the navy of her offenses. Merely to've told prior to sticking her the names and skippers of the ships she'd sunk would've been to stretch her life into the menopause; therefore I spent no wind on items; simply I demanded before I killed her: 'With your last breath tell me: Why?' " ' " '

" '(" (((("What?")))') (")'

" ' " ' " 'Why?' I repeated," I repeated,' I repeated," I repeated,' I repeated," I repeat. " ' " ' "And the woman, with a bride-shy smile and hushèd voice, replied: 'Why what?'

" ' " ' "Faster than Athena sealed beneath missile Sicily upstart Enceladus, Poseidon Nisyros mutine Polybutes, I sealed my would-widen eyes; snugger than Porces Laocoön, Heracles Antaeus, I held to my point interrogative Helen, to whom as about us combusted nightlong Ilion I rehearsed our history horse to horse, driving at last as eveningly myself to the seed and omphalos of all. . . ."(?((?((((?))))))

7

" ' " ' " 'By Zeus out of Leda,' I commenced, as though I weren't Menelaus, Helen Helen, 'egg-born Helen was a beauty desired by all men on earth. When Tyndareus declared she might wed whom she chose, every bachelor-prince in the peninsula camped on her stoop. Odysseus was there, mighty Ajax, Athenian Menestheus, cunning Diomedes: men great of arm, heart, wit, fame, purse; fit mates for the fairest. Menelaus alone paid the maid no court, though his brother Agamemnon, wed already to her fatal sister, sued for form's sake on his behalf. Less clever than Odysseus, fierce than Achilles, muscled than either Ajax, Menelaus excelled in no particular unless the doggedness with which he clung to the dream of embracing despite all Helen. He knew who others were—Odysseus resourceful, great Great Ajax, and the rest. Who was he? Whose eyes, at the wedding of Agamemnon and Clytemnestra, had laid hold of bridesmaid Helen's image and never since let go? While others wooed he brooded, played at princing, grappled idly with the truth that those within his imagination's grasp—which was to say, everyone but Menelaus—seemed to him finally imaginary, and he alone, ungraspable, real.

 " ' " ' " 'Imagine what he felt, then, when news reached him one spring forenoon that of all the men in Greece, hatchèd Helen had chosen him! Despite the bright hour he was asleep, dreaming as always of that faultless form; his brother's messenger strode in, bestowed without a word the wreath of Helen's choice, withdrew. Menelaus held shut his eyes and clung to the dream—which however for the first time slipped his grip. Dismayed, he woke to find his brow now fraught with the crown of love.' " ' " '

" 'Ah.'

" ' " ' " 'In terror he applied to the messenger: "Menelaus? Menelaus? Why of all princes Menelaus?" And the fellow answered: "Don't ask me."

" ' " ' " 'Then imagine what he felt in Tyndareus's court, pledge-horse disjoint and ready to be sworn on, his beaten betters gruntling about, when he traded Agamemnon the same question for ditto answer. Sly Odysseus held the princes to their pledge; all stood on the membered horse while Menelaus played the grateful winner, modest in election, wondering as he thanked: Could he play the lover too? Who was it wondered? Who is it asks?

" ' " ' " 'Imagine then what he felt on the nuptial night, when feast and sacrifice were done, carousers gone, and he faced his bedaydreamed in the waking flesh! Dreamisher yet, she'd betrothed him wordless, wordless wed; now without a word she led him to her chamber, let go her gold gown, stood golder before him. Not to die of her beauty he shut his eyes; of not beholding her embraced her. Imagine what he felt then!' " ' " '

" 'Two questions,' interjected Peisistratus—

" 'One! One! " ' " 'There the bedstead stood; as he swooning tipped her to it his throat croaked "Why?" ' "

" ' " ' "Why?" asked Eidothea.'

" ' " 'Why why?' Proteus echoed." '

" 'My own questions,' Peisistratus insisted, 'had to do with mannered rhetoric and your shift of narrative viewpoint.'

" ' " 'Ignore that fool!' Proteus ordered from the beach." '

" 'How can Proteus—' 'Seer.' 'So.' 'The opinions echoed in these speeches aren't necessarily the speaker's.

" ' " ' " ' "Why'd you wed me?" Menelaus asked his wife,' I told my wife. ' "Less crafty than Diomedes, artful than Teucer, et cetera?" She placed on her left breast his right hand.

" ' " ' " ' "Why me?" he cried again. "Less lipless than Achilles, et cetera!" The way she put on her other his other would have fired a stone.

" " " " " " "Speak!" he commanded. She whispered: "Love."

" ' " ' " 'Unimaginable notion! He was fetched up short. How could Helen love a man less gooded than Philoctetes, et cetera, and whom besides she'd glimpsed but once prior to wedding and not spoken to till that hour? But she'd say no more; the harder he pressed the cooler she turned, who'd been ardor itself till he put his query. He therefore forebore, but curiosity undid him; how could he know her and not know how he knew?' " '

" ' " 'Come to the point!'

" ' " ' "Hold on!"

" ' " ' " 'He held her fast; she took him willy-nilly to her; I feel her yet, one endless instant, Menelaus was no more, never has been since. In his red ear then she whispered: "Why'd I wed you, less what than who, et cetera?" ' " ' "

" ' "My very question."

" ' " ' " ' "Speak!" Menelaus cried to Helen on the bridal bed,' I reminded Helen in her Trojan bedroom," I confessed to Eidothea on the beach,' I declared to Proteus in the cavemouth," I vouchsafed to Helen on the ship,' I told Peisistratus at least in my Spartan hall," I say to whoever and where- I am. And Helen answered:

" ' " ' " ' "Love!" ' " ' " ' "

!

" ' " ' " 'He complied, he complied, as to an order. She took his corse once more to Elysium, to fade forever among the faceless asphodel; his curious fancy alone remained unlaid; when he came to himself it still asked softly: "Why?" ' " ' " ' " "

And don't I cry out to me every hour since, "Be sure you demanded of Peisistratus (and Telemachus), 'Didn't I exclaim to salvaged Helen, "Believe me that I here queried Proteus, 'Won't you ask of Eidothea herself whether or not I shouted at her, "Sheathed were my eyes, unsheathed my sword what time I challenged Troy-lit Helen, 'Think you not that Menelaus and his bride as one cried, *Love!*"?'"?'"?'"?'"?

" ' " ' " 'So the night went, and the days and nights: sex

and riddles. She burned him up, he played husband till he wasted, only his voice still diddled: "Why?" ' "

" ' " ' "What a question!" ' " '

" 'What's the answer?'

" ' " ' " 'Seven years of this, more or less, not much conversation, something wrong with the marriage. Helen he could hold; how hold Menelaus? To love is easy; to be loved, as if one were real, on the order of others: fearsome mystery! Unbearable responsibility! To her, *Menelaus* signified something recognizable, as *Helen* him. Whatever was it? They begot a child . . .' " ' "

" ' "I beg your pardon," Helen interrupted from the poop a quarter-century later. "Father Zeus got Hermione on me, disguised as you. That's the way he is, as everyone knows; there's no use pouting or pretending . . ."

" 'I begged her pardon, but insisted, as in Troy: " ' " 'It wasn't Zeus disguised as Menelaus who begot her, any more than Menelaus disguised as Zeus; it was Menelaus disguised as Menelaus, a mask masking less and less. Husband, father, lord, and host he played, grip slipping; he could imagine anyone loved, no accounting for tastes, but his cipher self. In his cups he asked on the sly their house guests: "Why'd she wed me, less horsed than Diomedes, et cetera?" None said. A night came when this misdoubt stayed him from her bed. Another . . .' " ' " ' "

Respite. I beg your pardon.

" ' " ' " 'Presently she asked him: et cetera. If only she'd declared, "Menelaus, I wed you because, of all the gilt clowns of my acquaintance, I judged you least likely to distract me from my lovers, of whom I've maintained a continuous and overlapping series since before we met." Wouldn't that have cleared the Lacedemonian air! In a rage of shame he'd've burned up the bed with her! Or had she said: "I truly am fond of you, Menelaus; would've wed no other. What one seeks in the husband way is a good provider, gentle companion, fit father for one's children whoever their sire—a blend in brief of brother, daddy, pal. What one doesn't wish are the traits of one's lovers, exciting by night, impossible by day: I mean peremptory desire, unexpectedness, rough play, high-pitched emotions of every sort. Of these, happily, you're free." Wouldn't that have stoked and drafted him! But "Love!" What was a man to do?'

" "(("((("((" 'Well . . .' ")))")))"")'

" ' " ' " 'He asked Prince Paris—' 'You didn't!' " "By Zeus!" ' 'By Zeus!" ' "You didn't!" ' 'Did you really?' " "By Zeus," I tell me I told all except pointed Helen, "I did.

" ' " ' " 'By Zeus,' I told pointed Helen, 'he did. Oh, he knew the wretch was eyes and hands for Helen; he wasn't blind; eight days they'd feasted him since he'd dropped in uninvited, all which while he'd hot-eyed the hostess, drunk from her goblet, teased out winy missives on the table top. On the ninth she begged Menelaus to turn him from the palace. But he confessed,' I confessed," I confessed,' I confessed," et cetera, " ' " 'he liked the scoundrel after all . . .' " ' " '

" 'Zeus! Zeus!'

" ' " ' " 'Young, rich, handsome he was, King Priam's son; a charmer, easy in the world . . .' " ' "

" ' "Don't remind us!"

" ' " ' "One night Helen went early to her chamber, second on one's left et cetera, and the two men drank alone. Menelaus watched Paris watch her go and abruptly put his question, how it was that one less this than that had been the other, and what might be the import of his wife's reply. "A proper mystery," Paris agreed; "you say the one thing she says is what?" Menelaus pointed to the word his nemesis, by Paris idly drawn at dinner in red Sardonic.

" ' " ' " ' "Consult an oracle," Paris advised. "There's a good one at Delphi." "I'm off to Crete," Menelaus told breakfast Helen. "Grandfather died. Catreus. Take care of things."

" ' " ' " ' "Love!" she pled, tearing wide her gown. Menelaus clapped shut his eyes and ears, ran for the north.' " ' " '

" 'North to Crete?' 'Delphi, Delphi, " ' " 'where he asked the oracle: "Why et cetera?" and was told: *No other can as well espouse her.*"

" ' " ' " ' " "How now!" Menelaus cried,' I ditto," et cetera " ' "Espouse? Espouse her? As lover? Advocate? Husband? Can't you speak more plainly? Who am I?"

" ' " ' " ' "   " ' " ' " ' "

. . .
" ' " ' " 'Post-haste he returned to Lacedemon, done with questions. He'd re-embrace his terrifying chooser, clasp her past speech, never let go, frig understanding; it would be bride-night, endless; their tale would rebegin. "Menelaus here!" His shout shook the wifeless hall.

7

" ' " ' " 'Odysseus outsmarted, unsmocked Achilles, mustered Agamemnon—all said: "Let her go." Said Menelaus: "Can't." What did he feel? Epic perplexity. That she'd left him for Paris wasn't the point. War not love. Ten years he played outraged spouse, clung ireful-limpetlike to Priam's west curtain, warwhooped the field of Ares. Never mind her promenading the bartizans arm in arm with her Troyish sport; no matter his seeing summerly her belly fill with love-tot. Curiosity was his passion, that too grew mild. When at last in the war's ninth year he faced Paris in single combat, it was purely for the sake of form. "I don't ask why she went with you," he paused to say. "But tell me, as I spear you: did Helen ever mention, while you clipped and tumbled, how she happened to choose me in the first place?" Paris grinned and whispered through his shivers: "Love." Aphrodite whisked him from the door of death; no smarterly than that old word did smirking Pandarus pierce Menelaus's side. War resumed.
" ' " ' " 'Came dark-horse-night; Paris dead, it was with her new mate Deiphobus Helen sallied forth to mock. When she had done playing each Greek's Mrs., in her own voice she called: "Are you there, Menelaus? Then hear this: the night you left me I left you, sailed off with Paris and your wealth.

At our first berthing I became his passion's harbor; to Aphrodite the Uniter we raised shrines. I was princess of desire, he prince; from Greece to Egypt, Egypt Troy, our love wore out the rowing-benches. By charms and potions I kept his passion nine years firm, made all Troy and its beleaguerers burn for me. Pederast Achilles pronged me in his dreams; before killed Paris cooled, hot Deiphobus climbed into his place: he who, roused by this wooden ruse, stone-horses your Helen even as she speaks. To whom did slick Odysseus not long since slip, and whisper all the while he wooed dirty Greek, welcome to my Troy-cloyed ear? Down, godlike Deiphobus! Ah!"

" ' " ' " 'Heart-burst, Menelaus had cracked with woe the Epeian barrel and his own, had not far-sight Odysseus caulked and coopered him, saying: "The whore played Clytemnestra's part and my Penelope's; now she plays Helen." So they sat in silence, murderous, until the gods who smile on Troy wearied of this game and rechambered the lovers. Then Odysseus unpalmed the mouth of Menelaus and declared: "She must die." Menelaus spat. "Stick her yourself," went on the Ithacan: "play the man."

" ' " ' " 'The death-horse dunged the town with Greeks; Menelaus ground his teeth, drew sword, changed point of view. Taking his wrongèd part, I invite one word before I cut your perfect throat. What did the lieless oracle intend? Why'd you you-know-what ditto-whom et cetera?'

6

" ' " ' "Replied my wife in a huskish whisper: 'You know why.'

" ' " ' "I chucked my sword, she hooked her gown, I fetched her shipward through the fire and curses, she crossed her legs, here I weep on the beach at Pharos, I wish I were dead, what'd you say your name was?"

5

" ' " 'Said Eidothea: "Eidothea." I hemmed, I hawed; "I'm not the man," I remarked, "I was." Shoulders shrugged. "I've advised disguise," she said. "If you find your falseface stinks, I advise ambrosia. My sixth advice is, not too much ambrosia; my seventh—" Frantic I recounted, lost track, where was I? "—ditto masks: when the hour's ripe, unhide yourself and jump." Her grabbèd dad, she declared, would turn first into animals, then into plants and wine-dark sea, then into no saying what. Let I go I'd be stuck forever; otherwise he'd return into Proteus and tell me what I craved to hear.

" ' " ' "Hang on," she said; "that's the main thing." I asked her wherefor her septuple aid; she only smiled, I hate that about women, paddled off. This noon, then, helped by her sealskins and deodorant, I jumped you. There you are. But you must have known all this already.'

4

" ' "Said Proteus in my voice: 'Never mind know. Loose me now, man, and I'll say what stands between you and your desire.' He talks that way. I wouldn't; he declared I had one virtue only, the snap-turtle's, who will beak fast though his head be severed. By way of preface to his lesson then, he broke my heart with news reports: how Agamemnon, Idomeneus, Diomedes were cuckolded by pacifists and serving-men; how Clytemnestra not only horned but axed my brother; how faithless Penelope, hearing Odysseus had slept a year with Circe, seven with Calypso, dishonored him by giving herself to all one hundred eight of her suitors, plus nine house-servants, Phemius the bard, and Melanthius the goat-herd . . ." '

" 'What's this?' cried Peisistratus. 'Telemachus swears they've had no word since he sailed from Troy!' 'Prophets get their tenses mixed,' I replied; 'not impossibly it's now that Mrs. Odysseus goes the rounds, while her son's away. But I think he knows what a tangled web his mother weaves; otherwise he'd not sit silent, but call me and Proteus false or run for Ithaca.' There I had him, someone; on with the story. 'On with the story. " 'On with the story,' I said to Proteus: 'Why can't I get off this beach, let go, go home again? I'm tired of holding Zeus knows what; the mussels on my legs are barnacled; my arms and mind have gone to sleep; our beards have grown together; your words, fishy as your breath, come from my mouth, in the voice of Menelaus. Why am I stuck with you? What is it makes all my winds north and chills my wife?'

" ' "Proteus answered: 'You ask too many questions. Not Athena, but Aphrodite is your besetter. Leave Helen with me here; go back to the mouth of River Egypt. There where the yeasting slime of green unspeakable jungle springs ferments the sea of your intoxicate Greek bards,' that's how the chap talks, 'make hecatombs to Aphrodite; beg Love's pardon for your want of faith. Helen chose you without reason because she loves you without cause; embrace her without question and watch your weather change. Let go.'

" ' "I tried; it wasn't easy; he swam and melted in the lesser Nile my tears. Then Eidothea surfaced just offshore, unless it was you . . ." Shipboard Helen. "Had he been Eidothea before? Had he turned Helen? Was I cuckold yet again, an old salt in my wound? Recollecting my hard homework I closed eyes, mouth, mind; set my teeth and Nileward course. It was a different river; on its crocodiled and dromedaried bank, to that goddess perversely polymorphous as her dam the sea or the shift Old Man Thereof, Menelaus sacrificed twin heifers, Curiosity, Common Sense. I no longer ask why you choose me, less tusked than Idomeneus, et cetera; should you declare it was love for me fetched you to Paris and broke the world, I'd raise neither eyebrow; 'Yes, well, so,' is what I'd say. I don't ask what's changed the wind, your opinion, me, why I hang here like, onto, and by my narrative. Gudgeon my pintle, step my mast, vessel me where you will. I believe all. I understand nothing. I love you."

3

" 'Snarled thwarted Helen: "Love!" Then added through our chorus groan: "Loving may waste us into Echoes, but it's being loved that kills. Endymion! Semele! Io! Adonis! Hyacinthus! Loving steers marine Odysseus; being loved turned poor Callisto into navigation-stars. Do you love me to punish me for loving you?"

" ' "I haven't heard so deep Greek since Delphi," I marveled. "But do I ask questions?"

" ' "I'll put this love of yours truly to the test," Helen said. Gently she revived me with cold water and pungents from her Nilish store. "I suppose you suppose," she declared then, "that I've been in Troy."

" 'So potent her medicaments, in no time at all I regained my breath and confessed I did.

" 'Severely she nodded. "And you suspect I've been unfaithful?"

" ' "It would be less than honest of me to say," I said, "that no fancy of that dirt-foot sort has ever grimed my imagination's marmor sill."

" ' "With Paris? And others as well?"

" ' "You wrest truth from me as Odysseus Astyanax Andromache."

" ' "In a word, you think yourself cuckold."

" 'I blushed. "To rash untowardly to conclusions ill becomes a man made wise by hard experience and time. Nevertheless, I grant that as I shivered in a Trojan ditch one autumn evening in the war's late years and watched you stroll with Paris on the bastions, a swart-hair infant at each breast and your belly swaggèd with another, the term you mention flit once across the ramparts of my mind like a bat through Ilion-dusk. Not impossibly the clever wound I'd got from Pandarus festered my judgment with my side . . ."

" 'Helen kissed my bilging tears and declared: "Husband, I have never been in Troy.

" ' "What's more," she added within the hour, before the boatswain could remobilize the crew, "I've never made love with any man but you."

" ' "Ah."

" 'She turned her pout lips portward. "You doubt me."

" ' "Too many years of unwomaned nights and combat
days," I explained, "gestate in our tenderer intelligences a
skeptic demon, that will drag dead Hector by the baldric till
his corpse-track moat the walls, and yet whisper when his
bones are ransomed: 'Hector lives.' Were one to say of
Menelaus at this present hour, 'That imp nips him,' one
would strike Truth's shield not very far off-boss."

" ' "Doubt no more," said Helen. "Your wife was never in
Troy. Out of love for you I left you when you left, but before
Paris could up-end me, Hermes whisked me on Father's orders to Egyptian Proteus and made a Helen out of clouds to
take my place.

" ' "All these years I've languished in Pharos, chaste and
comfy, waiting for you, while Paris, nothing wiser, fetched
Cloud-Helen off to Troy, made her his mistress, got on her
Bunomus, Aganus, Idaeus, and a little Helen, dearest of the
four. It wasn't I, but cold Cloud-Helen you fetched from Troy,
whom Proteus dissolved the noon you beached him. When
you then went off to account to Aphrodite, I slipped aboard.
Here I am. I love you."

" 'Not a quarter-hour later she asked of suspended me:
"Don't you believe me?"

" ' "What ground have I for doubt?" I whispered. "But that
imp aforementioned gives me no peace. 'How do you know, he
whispers with me, 'that the Helen you now hang onto isn't
the cloud-one? Why mayn't your actual spouse be back in

Troy, or fooling in naughty Egypt yet?' "

" ' "Or home in Lacedemon," Helen added, "where she's been all along, waiting for her husband."

" 'Presently my battle voice made clear from stem to stern my grown conviction that the entire holocaust at Troy, with its prior and subsequent fiascos, was but a dream of Zeus's conjure, visited upon me to lead me to Pharos and the recollection of my wife—or her nimbus like. For for all I knew I roared what I now gripped was but a further fiction, maybe Proteus himself, turned for sea-cow-respite to cuckold generals . . .

" ' "A likely story," Helen said. "Next thing, you'll say it was a cloud-Menelaus went fishing on the beach at Pharos! If I carry to my grave no heart-worm grudge at your decade vagrance, it's only that it irks me less just now than your present doubt. And that I happen to be not mortal. Yet so far from giving cut for cut, I'm obliged by Love and the one right action of your life to ease your mind entirely." Here she led me by the hand into her golden-Aphrodite's-grove, declaring: "If what's within your grasp is mere cloudy fiction, cast it to the wind; if fact then Helen's real, and really loves you. Espouse me without more carp! The senseless answer to our riddle woo, mad history's secret, base-fact and footer to the fiction crazy-house our life: imp-slayer love, terrific as the sun! Love! Love!"

" 'Who was I? Am? Mere Menelaus, if that: mote in the cauldron, splinter in the Troy-fire of her love! Does nail hold timber or timber nail? Held fast by his fast-held, consumed by what he feasted on, whatever was of Menelaus was no more. I must've done something right.

" ' " 'You'll not die in horsy Argos, son of Atreus . . .' " So quoted Proteus's last words to me my love-spiked wife. " 'The Olympic gods will west you in your latter days to a sweet estate where rain nor passion leaches, there to be your wife's undying advertisement, her espouser in the gods' slow time. Not fair-haired battleshouts or people-leading preserves you, but forasmuch as and only that you are beloved of Helen, they count you immortal as themselves.' "

" 'Lampreys and flat-fish wept for joy, squids danced on
the wave-tops, crab-choirs and minnow-anthems shook with
delight the opalescent welkin. As a sea-logged voyager
strives across the storm-shocked country of the sole, loses
ship and shipmates, poops to ground on alien shingle, gives
over struggling, and is whisked in a dream-dark boat, sleep-
skippered, to his shoaly home, there to wake next morning
with a wotless groan, wondering where he is and what fresh
lie must save him, until he recognizes with a heart-surge
whither he's come and hugs the home-coast to sweet oblivion.
So Menelaus, my best guess, flayed by love, steeved himself
snug in Helen's hold, was by her hatched and transport,
found as it were himself in no time Lacedemoned, where he
clings still stunned. She returned him to bride-bed; had he
ever been in Troy? Whence the brine he scents in her
ambrosial cave? Is it bedpost he clutches, or spruce horse rib?
He continues to hold on, but can no longer take the world seriously. Place and time, doer, done-to have lost their sense.
Am I stoppered in the equine bowel, asleep and dreaming? At
the Nile-fount, begging Love for mercy? Is it Telemachus I
hold, cold-hearth Peisistratus? No, no, I'm on the beach at
Pharos, must be forever. I'd thought my cave-work finished,
episode; re-entering Helen I understood that all subsequent
history is Proteus, making shift to slip me . . .'

" 'Beg pardon.'

" 'Telemachus? Come back?'

" 'To.'

" 'Thought I hadn't noticed, did you, how your fancy
strayed while I told of good-voyaging your father and the
rest? Don't I know Helen did the wine-trick? Are you the first
in forty years, d'you think, I ever thought I'd yarned till dawn
when in fact you'd slipped me?'

2

"Fagged Odysseus'-son responded: 'Your tale has held us fast
through a dark night, Menelaus, and will bring joy to

suitored Ithaca. Time to go. Wake up, Peisistratus. Our regards to Hermione, thanks to her magic mother.'

" 'Mine,' I replied, 'to chastest yours, muse and mistress
of the embroidrous art, to whom I commission you to retail
my round-trip story. Like yourself, let's say, she'll find it
short nor simple, though one dawn enlightens its dénoue-
ment. Her own, I'd guess, has similar abound of woof—yet
before your father's both will pale, what marvels and rich
mischances will have fetched him so late home! Beside that
night's fabrication this will stand as Lesser to Great Ajax.'

"So saying I gifted them off to Nestored Pylos and the pig-
fraught headlands dear to Odysseus, myself returning to my
unfooled narrate seat. There I found risen Helen, sleep-
gowned, replete, mulling twin cups at the new-coaxed coals. I
kissed her ear; she murmured 'Don't.' I stooped to embrace
her; 'Look out for the wine.' I pressed her, on, to home. 'Let
go, love.' I would not, ever, said so; she sighed and smiled,
women, I was taken in, it's a gift, a gift-horse, I shut my eyes,
here we go again, 'Hold fast to yourself, Menelaus.' Everything," I declare, "is now as day."

I

It was himself grasped undeceivèd Menelaus, solely, imper-
fectly. No man goes to the same Nile twice. When I understood that Proteus somewhere on the beach became
Menelaus holding the Old Man of the Sea, Menelaus ceased.
Then I understood further how Proteus thus also was as such
no more, being as possibly Menelaus's attempt to hold him,
the tale of that vain attempt, the voice that tells it. Ajax is
dead, Agamemnon, all my friends, but I can't die, worse luck;
Menelaus's carcass is long wormed, yet his voice yarns on
through everything, to itself. Not my voice, I am this voice, no
more, the rest has changed, re-changed, gone. The voice too,
even that changes, becomes hoarser, loses its magnetism,
grows screechy, incoherent, blank.

I'm not dismayed. Menelaus was lost on the beach at Pharos; he is no longer, and may be in no poor case as teller of his gripping history. For when the voice goes he'll turn tale, story of his life, to which he clings yet, whenever, how-, by whom-recounted. Then when as must at last every tale, all tellers, all told, Menelaus's story itself in ten or ten thousand years expires, yet I'll survive it, I, in Proteus's terrifying last disguise, Beauty's spouse's odd Elysium: the absurd, unending possibility of love.

The Balloon
Donald Barthelme

The balloon, beginning at a point on Fourteenth Street, the exact location of which I cannot reveal, expanded northward all one night, while people were sleeping, until it reached the Park. There, I stopped it; at dawn the northernmost edges lay over the Plaza; the free-hanging motion was frivolous and gentle. But experiencing a faint irritation at stopping, even to protect the trees, and seeing no reason the balloon should not be allowed to expand upward, over the parts of the city it was already covering, into the "air space" to be found there, I asked the engineers to see to it. This expansion took place throughout the morning, soft imperceptible sighing of gas through the valves. The balloon then covered forty-five blocks north-south and an irregular area east-west, as many as six crosstown blocks on either side of the Avenue in some places. That was the situation, then.

But it is wrong to speak of "situations," implying sets of circumstances leading to some resolution, some escape of tension; there were no situations, simply the balloon hanging there—muted heavy grays and browns for the most part, contrasting with walnut and soft yellows. A deliberate lack of finish, enhanced by skillful installation, gave the surface a rough, forgotten quality; sliding weights on the inside, carefully adjusted, anchored the great, vari-shaped mass at a number of points. Now we have had a flood of original ideas in all media, works of singular beauty as well as significant milestones in the history of inflation, but at that moment there was only *this balloon,* concrete particular, hanging there.

There were reactions. Some people found the balloon "interesting." As a response this seemed inadequate to the immensity of the balloon, the suddenness of its appearance over the city; on the other hand, in the absence of hysteria or other societally-induced anxiety, it must be judged a calm, "mature" one. There was a certain amount of initial argumentation about the "meaning" of the balloon; this subsided, because we have learned not to insist on meanings, and they are rarely even looked for now, except in cases involving the simplest, safest phenomena. It was agreed that since the meaning of the balloon could never be known absolutely, extended discussion was pointless, or at least less purposeful than the activities of those who, for example, hung green and blue paper lanterns from the warm gray underside, in certain streets, or seized the occasion to write messages on the surface, announcing their availability for the performance of unnatural acts, or the availability of acquaintances.

Daring children jumped, especially at those points where the balloon hovered close to a building, so that the gap between balloon and building was a matter of a few inches, or points where the balloon actually made contact, exerting an ever-so-slight pressure against the side of a building, so that balloon and building seemed a unity. The upper surface was so structured that a "landscape" was presented, small valleys as well as slight knolls, or mounds; once atop the balloon, a stroll was possible, or even a trip, from one place to another. There was pleasure in being able to run down an incline, then up the opposing slope, both gently graded, or in making a leap from one side to the other. Bouncing was possible, because of the pneumaticity of the surface, and even falling, if that was your wish. That all these varied motions, as well as others, were within one's possibilities, in experiencing the "up" side of the balloon, was extremely exciting for children, accustomed to the city's flat, hard skin. But the purpose of the balloon was not to amuse children.

Too, the number of people, children and adults, who took advantage of the opportunities described was not so large as it might have been: a certain timidity, lack of trust in the balloon, was seen. There was, furthermore, some hostility. Because we had hidden the pumps, which fed helium to the interior, and because the surface was so vast that the authorities could not determine the point of entry—that is, the point at which the gas was injected—a degree of frustration was evidenced by those city officers into whose province such manifestations normally fell. The apparent purposelessness of the balloon was vexing (as was the fact that it was "there" at all). Had we painted, in great letters, "LABORATORY TESTS PROVE" or "18% MORE EFFECTIVE" on the sides of the balloon, this difficulty would have been circumvented. But I could not bear to do so. On the whole, these officers were remarkably tolerant, considering the dimensions of the anomaly, this tolerance being the result of, first, secret tests conducted by night that convinced them that little or nothing could be done in the way of removing or destroying the balloon, and, secondly, a public warmth that arose (not uncolored by touches of the aforementioned hostility) toward the balloon, from ordinary citizens.

As a single balloon must stand for a lifetime of thinking about balloons, so each citizen expressed, in the attitude he chose, a complex of attitudes. One man might consider that the balloon had to do with the notion *sullied,* as in the sentence *The big balloon sullied the otherwise clear and radiant Manhattan sky.* That is, the balloon was, in this man's view, an imposture, something inferior to the sky that had formerly been there, something interposed between the people and their "sky." But in fact it was January, the sky was dark and ugly; it was not a sky you could look up into, lying on your back in the street, with pleasure, unless pleasure, for you, proceeded from having been threatened, from having been misused. And the underside of the balloon was a pleasure to look up into, we had seen to that, muted grays and browns for the most part, contrasted with walnut and soft, forgotten yellows. And so, while this man was thinking *sullied,* still there was an admixture of pleasurable cognition in his thinking, struggling with the original perception.

Another man, on the other hand, might view the balloon as if it were part of a system of unanticipated rewards, as when one's employer walks in and says, "Here, Henry, take this package of money I have wrapped for you, because we have been doing so well in the business here, and I admire the way you bruise the tulips, without which bruising your department would not be a success, or at least not the success that it is." For this man the balloon might be a brilliantly heroic "muscle and pluck" experience, even if an experience poorly understood.

Another man might say, "Without the example of — , it is doubtful that — would exist today in its present form," and find many to agree with him, or to argue with him. Ideas of "bloat" and "float" were introduced, as well as concepts of dream and responsibility. Others engaged in remarkably detailed fantasies having to do with a wish either to lose themselves in the balloon, or to engorge it. The private character of these wishes, of their origins, deeply buried and unknown, was such that they were not much spoken of; yet there is evidence that they were widespread. It was also argued that what was important was what you felt when you stood under the balloon; some people claimed that they felt sheltered, warmed, as never before, while enemies of the balloon felt, or reported feeling, constrained, a "heavy" feeling.

Critical opinion was divided:

"monstrous pourings"

"harp"

XXXXXXX "certain contrasts with darker
portions"

"inner joy"

"large, square corners"

"conservative eclecticism that has so far governed
modern balloon design"

::::::: "abnormal vigor"

"warm, soft, lazy passages"

"Has unity been sacrificed for a sprawling quality?"

"Quelle catastrophe!"

"munching"

People began, in a curious way, to locate themselves in relation to aspects of the balloon: "I'll be at that place where it dips down into Forty-seventh Street almost to the sidewalk, near the Alamo Chile House," or, "Why don't we go stand on top, and take the air, and maybe walk about a bit, where it forms a tight, curving line with the façade of the Gallery of Modern Art—" Marginal intersections offered entrances within a given time duration, as well as "warm, soft, lazy passages" in which . . . But it is wrong to speak of "marginal intersections," each intersection was crucial, none could be ignored (as if, walking there, you might not find someone capable of turning your attention, in a flash, from old exercises to new exercises, risks and escalations). Each intersection was crucial, meeting of balloon and building, meeting of balloon and man, meeting of balloon and balloon.

It was suggested that what was admired about the balloon was finally this: that it was not limited, or defined. Sometimes a bulge, blister, or subsection would carry all the way east to the river on its own initiative, in the manner of an army's movements on a map, as seen in a headquarters remote from the fighting. Then that part would be, as it were, thrown back again, or would withdraw into new dispositions; the next morning, that part would have made another sortie, or disappeared altogether. This ability of the balloon to shift its shape, to change, was very pleasing, especially to people whose lives were rather rigidly patterned, persons to whom change, although desired, was not available. The balloon, for the twenty-two days of its existence, offered the possibility, in its randomness, of mislocation of the self, in contradistinction to the grid of precise, rectangular pathways under our feet. The amount of specialized training currently needed, and the consequent desirability of long-term commitments, has been occasioned by the steadily growing importance of complex machinery, in virtually all kinds of operations; as this tendency increases, more and more people will turn, in bewildered inadequacy, to solutions for which the balloon may stand as a prototype, or "rough draft."

I met you under the balloon, on the occasion of your return from Norway; you asked if it was mine; I said it was. The balloon, I said, is a spontaneous autobiographical disclosure, having to do with the unease I felt at your absence, and with sexual deprivation, but now that your visit to Bergen has been terminated, it is no longer necessary or appropriate. Removal of the balloon was easy; trailer trucks carried away the depleted fabric, which is now stored in West Virginia, awaiting some other time of unhappiness, sometime, perhaps, when we are angry with one another.

You Must Remember This
Robert Coover

It is dark in Rick's apartment. Black leader dark, heavy and
abstract, silent but for a faint hoarse crackle like a voiceless
plaint, and brief as sleep. Then Rick opens the door and the
light from the hall scissors in like a bellboy to open up space,
deposit surfaces (there is a figure in the room), harbinger
event (it is Ilsa). Rick follows, too preoccupied to notice: his
café is closed, people have been shot, he has troubles. But
then, with a stroke, he lights a small lamp (such a glow! the
shadows retreat, *everything* retreats: where are the walls?)
and there she is, facing him, holding open the drapery at the
far window like the front of a nightgown, the light flickering
upon her white but determined face like static. Rick pauses
for a moment in astonishment. Ilsa lets the drapery and its
implications drop, takes a step forward into the strangely
fretted light, her eyes searching his.

"How did you get in?" he asks, though this is probably not
the question on his mind.

"The stairs from the street."

This answer seems to please him. He knows how vulnerable he is, after all, it's the way he lives—his doors are open,
his head is bare, his tuxedo jacket is snowy white—that's not
important. What matters is that by such a reply a kind of
destiny is being fulfilled. Sam has a song about it. "I told you
this morning you'd come around," he says, curling his lips as
if to advertise his appetite for punishment, "but this is a little
ahead of schedule." She faces him squarely, broad-shoul-
dered and narrow-hipped, a sash around her waist like a gun
belt, something shiny in her tensed left hand. He raises both
his own as if to show they are empty: "Well, won't you sit

69

down?"

His offer, whether in mockery or no, releases her. Her shoulders dip in relief, her breasts; she sweeps forward (it is only a small purse she is carrying: a toothbrush perhaps, cosmetics, her hotel key), her face softening: "Richard!" He starts back in alarm, hands moving to his hips. "I had to see you!"

"So you use Richard again!" His snarling retreat throws up a barrier between them. She stops. He pushes his hands into his pockets as though to reach for the right riposte: "We're back in Paris!"

That probably wasn't it. Their song seems to be leaking into the room from somewhere out in the night, or perhaps it has been there all the time—Sam maybe, down in the darkened bar, sending out soft percussive warnings in the manner of his African race: "Think twice, boss. Hearts fulla passion, you c'n rely. Jealousy, boss, an' hate. Le's go fishin'. Sam."

"*Please!*" she begs, staring at him intently, but he remains unmoved:

"Your unexpected visit isn't connected by any chance with the letters of transit?" He ducks his head, his upper lip swelling with bitterness and hurt. "It seems as long as I have those letters, I'll never be lonely."

Yet, needless to say, he will always be lonely—in fact, this is the confession ("You can ask any price you want," she is saying) only half-concealed in his muttered subjoinder: Rick Blaine is a loner, born and bred. Pity him. There is this lingering, almost primal image of him, sitting alone at a chessboard in his white tuxedo, smoking contemplatively in the midst of a raucous conniving crowd, a crowd he has himself assembled about him. He taps a pawn, moves a white knight, fondles a tall black queen while a sardonic smile plays on his lips. He seems to be toying, self-mockingly, with Fate itself, as indifferent toward Rick Blaine (never mind that he says— as he does now, turning away from her—that "*I'm* the only cause *I'm* interested in . . .") as toward the rest of the world. It's all shit, so who cares?

Ilsa is staring off into space, a space that a moment ago

Rick filled. She seems to be thinking something out. The ne-
gotiations are going badly; perhaps it is this she is worried
about. He has just refused her offer of "any price," ignored
her ultimatum ("You *must* giff me those letters!"), sneered at
her husband's heroism, and scoffed at the very cause that
first brought them together in Paris. How could he do that?
And now he has abruptly turned his back on her (does he
think it was just sex? what has happened to him since then?)
and walked away toward the balcony door, meaning, apparently, to turn her out. She takes a deep breath, presses her
lips together, and, clutching her tiny purse with both hands,
wheels about to pursue him: "Richard!" This has worked before, it works again: he turns to face her new approach: "We
luffed each other once . . ." Her voice catches in her throat,
tears come to her eyes. She is beautiful there in the slatted
shadows, her hair loosening around her ears, eyes glittering,
throat bare and vulnerable in the open V-neck of her ruffled
blouse. She's a good dresser. Even that little purse she
squeezes: so like the other one, so lovely, hidden away. She
shakes her head slightly in wistful appeal: "If those days
meant . . . anything at all to you . . ."

"I wouldn't bring up Paris if I were you," he says stonily.
"It's poor salesmanship."

She gasps (*she* didn't bring it up: is he a madman?),
tosses her head back: "Please! Please listen to me!" She closes
her eyes, her lower lip pushed forward as though bruised. "If
you knew what really happened, if you only knew the truth—!"

He stands over this display, impassive as a Moorish ex-
ecutioner (that's it! he's turning into one of these bloody Ar-
abs, she thinks). "I wouldn't believe you, no matter what you
told me," he says. In Ethiopia, after an attempt on the life of
an Italian officer, he saw 1600 Ethiopians get rounded up one
night and shot in reprisal. Many were friends of his. Or cli-
ents anyway. But somehow her deceit is worse. "You'd say
anything now, to get what you want." Again he turns his back
on her, strides away.

She stares at him in shocked silence, as though all that
had happened eighteen months ago in Paris were flashing

suddenly before her eyes, now made ugly by some terrible revelation. An exaggerated gasp escapes her like the breaking of wind: his head snaps up and he turns sharply to the right. She chases him, dogging his heels. "You want to feel sorry for yourself, don't you?" she cries and, surprised (he was just reaching for something on an ornamental table, the humidor perhaps), he turns back to her. "With so much at stake, all you can think off is your own feeling," she rails. Her lips are drawn back, her breathing labored, her eyes watering in anger and frustration. "One woman has hurt you, and you take your reffenge on the rest off the world!" She is choking, she can hardly speak. Her accent seems to have got worse. "You're a coward, und veakling, und—"

She gasps. What is she saying? He watches her, as though faintly amused. "No, Richard, I'm sorry!" Tears are flowing in earnest now: she's gone too far! This is the expression on her face. She's in a corner, struggling to get out. "I'm sorry, but—" She wipes the tears from her cheek, and calls once again on her husband, that great and courageous man whom they both admire, whom the whole world admires: "—you're our last hope! If you don't help us, Victor Laszlo will die in Casablanca!"

"What of it?" he says. He has been waiting for this opportunity. He plays with it now, stretching it out. He turns, reaches for a cigarette, his head haloed in the light from an arched doorway. "I'm gonna die in Casablanca. It's a good spot for it." This line is meant to be amusing, but Ilsa reacts with horror. Her eyes widen. She catches her breath, turns away. He lights up, pleased with himself, takes a practiced drag, blows smoke. "Now," he says, turning toward her, "if you'll—"

He pulls up short, squints: she has drawn a revolver on him. So much for toothbrushes and hotel keys. "All right. I tried to reason with you. I tried effrything. Now I want those letters." Distantly, a melodic line suggests a fight for love and glory, an ironic case of do or die. "Get them for me."

"I don't have to." He touches his jacket. "I got 'em right here."

"Put them on the table."

He smiles and shakes his head. "No." Smoke curls up from the cigarette he is holding at his side like the steam that enveloped the five o'clock train to Marseilles. Her eyes fill with tears. Even as she presses on ("For the last time . . . !"), she knows that "no" is final. There is, behind his ironic smile, a profound sadness, the fatalistic survivor's wistful acknowledgment that, in the end, the fundamental things apply. Time, going by, leaves nothing behind, not even moments like this. "If Laszlo and the cause mean so much," he says, taunting her with her own uncertainties, "you won't stop at anything . . ."

He seems almost to recede. The cigarette disappears, the smoke. His sorrow gives way to something not unlike eagerness. "All right, I'll make it easier for you," he says, and walks toward her. "Go ahead and shoot. You'll be doing me a favor."

She seems taken aback, her eyes damp, her lips swollen and parted. Light licks at her face. He gazes steadily at her from his superior moral position, smoke drifting up from his hand once more, his white tuxedo pressed against the revolver barrel. Her eyes close as the gun lowers, and she gasps his name: "Richard!" It is like an invocation. Or a profession of faith. "I tried to stay away," she sighs. She opens her eyes, peers up at him in abject surrender. A tear moves slowly down her cheek toward the corner of her mouth like secret writing. "I thought I would neffer see you again . . . that you were out off my life . . ." She blinks, cries out faintly—"Oh!"—and (he seems moved at last, his mask of disdain falling away like perspiration) turns away, her head wrenched to one side as though in pain.

Stricken with sudden concern, or what looks like concern, he steps up behind her, clasping her breasts with both hands, nuzzling in her hair. "The day you left Paris. . . !" she sobs, though she seems unsure of herself. One of his hands is already down between her legs, the other inside her blouse, pulling a breast out of its brassiere cup. "If you only knew . . . what I . . ." He is moaning, licking at one ear, the hand be-

tween her legs nearly lifting her off the floor, his pelvis bump-
ing at her buttocks. "Is this . . . right?" she gasps.

"I—I don't know!" he groans, massaging her breast, the
nipple between two fingers. "I can't think!"

"But . . . you *must* think!" she cries, squirming her hips.
Tears are streaming down her cheeks now. "For . . . for . . ."

"What?" he gasps, tearing her blouse open, pulling on her
breast as though to drag it over her shoulder where he might
kiss it. Or eat it: he seems ravenous suddenly.

"I . . . I can't remember!" she sobs. She reaches behind to
jerk at his fly (what else is she to do, for the love of Jesus?),
then rips away her sash, unfastens her skirt, her fingers
trembling.

"Holy shit!" he wheezes, pushing his hand inside her
girdle as her skirt falls. His cheeks too are wet with tears.
"Ilsa!"

"Richard!"

They fall to the floor, grabbing and pulling at each other's
clothing. He's trying to get her bra off which is tangled up
now with her blouse, she's struggling with his belt, yanking
at his black pants, wrenching them open. Buttons fly, straps
pop, there's the soft unfocused rip of silk, the jingle of buckles
and falling coins, grunts, gasps, whimpers of desire. He
strips the tangled skein of underthings away (all these straps
and stays—how does she get in and out of this crazy elastic?);
she works his pants down past his bucking hips, fumbles
with his shoes. *"Your elbow—!"*

"Mmmff!"

"Ah—!"

She pulls his pants and boxer shorts off, crawls round
and (he strokes her shimmering buttocks, swept by the light
from the airport tower, watching her full breasts sway above
him: it's all happening so fast, he'd like to slow it down, repeat some of the better bits—that view of her rippling
haunches on her hands and knees just now, for example, like
a 22, his lucky number—but there's a great urgency on them,
they can't wait) straddles him, easing him into her like a
train being guided into a station. *"I luff you, Richard!"* she

declares breathlessly, though she seems to be speaking, eyes squeezed shut and breasts heaving, not to him but to the ceiling, if there is one up there. His eyes too are closed now, his hands gripping her soft hips, pulling her down, his breath coming in short anguished snorts, his face puffy and damp with tears. There is, as always, something deeply wounded and vulnerable about the expression on his battered face, framed there against his Persian carpet: Rick Blaine, a man annealed by loneliness and betrayal, but flawed—hopelessly, it seems—by hope itself. He is, in the tragic sense, a true revolutionary: his gaping mouth bespeaks this, the spittle in the corners of his lips, his eyes, open now and staring into some infinite distance not unlike the future, his knitted brow. He heaves upward, impaling her to the very core: *"Oh, Gott!"* she screams, her back arching, mouth agape as though to commence "La Marseillaise."

Now, for a moment, they pause, feeling themselves thus conjoined, his organ luxuriating in the warm tub of her vagina, her enflamed womb closing around his pulsing penis like a mother embracing a lost child. "If you only knew. . . ," she seems to say, though perhaps she has said this before and only now it can be heard. He fondles her breasts; she rips his shirt open, strokes his chest, leans forward to kiss his lips, his nipples. This is not Victor inside her with his long thin rapier, all too rare in its embarrassed visits; this is not Yvonne with her cunning professional muscles, her hollow airy hole. This is love in all its clammy mystery, the ultimate connection, the squishy rub of truth, flesh as a self-consuming message. This is necessity, as in woman needs man, and man must have his mate. Even their identities seem to be dissolving; they have to whisper each other's name from time to time as though in recitative struggle against some ultimate enchantment from which there might be no return. Then slowly she begins to wriggle her hips above him, he to meet her gentle undulations with counterthrusts of his own. They hug each other close, panting, her breasts smashed against him, moving only from the waist down. She slides her thighs between his and squeezes his penis between them, as though to conceal it there, an underground member on the run, wounded but unbowed. He lifts his stockinged feet and plants them behind her knees as though in stirrups, her buttocks above pinching and opening, pinching and opening like a suction pump. And it is true about her vaunted radiance: she seems almost to glow from within, her flexing cheeks haloed in their own dazzling luster.

"It feels so good, Richard! In there . . . I've been so—*ah!*—so lonely. . . !"

"Yeah, me too, kid. *Ngh!* Don't talk."

She slips her thighs back over his and draws them up beside his waist like a child curling around her teddybear, knees against his ribs, her fanny gently bobbing on its pike like a mind caressing a cherished memory. He lies there passively for a moment, stretched out, eyes closed, accepting this warm rhythmical ablution as one might accept a nanny's teasing bath, a mother's care (a care, he's often said, denied him), in all its delicious innocence—or seemingly so: in fact, his whole body is faintly atremble, as though, with great difficulty, shedding the last of its pride and bitterness, its isolate neutrality. Then slowly his own hips begin to rock convulsively under hers, his knees to rise in involuntary surrender. She tongues his ear, her buttocks thumping more vigorously now, kisses his throat, his nose, his scarred lip, then rears up, arching her back, tossing her head back (her hair is looser now, wilder, a flush has crept into the distinctive pallor of her cheeks and throat, and what was before a fierce determination is now raw intensity, what vulnerability now a slack-jawed abandon), plunging him in more deeply than ever, his own buttocks bouncing up off the floor as though trying to take off like the next flight to Lisbon—"Gott in Himmel, *this is fonn!*" she cries. She reaches behind her back to clutch his testicles, he clasps her hand in both of his, his thighs spread, she falls forward, they roll over, he's pounding away now from above (he lacks her famous radiance: if anything his buttocks seem to suck in light, drawing a nostalgic murkiness around them like night fog, signaling a fundamental distance between them, and an irresistible attraction), she's clawing at his back under the white jacket, at his hips, his thighs, her voracious nether mouth leaping up at him from below and sliding back, over and over, like a frantic greased-pole climber. Faster and faster they slap their bodies together, submitting to this fierce rhythm as though to simplify themselves, emitting grunts and whinnies and helpless little farts, no longer Rick Blaine and Ilsa Lund, but some nameless conjunction somewhere between them, time, space, being itself getting redefined by the rapidly narrowing focus of their incandescent passion—then suddenly Rick rears back, his face seeming to puff out like a gourd, Ilsa cries out and kicks upward, crossing her ankles over Rick's clenched buttocks, for a moment they seem almost to float, suspended, unloosed from the earth's gravity, and then— *whumpf!*—they hit the floor again, their bodies continuing to hammer together, though less regularly, plunging, twitching, prolonging this exclamatory dialogue, drawing it out even as the intensity diminishes, even as it becomes more a declaration than a demand, more an inquiry than a declaration. Ilsa's feet uncross, slide slowly to the floor. "Fooff . . . *Gott!*" They lie there, cheek to cheek, clutching each other tightly, gasping for breath, their thighs quivering with the last involuntary spasms, the echoey reverberations, deep in their loins, of pleasure's fading blasts.

"Jesus," Rick wheezes, "I've been saving that one for a goddamn year and a half. . . !"

"It was the best fokk I effer haff," Ilsa replies with a tremulous sigh, and kisses his ear, runs her fingers in his hair. He starts to roll off her, but she clasps him closely: "No . . . wait. . . !" A deeper thicker pleasure, not so ecstatic, yet somehow more moving, seems to well up from far inside her to embrace the swollen visitor snuggled moistly in her womb, once a familiar friend, a comrade loved and trusted, now almost a stranger, like one resurrected from the dead.

"Ah—!" he gasps. God, it's almost like she's milking it! Then she lets go, surrounding him spongily with a kind of warm wet pulsating gratitude. "Ah . . ."

He lies there between Ilsa's damp silky thighs, feeling his

weight thicken, his mind soften and spread. His will drains
away as if it were some kind of morbid affection, lethargy
overtaking him like an invading army. Even his jaw goes
slack, his fingers (three sprawl idly on a dark-tipped breast)
limp. He wears his snowy white tuxedo jacket still, his shiny
black socks, which, together with the parentheses of Ilsa's
white thighs, make his melancholy buttocks—beaten in
childhood, lashed at sea, run lean in union skirmishes, sun-
burned in Ethiopia, and shot at in Spain—look gloomier than
ever, swarthy and self-pitying, agape now with a kind of heroic sadness. A violent tenderness. These buttocks are, it
could be said, what the pose of isolation looks like at its best:
proud, bitter, mournful, and, as the prefect of police might
have put it, tremendously attractive. Though his penis has
slipped out of its vaginal pocket to lie limply like a fat little
toe against her slowly pursing lips, she clasps him close still,
clinging to something she cannot quite define, something like
a spacious dream of freedom, or a monastery garden, or the
discovery of electricity. "Do you have a gramophone on, Richard?"

"What—?!" Her question has startled him. His haunches
snap shut, his head rears up, snorting, he seems to be reaching for the letters of transit. "Ah . . . no . . ." He relaxes again,
letting his weight fall back, though sliding one thigh over
hers now, stretching his arms out as though to unkink them,
turning his face away. His scrotum bulges up on her thigh
like an emblem of his inner serenity and generosity, all too
often concealed, much as an authentic decency might shine
through a mask of cynicism and despair. He takes a deep
breath. (A kiss is just a kiss is what the music is insinuating.
A sigh . . .) "That's probably Sam . . ."

She sighs (. . . and so forth), gazing up at the ceiling above
her, patterned with overlapping circles of light from the
room's lamps and swept periodically by the wheeling airport
beacon, coming and going impatiently, yet reliably, like desire itself. "He hates me, I think."

"Sam? No, he's a pal. What I think, he thinks."

"When we came into the bar last night, he started playing

'Luff for Sale.' Effryone turned and looked at me."

"It wasn't the song, sweetheart, it was the way you two were dressed. Nobody in Casablanca—"

"Then he tried to chase me away. He said I was bad luck to you." She can still see the way he rolled his white eyes at her, like some kind of crazy voodoo zombie.

Richard grunts ambiguously. "Maybe you should stop calling him 'boy.' "

Was that it? "But in all the moofies—" Well, a translation problem probably, a difficulty she has known often in her life. Language can sometimes be stiff as a board. Like what's under her now. She loves Richard's relaxed weight on her, the beat of his heart next to her breast, the soft lumpy pouch of his genitals squashed against her thigh, but the floor seems to be hardening under her like some kind of stern Calvinist rebuke and there is a disagreeable airy stickiness between her legs, now that he has slid away from there. "Do you haff a bidet, Richard?"

"Sure, kid." He slides to one side with a lazy grunt, rolls over. He's thinking vaguely about the pleasure he's just had, what it's likely to cost him (he doesn't care), and wondering where he'll find the strength to get up off his ass and go look for a cigarette. He stretches his shirttail down and wipes his crotch with it, nods back over the top of his head. "In there."

She is sitting up, peering between her spread legs. "I am afraid we haff stained your nice carpet, Richard."

"What of it? Put it down as a gesture to love. Want a drink?"

"Yes, that would be good." She leans over and kisses him, her face still flushed and eyes damp, but smiling now, then stands and gathers up an armload of tangled clothing. "Do I smell something burning?"

"What—?!" He rears up. "My goddamn cigarette! I musta dropped it on the couch!" He crawls over, brushes at it: it's gone out, but there's a big hole there now, dark-edged like ringworm. "Shit." He staggers to his feet, stumbles over to the humidor to light up a fresh smoke. Nothing's ever free, he thinks, feeling a bit light-headed. "What's your poison, kid?"

"I haff downstairs been drinking Cointreau," she calls out over the running water in the next room. He pours himself a large whiskey, tosses it down neat (light, sliding by, catches his furrowed brow as he tips his head back: what is wrong?), pours another, finds a decanter of Grand Marnier. She won't know the difference. In Paris she confused champagne with sparkling cider, ordered a Pommard thinking she was getting a rosé, drank gin because she couldn't taste it. He fits the half-burned cigarette between his lips, tucks a spare over his ear, then carries the drinks into the bathroom. She sits, straddling the bidet, churning water up between her legs like the wake of a pleasure boat. The beacon doesn't reach in here: it's as though he's stepped out of its line of sight, but that doesn't make him feel easier (something is nagging at him, has been for some time now). He holds the drink to her mouth for her, and she sips, looking mischievously up at him, one wet hand braced momentarily on his hipbone. Even in Paris she seemed to think drinking was naughtier than sex. Which made her on occasion something of a souse. She tips her chin, and he sets her drink down on the sink. "I wish I didn't luff you so much," she says casually, licking her lips, and commences to work up a lather between her legs with a bar of soap.

"Listen, what did you mean," he asks around the cigarette (this is it, or part of it: he glances back over his shoulder apprehensively, as though to find some answer to his question staring him in the face—or what, from the rear, is passing for his face), "when you said, 'Is this right?' "

"When. . . ?"

"A while ago, when I grabbed your, you know—"

"Oh, I don't know, darling. Yust a strange feeling, I don't exactly remember." She spreads the suds up her smooth belly and down the insides of her thighs, runs the soap up under her behind. "Like things were happening too fast or something."

He takes a contemplative drag on the cigarette, flips the butt into the toilet. "Yeah, that's it." Smoke curls out his nostrils like balloons of speech in a comic strip. "*All* this seems strange somehow. Like something that shouldn't have—"

"Well, I *am* a married woman, Richard."

"I don't mean that." But maybe he does mean that. She's rinsing now, her breasts flopping gaily above her splashing, it's hard to keep his mind on things. But he's not only been pronging some other guy's wife, this is the wife of Victor Laszlo of the International Underground, one of his goddamn heroes. One of the world's. Does that matter? He shoves his free hand in a jacket pocket, having no other, tosses back the drink. "Anyway," he wheezes, "from what you tell me, you were married already when we met in Paris, so that's not—"

"Come here, Richard," Ilsa interrupts with gentle but firm Teutonic insistence. *Komm' hier.* His back straightens, his eyes narrow, and for a moment the old Rick Blaine returns, the lonely American warrior, incorruptible, melancholy, master of his own fate, beholden to no one—but then she reaches forward and, like destiny, takes a hand. "Don't try to escape," she murmurs, pulling him up to the bidet between her knees. "You will neffer succeed."

She continues to hold him with one hand (he is growing there, stretching and filling in her hand with soft warm pulsations, and more than anything else that has happened to her since she came to Casablanca, more even than Sam's song, it is this sensation that takes her back to their days in Paris: wherever they went, from the circus to the movies, from excursion boats to dancehalls, it swelled in her hand, just like this), while soaping him up with the other. "Why are you circumcised, Richard?" she asks, as the engorged head (when it flushes, it seems to flush blue) pushes out between her thumb and index finger. There was something he always said in Paris when it poked up at her like that. She peers wistfully at it, smiling to herself.

"My old man was a sawbones," he says, and takes a deep breath. He sets his empty glass down, reaches for the spare fag. It seems to have vanished. "He thought it was hygienic."

"Fictor still has his. Off course in Europe it is often important not to be mistaken for a Chew." She takes up the fragrant bar of soap (black market, the best, Ferrari gets it for him) and buffs the shaft with it, then thumbs the head with her sudsy hands as though, gently, trying to uncap it. The first day he met her, she opened his pants and jerked him off in his top-down convertible right under the Arc de Triomphe, then, almost without transition, or so it seemed to him, blew him spectacularly in the Bois de Boulogne. He remembers every detail, or anyway the best parts. And it was never— ever—any better than that. Until tonight.

She rinses the soap away, pours the rest of the Grand Marnier (she thinks: Cointreau) over his gleaming organ like a sort of libation, working the excess around as though lightly basting it (he thinks: priming it). A faint sad smile seems to be playing at the corners of her lips. "Say it once, Richard . . ."

"What—?"

She's smiling sweetly, but: is that a tear in her eye? "For old times' sake. Say it . . ."

"Ah." Yes, he'd forgotten. He's out of practice. He grunts, runs his hand down her damp cheek and behind her ear. "Here's lookin' at you, kid . . ."

She puckers her lips and kisses the tip, smiling cross-eyed at it, then, opening her mouth wide, takes it in, all of it at once. "Oh, Christ!" he groans, feeling himself awash in the thick muscular foam of her saliva, "I'm crazy about you, baby!"

"Mmmm!" she moans. He has said that to her before, more than once no doubt (she wraps her arms around his hips under the jacket and hugs him close), but the time she is thinking about was at the cinema one afternoon in Paris. They had gone to see an American detective movie that was popular at the time, but there was a newsreel on before showing the Nazi conquests that month of Copenhagen, Oslo, Luxembourg, Amsterdam, and Brussels. "The Fall of Five Capitals," it was called. And the scenes from Oslo, though brief, showing the Gestapo goose-stepping through the storied streets of her childhood filled her with such terror and nostalgia (something inside her was screaming, "Who *am* I?"), that she reached impulsively for Richard's hand, grabbing what Victor calls "the old fellow" instead. She started to pull her hand back, but he held it there, and the next thing she knew she had her head in his lap, weeping and sucking as though at her dead mother's breast, the terrible roar of the German blitzkrieg pounding in her ears, Richard kneading her nape as her father used to do before he died (and as Richard is doing now, his buttocks knotted up under her arms, his penis fluttering in her mouth like a frightened bird), the Frenchmen in the theater shouting out obscenities, her own heart pounding like cannon fire. "God! I'm crazy about you, baby!" Richard whinnied as he came (now, as his knees buckle against hers and her mouth fills with the shockingly familiar unfamiliarity of his spurting seed, it is just a desperate "Oh fuck! Don't let go. . . !"), and when she sat up, teary-eyed and drooling and gasping for breath (it is not all that easy to breathe now, as he clasps her face close to his hairy belly, whimpering gratefully, his body sagging, her mouth filling), what she saw on the screen were happy Germans, celebrating their victories, taking springtime strolls through overflowing flower and vegetable markets, going to the theater to see translations of Shakespeare, snapping photographs of their children. "Oh Gott," she sniffled then (now she swallows, sucks and swallows, as though to draw out from this almost impalpable essence some vast structure of recollection), "it's too much!" Whereupon the man behind them leaned over and said: "Then try mine, mademoiselle. As you can see, it is not so grand as your Nazi friend's, but here in France, we grow men not pricks!" Richard's French was terrible, but it was good enough to understand "your Nazi friend": he hadn't even put his penis back in his pants (now it slides greasily past her chin, flops down her chest, his buttocks in her hugging arms going soft as butter, like a delicious half-grasped memory losing its clear outlines, melting into mere sensation), but just leapt up and took a swing at the Frenchman. With that, the cinema broke into an uproar with everybody calling everyone else a fascist or a whore. They were thrown out of the theater of course, the police put Richard on their blacklist as an exhibitionist, and they never

did get to see the detective movie. Ah well, they could laugh
about it then . . .

He sits now on the front lip of the bidet, his knees knuck-
led under hers, shirttails in the water, his cheek fallen on her
broad shoulder, arms loosely around her, feeling wonderfully
unwound, mellow as an old tune (which is still there somewhere, moonlight and love songs, same old story—maybe it's
coming up through the pipes), needing only a smoke to make
things perfect. The one he stuck over his ear is floating in the
scummy pool beneath them, he sees. Ilsa idly splashes his
drooping organ as though christening it. Only one answer,
she once said, peeling off that lovely satin gown of hers like a
French letter, will take care of all our questions, and she was
right. As always. He's the one who's made a balls-up of things
with his complicated moral poses and insufferable pride—a
diseased romantic, Louis once called him, and he didn't know
the half of it. She's the only realist in town; he's got to start
paying attention. Even now she's making sense: "My rump is
getting dumb, Richard. Dry me off and let's go back in the
other room."

But when he tries to stand, his knees feel like toothpaste,
and he has to sit again. Right back in the bidet, as it turns
out, dipping his ass like doughnuts in tea. She smiles under-
standingly, drapes a bath towel around her shoulders, pokes
through the medicine cabinet until she finds a jar of Yvonne's
cold cream, then takes him by the elbow. "Come on, Richard.
You can do it, yust lean on me." Which reminds him (his mind
at least is still working, more or less) of a night in Spain,
halfway up (or down) Suicide Hill in the Jarama valley, a
night he thought was to be his last, when he said that to
someone, or someone said it to him. God, what if he'd got it
shot off there? And missed this? An expression compounded
of hope and anguish, skepticism and awe, crosses his weary
face (thirty-eight at Christmas, if Strasser is right—oh
mother of God, it *is* going by!), picked up by the wheeling airport beacon. She removes his dripping jacket, his shirt as
well, and towels his behind before letting him collapse onto
the couch, then crosses to the ornamental table for a ciga-

rette from the humidor. She wears the towel like a cape, her haunches under it glittering as though sequined. She is, as always, a kind of walking light show, no less spectacular from the front as she turns back now toward the sofa, the nubbly texture of the towel contrasting subtly with the soft glow of her throat and breast, the sleek wet gleam of her belly.

She fits two cigarettes in her lips, lights them both (there's a bit of fumbling with the lighter, she's not very mechanical), and gazing soulfully down at Rick, passes him one of them. He grins. "Hey, where'd you learn that, kid?" She shrugs enigmatically, hands him the towel, and steps up between his knees. As he rubs her breasts, her belly, her thighs with the towel, the cigarette dangling in his lips, she gazes around at the chalky rough-plastered walls of his apartment, the Moorish furniture with its filigrees and inlaid patterns, the little bits of erotic art (there is a statue of a camel on the sideboard that looks like a man's wet penis on legs, and a strange nude statuette that might be a boy, or a girl, or something in between), the alabaster lamps and potted plants, those slatted wooden blinds, so exotic to her Northern eyes: he has style, she thinks, rubbing cold cream into her neck and shoulder with her free hand, he always did have . . .

She lifts one leg for him to dry and then the other, gasping inwardly (outwardly, she chokes and wheezes, having inhaled the cigarette by mistake: he stubs out his own with a sympathetic grin, takes what is left of hers) when he rubs the towel briskly between them, then she turns and bends over, bracing herself on the coffee table. Rick, the towel in his hands, pauses a moment, gazing thoughtfully through the drifting cigarette haze at these luminous buttocks, finding something almost otherworldly about them, like archways to heaven or an image of eternity. Has he seen them like this earlier tonight? Maybe, he can't remember. Certainly now he's able to savor the sight, no longer crazed by rut. They are, quite literally, a dream come true: he has whacked off to their memory so often during the last year and a half that it almost feels more appropriate to touch himself than this present manifestation. As he reaches toward them with the towel, he

seems to be crossing some strange threshold, as though passing from one medium into another. He senses the supple
buoyancy of them bouncing back against his hand as he
wipes them, yet, though flesh, they remain somehow immate-
rial, untouchable even when touched, objects whose very
presence is a kind of absence. If Rick Blaine were to believe
in angels, Ilsa's transcendent bottom is what they would look
like.

"Is this how you, uh, imagined things turning out tonight?" he asks around the butt, smoke curling out his nose
like thought's reek. Her cheeks seem to pop alight like his
Café Américain sign each time the airport beacon sweeps
past, shifting slightly like a sequence of film frames. Time itself may be like that, he knows: not a ceaseless flow, but a
rapid series of electrical leaps across tiny gaps between dis-
continuous bits. It's what he likes to call his link-and-claw
theory of time, though of course the theory is not his . . .

"Well, it may not be perfect, Richard, but it is better than
if I haff shot you, isn't it?"

"No, I meant . . ." Well, let it be. She's right, it beats eating a goddamn bullet. In fact it beats anything he can imagine. He douses his cigarette in the wet towel, tosses it aside,
wraps his arms around her thighs and pulls her buttocks (he
is still thinking about time as a pulsing sequence of film
frames, and not so much about the frames, their useless
dated content, as the gaps between: infinitesimally small
when looked at two-dimensionally, yet in their third dimension as deep and mysterious as the cosmos) toward his face,
pressing against them like a child trying to see through a
foggy window. He kisses and nibbles at each fresh-washed
cheek (and what if one were to slip *between* two of those
frames? he wonders—), runs his tongue into (—where would
he be then?) her anus, kneading the flesh on her pubic knoll
between his fingers all the while like little lumps of stiff taffy.
She raises one knee up onto the cushions, then the other, low-
ering her elbows to the floor (oh! she thinks as the blood
rushes in two directions at once, spreading into her head and
sex as though filling empty frames, her heart the gap be-

tween: what a strange dizzying dream time is!), thus lifting
to his contemplative scrutiny what looks like a clinging sea
anemone between her thighs, a thick woolly pod, a cloven
chinchilla, open purse, split fruit. But it is not the appearance of it that moves him (except to the invention of these
fanciful catalogues), it is the smell. It is this which catapults
him suddenly and wholly back to Paris, a Paris he'd lost until
this moment (she is not in Paris, she is in some vast dimen-
sionless region she associates with childhood, a nighttime
glow in her midsummer room, featherbedding between her
legs) but now has back again. Now and for all time. As he
runs his tongue up and down the spongy groove, pinching the
lips tenderly between his tongue and stiff upper lip (an old
war wound), feeling it engorge, pulsate, almost pucker up to
kiss him back, he seems to see—as though it were fading in
on the blank screen of her gently rolling bottom—that night
at her apartment in Paris when she first asked him to "Kiss
me, Richard, here. My other mouth wants to luff you, too . . ."
He'd never done that before. He had been all over the world,
had fought in wars, battled cops, been jailed and tortured,
hid out in whorehouses, parachuted out of airplanes, had
eaten and drunk just about everything, had been blown off
the decks of ships, killed more men than he'd like to count,
and had banged every kind and color of woman on earth, but
he had never tasted one of these things before. Other women
had sucked him off, of course, before Ilsa nearly caused him
to wreck his car that day in the Bois de Boulogne, but he had
always thought of that as a service due him, something he'd
paid for in effect—he was the man, after all. But reciproca-
tion, sucking back—well, that always struck him as vaguely
queer, something guys, manly guys anyway, didn't do. That
night, though, he'd had a lot of champagne and he was—this
was the simple truth, and it was an experience as exotic to
Rick Blaine as the taste of a cunt—madly in love. He had
been an unhappy misfit all his life, at best a romantic drifter,
at worst and in the eyes of most a sleazy gunrunner and
chickenshit mercenary (though God knows he'd hoped for
more), a whoremonger and brawler and miserable gutter

drunk: nothing like Ilsa Lund had ever happened to him, and he could hardly believe it was happening to him that night. His immediate reaction—he admits this, sucking greedily at it now (she is galloping her father's horse through the woods of the north, canopy-dark and sunlight-blinding at the same time, pushing the beast beneath her, racing toward what she believed to be God's truth, flushing through her from the saddle up as eternity might when the saints were called), while watching himself, on the cinescreen of her billowing behind, kneel to it that first time like an atheist falling squeamishly into conversion—was not instant rapture. No, like olives, home brew, and Arab cooking, it took a little getting used to. But she taught him how to stroke the vulva with his tongue, where to find the nun's cap ("my little sister," she called it, which struck him as odd) and how to draw it out, how to use his fingers, nose, chin, even his hair and ears, and the more he practiced for her sake, the more he liked it for his own, her pleasure (he could *see* it: it bloomed right under his nose, filling his grimy life with colors he'd never even thought of before!) augmenting his, until he found his appetite for it almost insatiable. God, the boys on the block back in New York would laugh their asses off to see how far he'd fallen! And though he has tried others since, it is still the only one he really likes. Yvonne's is terrible, bitter and pomaded (she seems to sense this, gets no pleasure from it at all, often turns fidgety and mean when he goes down on her, even had a kind of biting, scratching fit once: "Don' you lak to *fuck?*" she'd screamed), which is the main reason he's lost interest in her. That and her hairy legs.

His screen is shrinking (her knees have climbed to his shoulders, scrunching her hips into little bumps and bringing her shoulderblades into view, down near the floor, where she is gasping and whimpering and sucking the carpet), but his vision of the past is expanding, as though her pumping cheeks were a chubby bellows, opening and closing, opening and closing, inflating his memories. Indeed, he no longer needs a screen for them, for it is not this or that conquest that he recalls now, this or that event, not what she wore or what she said, what he said, but something more profound than that, something experienced in the way that a blind man sees or an amputee touches. Texture returns to him, ambience, impressions of radiance, of coalescence, the foamy taste of the ineffable on his tongue, the downy nap of time-lessness, the tooth of now. All this he finds in Ilsa's juicy bouncing cunt—and more: love's pungent illusions of consub-stantiation and infinitude (oh, he knows what he lost that day in the rain in the Gare de Lyon!), the bittersweet fall into actuality, space's secret folds wherein one might lose one's ego, one's desperate sense of isolation, Paris, rediscovered here as pure aura, effervescent and allusive, La Belle Aurore as immanence's theater, sacred showplace—

Oh hell, he thinks as Ilsa's pounding hips drive him to his back on the couch, her thighs slapping against his ears (as she rises, her blood in riptide against her mounting excite-ment, the airport beacon touching her in its passing like bursts of inspiration, she thinks: childhood is a place apart, needing the adult world to exist at all: without Victor there could *be* no Rick!—and then she cannot think at all), La Belle Aurore! She broke his goddamn heart at La Belle Aurore. "Kiss me," she said, holding herself with both hands as though to keep the pain from spilling out down there, "one last time," and he did, for her, Henri didn't care, merde alors, the Germans were coming anyway, and the other patrons thought it was just part of the entertainment; only Sam was offended and went off to the john till it was over. And then she left him. Forever. Or anyway until she turned up here a night ago with Laszlo. God, he remembers everything about that day in the Belle Aurore, what she was wearing, what the Germans were wearing, what Henri was wearing. It was not an easy day to forget. The Germans were at the very edge of the city, they were bombing the bejesus out of the place and everything was literally falling down around their ears (she's smothering him now with her bucking arse, her scissoring thighs: he heaves her over onto her back and pushes his arms between her thighs to spread them); they'd had to crawl over rubble and dead bodies, push through barricades, just to reach the damned café. No chance to get out by car, he was lucky there was enough left in his "F.Y. Fund" to buy them all train tickets. And then the betrayal: "I can' find her, Mr. Richard. She's checked outa de hotel. But dis note come jus' after you lef'!" Oh shit, even now it makes him cry. "I cannot go with you or ever see you again." In perfect Palmer Method handwriting, as though to exult in her power over him. He kicked poor Sam's ass up and down that train all the way to Marseilles, convinced it was somehow his fault. Even a hex maybe, that day he could have believed anything. Now, with her hips bouncing frantically up against his mouth, her bush grown to an astonishing size, the lips out and flapping like flags, the trench between them awash in a fragrant ooze like oily air, he lifts his head and asks: "Why weren't you honest with me? Why did you keep your marriage a secret?"

"Oh Gott, Richard! Not *now*—!"

She's right, it doesn't seem the right moment for it, but then nothing has seemed right since she turned up in this godforsaken town: it's almost as though two completely different places, two completely different times, are being forced to mesh, to intersect where no intersection is possible, causing a kind of warp in the universe. In his own private universe anyway. He gazes down on this lost love, this faithless wife, this trusting child, her own hands between her legs now, her hips still jerking out of control ("Please, Richard!" she is begging softly through clenched teeth, tears in her eyes), thinking: It's still a story without an ending. But more than that: the beginning and middle bits aren't all there either. Her face is drained as though all the blood has rushed away to other parts, but her throat between the heaving white breasts is almost literally alight with its vivid blush. He touches it, strokes the soft bubbles to either side, watching the dark little nipples rise like patriots—and suddenly the answer to all his questions seems (yet another one, that is—answers, in the end, are easy) to suggest itself. "Listen kid, would it be all right if I—?"

"Oh yes! yes!—*but hurry!*"

He finds the cold cream (at last! he is so slow!), lathers it on, and slips into her cleavage, his knees over her shoulders like a yoke. She guides his head back into that tropical explosion between her legs, then clasps her arms around his hips, already beginning to thump at her chest like a resuscitator, popping little gasps from her throat. She tries to concentrate on his bouncing buttocks, but they communicate to her such a touching blend of cynicism and honesty, weariness and generosity, that they nearly break her heart, making her more light-headed than ever. The dark little hole between them bobs like a lonely survivor in a tragically divided world. It is he! "Oh Gott!" she whimpers. And she! The tension between her legs is almost unbearable. "I can't fight it anymore!" Everything starts to come apart. She feels herself falling as though through some rift in the universe (she cannot wait for him, and anyway, where she is going he cannot follow), out of time and matter into some wondrous radiance, the wheeling beacon flashing across her stricken vision now like intermittent star bursts, the music swelling, *everything* swelling, her eyes bursting, ears popping, teeth ringing in their sockets— "Oh Richard! Oh fokk! *I luff you so much!*"

He plunges his face deep into Ilsa's ambrosial pudding, lapping at its sweet sweat, feeling her loins snap and convulse violently around him, knowing that with a little inducement she can spasm like this for minutes on end, and meanwhile pumping away between her breasts now like a madman, no longer obliged to hold back, seeking purely his own pleasure. This pleasure is tempered only by (and maybe enhanced by as well) his pity for her husband, that heroic sonuvabitch. God, Victor Laszlo is almost a father figure to him, really. And while Laszlo is off at the underground meeting in the Caverne du Roi, no doubt getting his saintly ass shot to shit, here he is—Rick Blaine, the Yankee smart aleck and general jerk-off—safely closeted off in his rooms over the town saloon, tit-fucking the hero's wife, his callous nose up her own royal grotto like an advance scout for a squad of storm troopers. It's not fair, goddamn it, he thinks, and laughs at this even as he comes, squirting jism down her sleek belly and under his own, his head locked in her clamped thighs, her arms hugging him tightly as though to squeeze the juices out.

He is lying, completely still, his face between Ilsa's flaccid thighs, knees over her shoulders, arms around her lower body, which sprawls loosely now beneath him. He can feel her hands resting lightly on his hips, her warm breath against his leg. He doesn't remember when they stopped moving. Maybe he's been sleeping. Has he dreamt it all? No, he shifts slightly and feels the spill of semen, pooled gummily between their conjoined navels. His movement wakes Ilsa: she snorts faintly, sighs, kisses the inside of his leg, strokes one buttock idly. "That soap smells nice," she murmurs. "I bet effry girl in Casablanca wishes to haff a bath here."

"Yeah, well, I run it as a kind of public service," he grunts, chewing the words around a strand or two of pubic hair. He's always told Louis—and anyone else who wanted to know—that he sticks his neck out for nobody. But in the end, shit, he thinks, I stick it out for everybody. "I'm basically a civic-minded guy."

Cynic-minded, more like, she thinks, but keeps the thought to herself. She cannot risk offending him, not just now. She is still returning from wherever it is orgasm has taken her, and it has been an experience so profound and powerful, yet so remote from its immediate cause—his muscular tongue at the other end of this morosely puckered hole in front of her nose—that it has left her feeling very insecure, unsure of who or what she is, or even where. She knows of course that her role as the well-dressed wife of a courageous underground leader is just pretense, that beneath this charade she is certainly someone—or something—else. Richard's lover, for example. Or a little orphan girl who lost her mother, father, and adoptive aunt, all before she'd even started menstruating—that's who she often is, or feels like she is, especially at moments like this. But if her life as Victor Laszlo's wife is not real, are these others any more so? Is she one person, several—or no one at all? What was that thought she'd had about childhood? She lies there, hugging Richard's hairy cheeks (are they Richard's? are they cheeks?), her pale face framed by his spraddled legs, trying to puzzle it all out. Since the moment she arrived in Casablanca, she and Richard have been trying to tell each other stories, not very funny stories, as Richard has remarked, but maybe not very true ones either. Maybe memory itself is a kind of trick, something that turns illusion into reality and makes the real world vanish before everyone's eyes like magic. One can certainly sink away there and miss everything, she knows. Hasn't Victor, the wise one, often warned her of that? But Victor is a hero. Maybe the real world is too much for most people. Maybe making up stories is a way to keep them all from going insane. A tear forms in the corner of one eye. She blinks (and what are these unlikely configurations called "Paris" and "Casablanca," where in all the universe is she, and what is "where"?), and the tear trickles into the hollow between cheekbone and nose, then bends its course toward the middle of her cheek. There is a line in their song (yes, it is still there, tinkling away somewhere like mice in the walls: is someone trying to drive her crazy?) that goes, "This day and age we're living in gives cause for apprehension,/With speed and new invention and things like third dimension . . ." She always thought that was a stupid mistake of the lyricist, but now she is not so sure. For the real mystery—she sees this now, or *feels* it rather—is not the fourth dimension as she'd always supposed (the tear stops halfway down her cheek, begins to fade), or the third either for that matter . . . but the *first*.

"You never finished answering my question . . ."

There is a pause. Perhaps she is daydreaming. "What question, Richard?"

"A while ago. In the bathroom . . ." He, too, has been mulling over recent events, wondering not only about the events themselves (wondrous in their own right, of course: he's not enjoyed multiple orgasms like this since he hauled his broken-down blacklisted ass out of Paris a year and a half ago, and that's just for starters), but also about their "recentness": When did they really happen? Is "happen" the right word, or were they more like fleeting conjunctions with the Absolute, that *other* Other, boundless and immutable as number? And, if so, what now is "when"? How much time has elapsed, for example, since he opened the door and found her in this room? Has *any* time elapsed? "I asked you what you meant when you said, 'Is this right?'"

"Oh, Richard, I don't know what's right any longer." She lifts one thigh in front of his face, as though to erase his dark imaginings. He strokes it, thinking: well, what the hell, it probably doesn't amount to a hill of beans, anyway. "Do you think I can haff another drink now?"

"Sure, kid. Why not." He sits up beside her, shakes the butt out of the damp towel, wipes his belly off, hands the towel to her. "More of the same?"

"Champagne would be nice, if it is possible. It always makes me think of Paris . . . and you . . ."

"You got it, sweetheart." He pushes himself to his feet and thumps across the room, pausing at the humidor to light up a fresh smoke. "If there's any left. Your old man's been going through my stock like Vichy water." Not for the first time, he has the impression of being watched. Laszlo? Who knows, maybe the underground meeting was just a ruse; it certainly seemed like a dumb thing to do on the face of it, especially with Strasser in town. There's a bottle of champagne in his icebox, okay, but no ice. He touches the bottle: not cold, but cool enough. It occurs to him the sonuvabitch might be out on the balcony right now, taking it all in, he and all his goddamn underground. Europeans can be pretty screwy, especially these rich stiffs with titles. As he carries the champagne and glasses over to the coffee table, the cigarette like a dart between his lips, his bare ass feels suddenly both hot and chilly at the same time. "Does your husband ever get violent?" he asks around the smoke and snaps the metal clamp off the champagne bottle, takes a grip on the cork.

"No. He has killed some people, but he is not fiolent." She is rubbing her tummy off, smiling thoughtfully. The light from the airport beacon, wheeling past, picks up a varnish-like glaze still between her breasts, a tooth's wet twinkle in her open mouth, an unwonted shine on her nose. The cork pops, champagne spews out over the table top, some of it get-

ting into the glasses. This seems to suggest somehow a revelation. Or another memory. The tune, as though released,
rides up once more around them. "Gott, Richard," she sighs,
pushing irritably to her feet. "That music is getting on my
nerfs!"

"Yeah, I know." It's almost as bad in its way as the
German blitzkrieg hammering in around their romance in
Paris—sometimes it seemed to get right between their embraces. Gave him a goddamn headache. Now the music is doing much the same thing, even trying to tell them when to
kiss and when not to. He can stand it, though, he thinks,
tucking the cigarette back in his lips, if she can. He picks up
the two champagne glasses, offers her one. "Forget it, kid.
Drown it out with this." He raises his glass. "Uh, here's
lookin'—"

She gulps it down absently, not waiting for his toast.
"And that light from the airport," she goes on, batting at it as
it passes as though to shoo it away. "How can you effer sleep
here?"

"No one's supposed to sleep well in Casablanca," he replies with a worldly grimace. It's his best expression, he
knows, but she isn't paying any attention. He stubs out the
cigarette, refills her glass, blowing a melancholy whiff of
smoke over it. "Hey, kid here's—"

"No, wait!" she insists, her ear cocked. "*Is* it?"

"Is what?" Ah well, forget the fancy stuff. He drinks off
the champagne in his glass, reaches down for a refill.

"Time. Is it going by? Like the song is saying?"

He looks up, startled. "That's funny, I was just—!"

"What time do you haff, Richard?"

He sets the bottle down, glances at his empty wrist. "I
dunno. My watch must have got torn off when we . . ."

"Mine is gone, too."

They stare at each other a moment, Rick scowling
slightly in the old style, Ilsa's lips parted as though saying
"story," or "glory." Then the airport beacon sweeps past like a
prompter, and Rick, blinking, says: "Wait a minute—there's a
clock down in the bar!" He strides purposefully over to the

door in his stocking feet, pausing there a moment, one hand on the knob, to take a deep breath. "I'll be right back," he announces, then opens the door and (she seems about to call out to him) steps out on the landing. He steps right back in again. He pushes the door closed, leans against it, his face ashen. "They're all down there," he says.

"What? Who's down there?"

"Karl, Sam, Abdul, that Norwegian—"

"Fictor?!"

"Yes, everybody! Strasser, those goddamn Bulgarians, Sasha, Louis—"

"Yffonne?"

Why the hell did she ask about Yvonne? "I said everybody! They're just standing down there! Like they're waiting for something! But . . . for what?!" He can't seem to stop his goddamn voice from squeaking. He wants to remain cool and ironically detached, cynical even, because he knows it's expected of him, not least of all by himself, but he's still shaken by what he's seen down in the bar. Of course it might help if he had his pants on. At least he'd have some pockets to shove his hands into. For some reason, Ilsa is staring at his crotch, as though the real horror of it all were to be found there. Or maybe she's trying to see through to the silent crowd below. "It's, I dunno, like the place has sprung a goddamn leak or something!"

She crosses her hands to her shoulders, pinching her elbows in, hugging her breasts. She seems to have gone flat-footed, her feet splayed, her bottom, lost somewhat in the slatted shadows, drooping, her spine bent. "A leak?" she asks meaninglessly in her soft Scandinavian accent. She looks like a swimmer out of water in chilled air. Richard, slumping against the far door, stares at her as though at a total stranger. Or perhaps a mirror. He seems older somehow, tired, his chest sunken and belly out, legs bowed, his genitals shriveled up between them like dried fruit. It is not a beautiful sight. Of course Richard is not a beautiful man. He is short and bad-tempered and rather smashed up. Victor calls him riffraff. He says Richard makes him feel greasy. And it is true, there is something common about him. Around Victor she always feels crisp and white, but around Richard like a sweating pig. So how did she get mixed up with him, in the first place? Well, she was lonely, she had nothing, not even hope, and he seemed so happy when she took hold of his penis. As Victor has often said, each of us has a destiny, for good or for evil, and her destiny was Richard. Now that destiny seems confirmed—or sealed—by all those people downstairs. "They are not waiting for anything," she says, as the realization comes to her. It is over.

Richard grunts in reply. He probably hasn't heard her. She feels a terrible sense of loss. He shuffles in his black socks over to the humidor. "Shit, even the fags are gone," he mutters gloomily. "Why'd you have to come to Casablanca anyway, goddamn it; there are other places . . ." The airport beacon, sliding by, picks up an expression of intense concentration on his haggard face. She knows he is trying to understand what cannot be understood, to resolve what has no resolution. Americans are like that. In Paris he was always wondering how it was they kept getting from one place to another so quickly. "It's like everything is all speeded up," he would gasp, reaching deliriously between her legs as her apartment welled up around them. Now he is probably wondering why there seems to be no place to go and why time suddenly is just about all they have. He is an innocent man, after all; this is probably his first affair.

"I would not haff come if I haff known . . ." She releases her shoulders, picks up her ruffled blouse (the buttons arc gone), pulls it on like a wrap. As the beacon wheels by, the room seems to expand with light as though it were breathing. "Do you see my skirt? It was here, but—is it getting dark or something?"

"I mean, of all the gin joints in all the towns in all the—!" He pauses, looks up. "What did you say?"

"I said, is it—?"

"Yeah, I know . . ."

They gaze about uneasily. "It seems like effry time that light goes past . . ."

"Yeah . . ." He stares at her, slumped there at the foot of the couch, working her garter belt like rosary beads, looking like somebody had just pulled her plug. "The world will always welcome lovers," the music is suggesting, not so much in mockery as in sorrow. He's thinking of all those people downstairs, so hushed, so motionless: it's almost how he feels inside. Like something dying. Or something dead revealed. Oh shit. Has this happened before? Ilsa seems almost wraith-like in the pale staticky light, as though she were wearing her own ghost on her skin. And which is it he's been in love with? he wonders. He sees she is trembling, and a tear slides down the side of her nose, or seems to, it's hard to tell. He feels like he's going blind. "Listen. Maybe if we started over . . ."

"I'm too tired, Richard . . ."

"No, I mean, go back to where you came in, see—the letters of transit and all that. Maybe we made some kinda mistake, I dunno, like when I put my hands on your jugs or something, and if—"

"A mistake? You think putting your hands on my yugs was a mistake—?"

"Don't get offended, sweetheart. I only meant—"

"Maybe my bringing my yugs *here* tonight was a mistake! Maybe my not shooting the *trigger* was a mistake!"

"Come on, don't get your tail in an uproar, goddamn it! I'm just trying to—"

"Oh, what a fool I was to fall . . . to fall . . ."

"Jesus, Ilsa, are you crying. . . ? Ilsa. . . ?" He sighs irritably. He is never going to understand women. Her head is bowed as though in resignation: one has seen her like this often when Laszlo is near. She seems to be staring at the empty buttonholes in her blouse. Maybe she's stupider than he thought. When the dimming light swings past, tears glint in the corners of her eyes, little points of light in the gathering shadows on her face. "Hey, dry up, kid! All I want you to do is go over there by the curtains where you were when I—"

"Can I tell you a . . . story, Richard?"

"Not *now*, Ilsa! Christ! The light's almost gone and—"

"Anyway, it wouldn't work."

"What?"

"Trying to do it all again. It wouldn't work. It wouldn't be the same. I won't even haff my girdle on."

"That doesn't matter. Who's gonna know? Come on, we can at least—"

"No, Richard. It is impossible. You are different, I am different. You haff cold cream on your penis—"

"But—!"

"My makeup is gone, there are stains on the carpet. And I would need the pistol—how could we effer find it in the dark? No, it's useless, Richard. Belief me. Time goes by."

"But maybe that's just it . . ."

"Or what about your tsigarette? Eh? Can you imagine going through that without your tsigarette? Richard? I am laughing! Where are you, Richard . . . ?"

"Take it easy, I'm over here. By the balcony. Just lemme think."

"Efen the airport light has stopped."

"Yeah. I can't see a fucking thing out there."

"Well, you always said you wanted a wow finish . . . Maybe . . ."

"What?"

"What?"

"What did you say?"

"I said, maybe this is . . . you know, what we always wanted . . . Like a dream come true . . ."

"Speak up, kid. It's getting hard to hear you."

"I said, *when we are fokking—*"

"Nah, that won't do any good, sweetheart, I know that now. We gotta get back into the goddamn world somehow. If we don't, we'll regret it. Maybe not today—"

"What? We'll forget it?"

"No, I said—"

"What?"

"Never mind."

"Forget what, Richard?"

"I said I think I shoulda gone fishing with Sam when I had the chance."

"I can't seem to hear you . . ."

"No, wait a minute! Maybe you're right! Maybe going back isn't the right idea . . ."

"Richard . . . ?"

"Instead, maybe we gotta think ahead . . ."

"Richard, I am afraid . . ."

"Yeah, like you could sit there on the couch, see, we've been fucking, that's all right, who cares, now we're having some champagne—"

"I think I am *already* forgetting . . ."

"And you can tell me that story you've been wanting to tell—are you listening? A good story, that may do it—anything that *moves!* And meanwhile, lemme think, I'll, let's see, I'll sit down—no, I'll sort of lean here in the doorway and—*oof!*—shit! I think they moved it!"

"Richard . . . ?"

"Who the hell rearranged the—*ungh!*—goddamn geography?"

"Richard, it's a crazy world . . ."

"Ah, here! this feels like it. Something like it. Now what was I—? Right! You're telling a story, so, uh, I'll say . . ."

"But wherever you are . . ."

"*And then*—*?* Yeah, that's good. It's almost like I'm remembering this. You've stopped, see, but I want you to go on, I want you to keep spilling what's on your mind, I'm filling in all the blanks . . ."

". . . whatever happens . . ."

"So I say: *And then*—*?* C'mon, kid, can you hear me? Remember all those people downstairs! They're depending on us! Just think it: if you think it, you'll do it! *And then*—*?*"

". . . I want you to know . . ."

"*And then* . . . *?* Oh shit, Ilsa . . . ? Where are you? And then . . . ?"

". . . I luff you . . ."

"And then . . . ? Ilsa . . . ? And *then* . . . *?*"

Szyrk v. Village of Tatamount et al., U.S. District Court, Southern District of Virginia No. 105-87

William Gaddis

OPINION

CREASE, J.

The facts are not in dispute. On the morning of September 30 while running at large in the Village a dog identified as Spot entered under and therewith became entrapped in the lower reaches of a towering steel sculpture known as Cyclone Seven which dominates the plaza overlooking and adjoining the depot of the Norfolk & Pee Dee Railroad. Searching for his charge, the dog's master James B who is seven years old was alerted by its whines and yelps to discover its plight, whereupon his own vain efforts to deliver it attracted those of a passerby soon joined by others whose combined attempts to wheedle, cajole, and intimidate the unfortunate animal forth served rather to compound its predicament, driving it deeper into the structure. These futile activities soon assembled a good cross section of the local population, from the usual idlers and senior citizens to members of the Village Board, the Sheriff's office, the Fire Department, and, not surprisingly, the victim's own kind, until by nightfall word having spread to neighboring hamlets attracted not only them in numbers sufficient to cause an extensive traffic jam but members of the local press and an enterprising television crew. Notwithstanding means successfully devised to assuage the dog's pangs of hunger, those of its confinement continued well into the following day when the decision was taken by the full Village Board to engage the Fire Department to enter the structure employing acetylene torches to effect its safe delivery, without considering the good likelihood of precipitating an action for damages by the creator of Cyclone Seven, Mr Szyrk, a sculptor of some wide reputation in artistic circles.

Alerted by the media to the threat posed to his creation, Mr Szyrk moved promptly from his SoHo studio in New York to file for a temporary restraining order 'on a summary showing of its necessity to prevent immediate and irreparable injury' to his sculptural work, which was issued ex parte even as the torches of deliverance were being kindled. All this occurred four days ago.

Given the widespread response provoked by this confrontation in the media at large and echoing as far distant as the deeper South and even Arkansas but more immediately at the site itself, where energies generated by opposing sympathies further aroused by the police presence and that of the Fire Department in full array, the floodlights, vans, and other paraphernalia incident to a fiercely competitive television environment bringing in its train the inevitable placards and displays of the American flag, the venders of food and novelty items, all enhanced by the barks and cries of the victim's own local acquaintance, have erupted in shoving matches, fistfights, and related hostilities with distinctly racial overtones (the dog's master James B and his family are black), and finally in rocks and beer cans hurled at the sculpture Cyclone Seven itself, the court finds sufficient urgency in the main action of this proceeding to reject defendants' assertions and cross motions for the reasons set forth below and grants summary judgment to plaintiff on the issue of his motion for a preliminary injunction to supersede the temporary restraining order now in place.

To grant summary judgment, as explicated by Judge Stanton in Steinberg v. Columbia Pictures et al., Fed. R. Civ. P. 56 requires a court to find that 'there is no genuine issue as to any material fact and that the moving party is entitled to a judgment as a matter of law.' In reaching its decision the court must 'assess whether there are any factual issues to be tried, while resolving ambiguities and drawing reasonable inferences against the moving party' (Knight v. U.S. Fire Ins. Co., 804 F.2d 9, 11, 2d Circ., 1986, citing Anderson v. Liberty Lobby, 106 S.Ct. 2505, 2509-11, 1986). In plaintiff's filing for a restraining order his complaint alleges, by counts, courses of action to which defendants have filed answers and cross claims opposing motion for a preliminary injunction. The voluminous submissions accompanying these cross motions leave no factual issues concerning which further evidence is likely to be presented at a trial. Moreover, the factual determinations necessary to this decision do not involve conflicts in testimony that would depend for their resolution on an assessment of witness credibility as cited infra. The interests of judicial economy being served by deciding the case at its present stage, summary judgment is therefore appropriate.

Naming as defendants the Village Board, the dog's master James B through his guardian ad litem, 'and such other parties and entities as may emerge in the course of this proceeding,' Mr Szyrk first alleges animal trespass, summoning in support of this charge a citation from early law holding that 'where my beasts of their own wrong without my will and knowledge break another's close I shall be punished, for I am the trespasser with my beasts' (12 Henry VII, Kielwey 3b), which exhibit the court, finding no clear parallel in the laws of this Commonwealth, dismisses as ornamental. Concerning plaintiff's further exhibit of Village Code 21 para. 6b (known as 'the leash law'), we take judicial notice of defendants' response alleging that, however specific in wording and intent, this ordinance appears more honored in the breach, in that on any pleasant day well known members of the local dog community are to be observed in all their disparity of size, breed, and other particulars ambling in the raffish camaraderie of sailors ashore down the Village main street and thence wherever habit and appetite may take them undeterred by any citizen or arm of the law. Spot, so named for the liver colored marking prominent on his loin, is described as of mixed breed wherein, from his reduced stature, silken coat, and 'soulful' eyes, that of spaniel appears to prevail. His age is found to be under one year. Whereas in distinguishing between animals as either mansuetae or ferae naturae Spot is clearly to be discovered among the former 'by custom devoted to the service of mankind at the time and in the place in which it is kept' and thus granted the indulgence customarily accorded such domestic pets, and further whereas as in the instant case scienter is not required (Weaver v. National Biscuit Co., 125 F.2d 463, 7th Circ., 1942; Parsons v. Manser, 119 Iowa 88, 93 N.W. 86, 1903), such indulgence is indicative of the courts' retreat over the past century from strict liability for trespass (Sanders v. Teape & Swan, 51 L.T. 263, 1884; Olson v. Pederson, 206 Minn. 415, 288 N.W. 856,1939), we find plaintiff's allegation on this count without merit (citation omitted).

On the related charge of damages brought by plaintiff the standard for preliminary relief must first be addressed. Were it to be found for plaintiff that irreparable harm has indeed been inflicted upon his creation, and that adequate remedy at law should suffice in the form of money damages, in such event the court takes judicial notice in directing such claim to be made against the Village Board and the dog's master in tandem, since as in the question posed by the Merchant of Venice (I, iii, 122) 'Hath a dog money?' the answer must be that it does not. However, as regards the claim that the dog Spot, endowed with little more than milk teeth however sharp, and however extreme the throes of his despair, can have wreaked irreparable harm upon his steel confines this appears to be without foundation. Further to this charge, defendants respond, and the court concurs, citing plaintiff's original artistic intentions, that these steel surfaces have become pitted and acquired a heavy patina of rust following plaintiff's stated provision that his creation stand freely exposed to the mercy or lack thereof of natural forces, wherewith we may observe that a dog is not a boy, much less a fireman brandishing an acetylene torch, but nearer in its indifferent ignorance to those very forces embraced in the pathetic fallacy and so to be numbered among them. We have finally no more than a presumption of damage due to the inaccessibility of this inadvertent captive's immediate vicinity, and failing such evidentiary facts we find that the standards for preliminary relief have not been met and hold this point moot.

Here we take judicial notice of counterclaims filed on behalf of defendant James B seeking to have this court hold both plaintiff and the Village and other parties thereto liable for wilfully creating, installing and maintaining an attractive nuisance which by its very nature and freedom of access constitutes an allurement to trespass, thus enticing the dog into its present allegedly dangerous predicament. Here plaintiff demurs, the Village joining in his demurrer, offering in exhibit similar structures of which Cyclone Seven is one of a series occupying sites elsewhere in the land, wherein among the four and on only one occasion a similar event occurred at a Long Island, New York, site in the form of a boy similarly entrapped and provoking a similar outcry until a proffered ten dollar bill brought him forth little the worse. However, a boy is not a dog, and whereas in the instant case Cyclone Seven posed initially a kind of ornate 'jungle gym' to assorted younger members of the community, we may find on the part of Spot absent his testimony neither a perception of challenge to his prowess at climbing nor any aesthetic sensibility luring him into harm's way requiring a capacity to distinguish Cyclone Seven as a work of art from his usual environs in the junk yard presided over by defendant James B's father and guardian ad litem, where the progeny of man's inventiveness embraces three acres of rusting testimony thereto, and that hence his trespass was entirely inadvertent and in good likelihood dictated by a mere call of nature as abounding evidence of similar casual missions on the part of other members of the local dog community in the sculpture's immediate vicinity attest.

In taking judicial notice of defendant's counterclaim charging allurement we hold this charge to be one of ordinary negligence liability, already found to be without merit in this proceeding; however, we extend this judicial notice to embrace that section of plaintiff's response to the related charge of dangerous nuisance wherein plaintiff alleges damage from the strong hence derogatory implication that his sculptural creation, with a particular view to its internal components, was designed and executed not merely to suggest but to actually convey menace, whereto he exhibits extensive dated and annotated sketches, drawings, and notes made, revised, and witnessed in correspondence, demonstrating that at no time was the work, in any way or ways as a whole or in any component part or parts or combinations thereof including but not limited to sharp planes, spirals, and serrated steel limbs bearing distinct resemblances to teeth, ever in any manner conceived or carried out with intent of entrapment and consequent physical torment, but to the contrary that its creation was inspired and dictated in its entirety by wholly artistic considerations embracing its component parts in an aesthetic synergy wherein the sum of these sharp planes, jagged edges and toothlike projections aforementioned stand as mere depictions and symbols being in the aggregate greater than the sum of the parts taken individually to serve the work as, here quoting the catalogue distributed at its unveiling, 'A testimony to man's indiminable [*sic*] spirit.'

We have in other words plaintiff claiming to act as an instrument of higher authority, namely 'art,' wherewith we may first cite its dictionary definition as '(1) Human effort to imitate, supplement, alter or counteract the work of nature.' Notwithstanding that Cyclone Seven clearly answers this description especially in its last emphasis, there remain certain fine distinctions posing some little difficulty for the average lay observer persuaded from habit and even education to regard sculptural art as beauty synonymous with truth in expressing harmony as visibly incarnate in the lineaments of Donatello's David, or as the very essence of the sublime manifest in the Milos Aphrodite, leaving him in the present instance quite unprepared to discriminate between sharp steel teeth as sharp steel teeth, and sharp steel teeth as artistic expressions of sharp steel teeth, obliging us for the purpose of this proceeding to confront the theory that in having become self referential art is in itself theory without which it has no more substance than Sir Arthur Eddington's famous step 'on a swarm of flies,' here present in further exhibits by plaintiff drawn from prestigious art publications and highly esteemed critics in the lay press, where they make their livings, recommending his sculptural creation in terms of slope, tangent, acceleration, force, energy and similar abstract extravagancies serving only a corresponding self referential confrontation of language with language and thereby, in reducing language itself to theory, rendering it a mere plaything, which exhibits the court finds frivolous. Having here in effect thrown the bathwater out with the baby, in the clear absence of any evidentiary facts to support defendants' countercharge 'dangerous nuisance,' we find it without merit.

We next turn to a related complaint contained in defendant James B's cross claim filed in rem Cyclone Seven charging plaintiff, the Village, 'and other parties and entities as their interests may appear' with erecting and maintaining a public nuisance in the form of 'an obstruction making use of passage inconvenient and unreasonably burdensome upon the general public' (Fugate v. Carter, 151 Va. 108, 144 S.E. 483, 1928; Regester v. Lincoln Oil Ref. Co., 95 Ind.App. 425, 183 N.E. 693, 1933). As specified in this complaint, Cyclone Seven stands 24 feet 8 inches high with an irregular base circumference of approximately 74 feet and weighs 24 tons, and in support of his allegation of public nuisance defendant cites a basic tenet of early English law defining such nuisance as that 'which obstructs or causes inconvenience or damage to the public in the exercise of rights common to all Her Majesty's subjects,' further citing such nuisance as that which 'injuriously affects the safety, health or morals of the public, or works some substantial annoyance, inconvenience or injury to the public' (Commonwealth v. South Covington & Cincinnati Street Railway Co., 181 Ky. 459, 463, 205 SW 581, 583, 6 A.L.R. 118, 1918). Depositions taken from selected Village residents and submitted in rem Cyclone Seven include: 'We'd used to be this nice peaceable town before this foreigner come in here putting up this [expletive] piece of [obscenity] brings in every [expletive] kind of riffraff, even see some out of state plates'; 'Since that [expletive] thing went up there I have to park my pickup way down by Ott's and walk all hell and gone just for a hoagie'; 'Let's just see you try and catch a train where you can't hardly see nothing for the rain and sleet and you got to detour way round that heap of [obscenity] to the depot to get there'; 'I just always used the men's room up there to the depot but now there's times when I don't hardly make it'; 'They want to throw away that kind of money I mean they'd have just better went and put us up another [expletive] church.'

Clearly from this and similar eloquent testimony certain members of the community have been subjected to annoyance and serious inconvenience in the pursuit of private errands of some urgency; however recalling to mind that vain and desperate effort to prevent construction of a subway kiosk in Cambridge, Massachusetts, enshrined decades ago in the news headline PRESIDENT LOWELL FIGHTS ERECTION IN HARVARD SQUARE, by definition the interests of the general public must not be confused with that of one or even several individuals (People v. Brooklyn & Queens Transit Corp., 258 App.Div. 753, 15 N.Y.S.2d 295,1939, affirmed 283 N.Y. 484, 28 N.E.2d 925, 1940); furthermore the obstruction is not so substantial as to preclude access (Holland v. Grant County, 208 Or. 50, 298 P.2d 832, 1956; Ayers v. Stidham, 260 Ala. 390, 71 So.2d 95, 1954), and in finding the former freedom of access to have been provided by mere default where no delineated path or thoroughfare was ever ordained or even contemplated this claim is denied.

On a lesser count charging private nuisance, H R Suggs Jr, joins himself to this proceeding via intervention naming all parties thereto in his complaint on grounds of harboring a dog 'which makes the night hideous with its howls' which the court severs from this action nonetheless taking judicial notice of intervener's right inseparable from ownership of the property bordering directly thereupon, to its undisturbed enjoyment thereof (Restatement of the Law, Second, Torts 2d,

822c), and remands to trial. Similarly, whereas none of the parties to this action has sought relief on behalf of the well being and indeed survival of the sculpture's unwilling resident, and whereas a life support system of sorts has been devised pro tem thereto, this matter is not at issue before the court, which nonetheless, taking judicial notice thereof should it arise in subsequent litigation, leaves it for adjudication to the courts of this local jurisdiction.

We have now cleared away the brambles and may proceed to the main action as set forth in plaintiff's petition for a preliminary injunction seeking to hold inviolable the artistic and actual integrity of his sculptural creation Cyclone Seven in situ against assault, invasion, alteration, or destruction or removal or any act posing irreparable harm by any person or persons or agencies thereof under any authority or no authority assembled for such purpose or purposes for any reason or for none, under threat of recovery for damages consonant with but not limited to its original costs. While proof of ownership is not at issue in this proceeding, parties agree that these costs, including those incident to its installation, in the neighborhood of fourteen million dollars, were borne by contributions from various private patrons and underwritten by such corporate entities as Martin Oil, Incidental Oil, Bush AFG Corp., Anco Steel, Norfolk & Pee Dee Railroad, Frito-Cola Bottling Co., and the Tobacco Council, further supported with cooperation from the National Arts Endowment and both state and regional Arts Councils. The site, theretofore a weed infested rubble strewn area serving for casual parking of vehicles and as an occasional dumping ground by day and trysting place by night, was donated under arrangements worked out between its proprietor Miller Feed Co. and the Village in consideration of taxes unpaid and accrued thereon over the preceding thirty-eight years. In re the selection of this specific site plaintiff exhibits drawings, photographs, notes and other pertinent materials accompanying his original applications to and discussions with the interested parties aforementioned singling out the said site as 'epitomizing that unique American environment of moral torpor and spiritual vacuity' requisite to his artistic enterprise, together with correspondence validating his intentions and applauding their results. Here we refer to plaintiff's exhibits drawn from contemporary accounts in the press of ceremonies inaugurating the installation of Cyclone Seven wherein it was envisioned as a compelling tourist attraction though not, in the light of current events, for the reasons it enjoys today. Quoted therein, plaintiff cites, among numerous contemporary expressions of local exuberance, comments by then presiding Village Board member J Harret Ruth at the ribbon cutting and reception held at nearby Mel's Kandy Kitchen with glowing photographic coverage, quoting therefrom 'the time, the place, and the dedication of all you assembled here from far and wide, the common people and captains of industry and the arts rubbing elbows in tribute to the patriotic ideals rising right here before our eyes in this great work of sculptural art.'

Responding to plaintiff's exhibits on this count, those of defendant appear drawn well after the fact up to and including the present day and provoked (here the court infers) by the prevailing emotional climate expressed in, and elicited by, the print and television media, appending thereto recently published statements by former Village official J Harret Ruth in his current pursuit of a seat on the federal judiciary referring to the sculptural work at the center of this action as 'a rusting travesty of our great nation's vision of itself' and while we may pause to marvel at his adroitness in ascertaining the direction of the parade before leaping in front to lead it we dismiss this and supporting testimony supra as contradictory and frivolous, and find plaintiff's exhibits in evidence persuasive.

Another count in plaintiff's action naming defendants both within and beyond this jurisdiction seeks remedy for defamation and consequent incalculable damage to his career and earning power derived therefrom (Reiman v. Pacific Development Soc., 132 Or. 82, 284 P. 575, 1930; Brauer v. Globe Newspaper Co., 351 Mass. 53, 217 N.E.2d 736, 1966). It is undisputed that plaintiff and his work, as here represented by the steel sculpture Cyclone Seven, have been held up to public ridicule both locally and given the wide ranging magic of the media, throughout the land, as witnessed in a cartoon published in the South Georgia Pilot crudely depicting a small dog pinioned under a junk heap comprising old bedsprings, chamber pots, and other household debris, and from the Arkansas Family Visitor an editorial denouncing plaintiff's country of origin as prominent in the Soviet bloc, thereby distinctly implying his mission among us to be one of atheistic subversion of our moral values as a Christian nation, whereas materials readily available elsewhere show plaintiff to have departed his birthplace at age three with his family who were in fact fleeing the then newly installed Communist regime. We take judicial notice of this exhibit as defamatory communication and libellous per se, tending 'to lower him in the estimation of the community or to deter third persons from associating or dealing with him' (Restatement of the Law, Second, Torts 2d, 559), but it remains for plaintiff to seek relief in the courts of those jurisdictions.

Similarly, where plaintiff alleges defamation in this and far wider jurisdictions through radio and television broadcast we are plunged still deeper into the morass of legal distinctions embracing libel and slander that have plagued the common law since the turn of the seventeenth century. As slander was gradually wrested from the jurisdiction of the ecclesiastical courts through tort actions seeking redress for temporal damage rather than spiritual offense, slander became actionable only with proof or the reasonable assumption of special damage of a pecuniary character. Throughout, slander retained its identity as spoken defamation, while with the rise of the printing press it became libel in the written or printed word, a distinction afflicting our own time in radio and television broadcasting wherein defamation has been held as libel if read from a script by the broadcaster (Hartmann v. Winchell, 296 N.Y. 296, N.E.2d 30, 1947; Hryhorijiv v. Winchell, 1943, 180 Misc. 574, 45 N.Y.S.2d 31, affirmed, 267 App.Div. 817, 47 N.Y.S.2d 102, 1944) but as slander if it is not. But see Restatement of the Law, Second,

Torts 2d, showing libel as 'broadcasting of defamatory matter by means of radio or television, whether or not it is read from a manuscript' (#568A). Along this tortuous route, our only landmark in this proceeding is the aforementioned proof or reasonable assumption of special damage of a pecuniary character and, plaintiff failing in these provisions, this remedy is denied.

In reaching these conclusions, the court acts from the conviction that risk of ridicule, of attracting defamatory attentions from his colleagues and even raucous demonstrations by an outraged public have ever been and remain the foreseeable lot of the serious artist, recalling among the most egregious examples Ruskin accusing Whistler of throwing a paint pot in the public's face, the initial scorn showered upon the Impressionists and, once they were digested, upon the Cubists, the derision greeting Bizet's musical innovations credited with bringing about his death of a broken heart, the public riots occasioned by the first performance of Stravinsky's Rite of Spring, and from the day Aristophanes labeled Euripides 'a maker of ragamuffin mannequins' the avalanche of disdain heaped upon writers: the press sending the author of Ode on a Grecian Urn 'back to plasters, pills, and ointment boxes,' finding Ibsen's Ghosts 'a loathsome sore unbandaged, a dirty act done publicly' and Tolstoy's Anna Karenina 'sentimental rubbish,' and in our own land the contempt accorded each succeeding work of Herman Melville, culminating in Moby Dick as 'a huge dose of hyperbolical slang, maudlin sentimentalism and tragic-comic bubble and squeak,' and since Melville's time upon writers too numerous to mention. All this must most arguably in deed and intent affect the sales of their books and the reputations whereon rest their hopes of advances and future royalties, yet to the court's knowledge none of this opprobrium however enviously and maliciously conceived and however stupid, careless, and ill informed in its publication has ever yet proved grounds for a successful action resulting in recovery from the marplot. In short, the artist is fair game and his cause is turmoil. To echo the words of Horace, Pictoribus atque poetis quidlibet audendi semper fuit aequa potestas, in this daring invention the artist comes among us not as the bearer of idées reçues embracing art as decoration or of the comfort of churchly beliefs enshrined in greeting card sentiments but rather in the aesthetic equivalent of one who comes on earth 'not to send peace, but a sword.'

The foregoing notwithstanding, before finding for plaintiff on the main action before the court set forth in his motion for a preliminary injunction barring interference of any sort by any means by any party or parties with the sculptural creation Cyclone Seven the court is compelled to address whether, following such a deliberate invasion for whatever purpose however merciful in intent, the work can be restored to its original look in keeping with the artist's unique talents and accomplishment or will suffer irreparable harm therefrom. Bowing to the familiar adage Cuilibet in arte sua perito est credendum, we hold the latter result to be an inevitable consequence of such invasion and such subsequent attempt at reconstitution at the hands of those assembled for such purposes in the form of members of the local Fire Department, whose training and talents such as they may be must be found to lie elsewhere, much in the manner of that obituary upon our finest poet of the century wherein one of his purest lines was reconstituted as 'I do not think they will sing to me' by a journalist trained to eliminate on sight the superfluous 'that.'

For the reasons set out above, summary judgment is granted to plaintiff as to preliminary injunction.

Is It Sexual Harassment Yet?

Cris Mazza

Even before the Imperial
Penthouse switched from a
staff of exclusively male
waiters and food handlers to
a crew of fifteen waitresses,
Terence Lovell was the floor
captain. Wearing a starched
ruffled shirt and black tails,
he embodied continental
grace and elegance as he
seated guests and, with a
toreador's flourish, produced
menus out of thin air. He
took all orders but did not
serve—except in the case of a
flaming meal or dessert, and
this duty, for over ten years,
was his alone. One of his
trademarks was to never be
seen striking the match—either the flaming platter was
swiftly paraded from the
kitchen or the dish would
seemingly spontaneously ignite on its cart beside the
table, a quiet explosion, then
a four-foot column of flame,
like a fountain with floodlights of changing colors.

There'd been many rea-
sons for small celebrations at
the Lovell home during the
past several years: Terence's
wife, Maggie, was able to
quit her job as a keypunch
operator when she finished
courses and was hired as a
part-time legal secretary. His
son was tested into the gifted
program at school. His daughter learned to swim before
she could walk. The news-
paper did a feature on the
Imperial Penthouse with a
half-page photo of Terence
holding a flaming shish-kebab.

Then one day on his way
to work, dressed as usual in
white tie and tails, Terence
Lovell found himself stopping off at a gun store.
For that moment, as he approached the glass-topped
counter, Terence said his biggest fear was that he might
somehow, despite his professional elegant manners, appear to the rest of the world
like a cowboy swaggering his
way up to the bar to order a
double. Terence purchased a
small hand gun—the style
that many cigarette lighters
resemble—and tucked it into
his red cummerbund.

It was six to eight months prior to Terence's purchase of the gun that the restaurant began to integrate wait-resses into the personnel. Over the next year or so, the floor staff was supposed to eventually evolve into one made up of all women with the exception of the floor cap-tain. It was still during the early weeks of the new staff, however, when Terence be-gan finding gifts in his locker. First there was a black lace and red satin garter. Terence pinned it to the bulletin board in case it had been put into the wrong locker, so the owner could claim it. But the flowers he found in his locker were more of a problem—they were taken from the vases on the tables. Each time that he found a single red rosebud threaded through the vents in his locker door, he found a table on the floor with an empty vase, so he al-ways put the flower back where it belonged. Terence spread the word through the busboys that the waitresses could take the roses off the tables each night *after* the restaurant was closed, but not before. But on the whole, he thought—admittedly on

I know they're going to ask about my previous sexual experiences. What counts as sexual? Holding hands? Wet kisses? A finger up my ass? Staring at a man's bulge? He wore incredibly tight pants. But before all this happened, I wasn't a virgin, and I wasn't a virgin in so many ways. I never had an abortion, I never had VD, never went into a toilet stall with a woman, never castrated a guy at the moment of climax. But I know enough to know. As soon as you feel like *some-one*, you're no one. Why am I doing this? *Why?*

So, you'll ask about my sexual history but won't think to inquire about the previous encounters I *almost* had, or *never* had: it wasn't the old ships-in-the-night tragedy, but let's say I had a ship, three or four years ago, the ship of love, okay? So once when I had a lot of wind in my sails (is this a previous sexual experience yet?), the captain sank the vessel when he started saying stuff like, "You're not ever going to be the most important thing in someone else's life unless it's something like he kills you— and then only if he hasn't retrospect—the atmosphere with the new waitresses seemed, for the first several weeks, amiable and unstressed.

Then one of the waitresses, Michelle Rae, reported to management that Terence had made inappropriate comments to her during her shift at work. Terence said he didn't know which of the waitresses had made the complaint, but also couldn't remember if management had withheld the name of the accuser, or if, when told the name at this point, he just didn't know which waitress she was. He said naturally there was a shift in decorum behind the door to the kitchen, but he wasn't aware that anything he said or did could have possibly been so misunderstood. He explained that his admonishments were never more than half-serious, to the waitresses as well as the waiters or busboys: "Move your butt," or "One more mix-up and you'll be looking at the happy end of a skewer." While he felt a food server should appear unruffled, even languid, on the floor, he pointed out that movement was brisk in the

killed anyone else yet nor knocked people off for a living—otherwise no one's the biggest deal in anyone's life but their own." Think about that. He may've been running my ship, but it turns out he was navigating by remote control. When the whole thing blew up, *he* was unscathed. Well, now I try to live as though I wrote that rule, as though it's *mine*. But that hasn't made me like it any better.

There are so many ways to humiliate someone. Make someone so low they leave a snail-trail. Someone makes a joke, you don't laugh. Someone tells a story—a personal story, something that mattered—you don't listen, you aren't moved. Someone wears a dance leotard to work, you don't notice. But underneath it all, you're planning the real humiliation. The symbolic humiliation. The humiliation of humiliations. Like I told you, I learned this before, I already know the *type:* he'll be remote, cool, distant—*seeming* to be gentle and tolerant but actually cruelly indifferent. It'll be great fun for him to be aloof or preoccupied when kitchen area, communication had to get the point across quickly, leaving no room for confusion or discussion. And while talking and joking on a personal level was not uncommon, Terence believed the waitresses had not been working there long enough for any conversations other than work-related, but these included light-hearted observations: a customer's disgusting eating habits, vacated tables that appeared more like battlegrounds than the remains of a fine dinner, untouched expensive meals, guessing games as to which couples were first dates and which were growing tired of each other, whose business was legitimate and whose probably dirty, who were wives and which were the mistresses, and, of course, the rude customers. Everyone always had rude-customer stories to trade. Terence had devised a weekly contest where each food server produced their best rude-customer story on a 3x5 card and submitted it each Friday. Terence then judged them and awarded the winner a specially made shish-kebab prepared after the restau-

someone is in love with him, genuflecting, practically prostrating herself. If he doesn't respond, she can't say he hurt her, she never got close enough. He'll go on a weekend ski trip with his friends. She'll do calisthenics, wash her hair, shave her legs, and wait for Monday. Well, not *this* time, no sir. Terence Lovell is messing with a sadder-but-wiser chick.

rant had closed, with all of the other waiters and waitresses providing parodied royal table service, even to the point of spreading the napkin across the winner's lap and dabbing the corners of his or her mouth after each bite.

The rude-customer contest was suspended after the complaint to management. However, the gifts in his locker multiplied during this time. He continued to tack the gifts to the bulletin board, whenever possible: the key chain with a tiny woman's high-heeled shoe, the 4x6 plaque with a poem printed over a misty photograph of a dense green moss-covered forest, the single black fishnet stocking. When he found a pair of women's underwear in his locker, instead of tacking them to the bulletin board, he hung them on the inside doorknob of the woman's restroom. That was the last gift he found in his locker for a while. Within a week he received in the mail the same pair of women's underwear.

Since the beginning of the new staff, the restaurant

Yes, I was one of the first five women to come in as food

manager had been talking about having a staff party to help the new employees feel welcome and at ease with the previous staff. But in the confusion of settling in, a date had never been set. Four or five months after the waitresses began work, the party had a new purpose: to ease the tension caused by the complaint against Terence. So far, nothing official had been done or said about Ms. Rae's allegations.

During the week before the party, which was to be held in an uptown nightclub with live music on a night the Imperial Penthouse was closed, Terence asked around to find out if Michelle Rae would be attending. All he discovered about her, however, was that she didn't seem to have any close friends on the floor staff.

Michelle did come to the party. She wore a green strapless dress which, Terence remembered, was unbecomingly tight and, as he put it, made her rump appear too ample. Her hair was in a style Terence described as finger-in-a-light-socket. Terence believed he probably would not have noticed

servers, and I expected the usual resistance—the dirty glasses and ash-strewn linen on our tables (before the customer was seated), planting long hairs in the salads, cold soup, busboys delivering tips that appeared to have been left on greasy plates or in puddles of gravy on the tablecloth. I could stand those things. It was like them saying, "We know you're here!" But no, not *him*. *He* didn't want to return to the days of his all-male staff. Why would he want that? Eventually he was going to be in charge of an all-woman floor. Sound familiar? A harem? A pimp's stable? He thought it was so hilarious, he started saying it every night: "Line up, girls, and pay the pimp." Time to split tips. See what I mean? But he only flirted a little with them to cover up the obviousness of what he was doing to me. Just a few weeks after I started, I put a card on the bulletin board announcing that I'm a qualified aerobic dance instructor and if anyone was interested, I would lead an exercise group before work. My card wasn't there three hours before someone (and I don't

Michelle at all that night if he were not aware of the complaint she had made. He recalled that her lipstick was the same shade of red as her hair and there were red tints in her eye shadow.

Terence planned to make it an early evening. He'd brought his wife, and, since this was the first formal staff party held by the Imperial Penthouse, had to spend most of the evening's conversation in introducing Maggie to his fellow employees. Like any ordinary party, however, he was unable to remember afterwards exactly what he did, who he talked to, or what they spoke about, but he knew that he did not introduce his wife to Michelle Rae.

Terence didn't see Maggie go into the restroom. It was down the hall, toward the kitchen. And he didn't see Michelle Rae follow her. In fact, no one did. Maggie returned to the dance area with her face flushed, breathing heavily, her eyes filled with tears, tugged at his arm and, with her voice shaking, begged Terence to take her home. It wasn't until they arrived home that Maggie told

need a detective) had crossed out "aerobic" and wrote "erotic," and he added a price per session! I had no intention of charging anything for it since I go through my routine everyday anyway, and the more the merrier is an aerobic dance motto—we like to share the pain. My phone number was clear as day on that card—if he was at all intrigued, he could've called and found out what I was offering. I've spent ten years exercising my brains out. Gyms, spas, classes, health clubs . . . no bars. He could've just once picked up the phone, I was always available, willing to talk this out, come to a settlement. He never even tried. Why should he? He was already king of Nob Hill. You know that lowlife bar he goes to? If anyone says how he was such an amiable and genial supervisor . . . you bet he was genial, he was halfway drunk. It's crap about him being a big family man. Unless his living room had a pool table, those beer mirrors on the wall, and the sticky brown bar itself— the wood doesn't even show through anymore, it's grime from people's hands, the kind

Terence how Michelle Rae had come into the restroom and threatened her. Michelle had warned Mrs. Lovell to stay away from Terence and informed her that she had a gun in her purse to help *keep* her away from Terence.

Terence repeated his wife's story to the restaurant manager. The manager thanked him. But, a week later, after Terence had heard of no further developments, he asked the manager what was going to be done about it. The manager said he'd spoken with both Ms. Rae and Mrs. Lovell, separately, but Ms. Rae denied the incident, and, as Mrs. Lovell did not actually see any gun, he couldn't fire an employee simply on the basis of what another employee's wife said about her, especially with the complaint already on file, how would that look? Terence asked, "But isn't there some law against this?" The manager gave Terence a few days off to cool down.

The Imperial Penthouse was closed on Mondays, and most Monday evenings Terence

of people who go there, the same way a car's steering wheel builds up that thick hard black layer which gets sticky when it rains and you can cut it with a knife. No, his house may not be like that, but he never spent a lot of time at his house. I know what I'm talking about. He'll say he doesn't remember, but I wasn't ten feet away while he was flashing his healthy salary (imported beer), and he looked right through me — no, *not* like I wasn't there. When a man looks at you the way he did at me, he's either ignoring you or undressing you with his eyes, but probably *both*. And that's just what he did and didn't stop there. He's not going to get away with it.

Wasn't it his idea to hire us in the first place? No, he wasn't there at the interview, went out with a group of friends to a local sports bar. Maggie Lovell taught piano lessons at home in the evenings, so it was their mutual agreement that Terence go out to a movie or, more often, to see a football game on television. On one such evening, Maggie received a phone call from a woman who said she was calling from the restaurant—there'd been a small fire in one of the storage rooms and the manager was requesting that Terence come to the restaurant and help survey the damage. Mrs. Lovell told the caller where Terence was.

The Imperial Penthouse never experienced any sort of fire, and Terence could only guess afterwards whether or not that was the same Monday evening that Michelle Rae came to the sports bar. At first he had considered speaking to her, to try to straighten out what was becoming an out-of-proportion misunderstanding. But he'd already been there for several hours—the game was almost over—and he'd had three or four beers. Because he was, therefore, not absolutely certain what the out-

but looked right at me my first day, just at me while he said, "You girls probably all want to be models or actresses. You don't give *this* profession enough respect. Well," he said, "you will." Didn't look at anyone else. He meant me. I didn't fail to notice, either, I was the only one with red hair. Not dull auburn . . . flaming red. They always assume, don't they? You know, the employee restrooms were one toilet each for men and women, all the customary holes drilled in the walls, stuffed with paper, but if one restroom was occupied, we could use the other, so the graffiti was heterosexual, a dialogue. It could've been healthy, but he never missed an opportunity. I'd just added my thoughts to an on-going discussion of the growing trend toward androgyny in male rock singers—they haven't yet added breasts and aren't quite at the point of cutting off their dicks—and an hour later, there it was, the thick black ink pen, the block letters: "Let's get one thing clear—do you women want it or *not?* Just what is the *thrust* of this conversation?" What do come would be if he talked to her, he checked his impulse to confront Ms. Rae, and, in fact, did not acknowledge her presence.

When a second complaint was made, again charging Terence with inappropriate behavior and, this time, humiliation, Terence offered to produce character witnesses, but before anything came of it, a rape charge was filed with the district attorney and Terence was brought in for questioning. The restaurant suspended Terence without pay for two weeks. All the waitresses, except Ms. Rae, were interviewed, as well as several ex-waitresses—by this time the restaurant was already experiencing some turnover of the new staff. Many of those interviewed reported that Michelle Rae had been asking them if they'd slept with Terence. In one case Ms. Rae was said to have told one of her colleagues that she, Michelle, knew all about her co-worker's affair with the floor captain. Some of the waitresses said that they'd received phone calls on Mondays; an unidentified female demanded to know if Terence

you *call* an attitude like that? And he gets *paid* for it! You know, after you split a tip with a busboy, bartender, and floor captain, there's not much left. *He* had an easy answer: earn bigger tips. *Earn* it, work your *ass* off for it, you know. But who's going to tip more than 15% unless . . . . Well, unless the waitress wears no underwear. He even said that the best thing about taking part of our tip money was it made us move our asses that much prettier. There was another thing he liked about how I had to earn bigger tips—reaching or bending. And then my skirt was "mysteriously," "accidentally" lifted from behind, baring my butt in front of the whole kitchen staff. He pretended he hadn't noticed. Then winked and smiled at me later when I gave him his share of my tips. Told me to keep up the good work. Used the word *ass* every chance he got in my presence for weeks afterwards. Isn't this sexual harassment yet?

Lovell was, at that moment, visiting them. A few of those waitresses assumed it was Michelle Rae while others said they'd thought the caller had been Mrs. Lovell.

When the district attorney dropped the rape charge for lack of evidence, Michelle Rae filed suit claiming harassment, naming the restaurant owner, manager and floor captain. Meanwhile Terence began getting a series of phone calls where the caller immediately hung up. Some days the phone seemed to ring incessantly. So once, in a rage of frustration, Terence grabbed the receiver and made a list of threats—the worst being, as he remembered it, "kicking her lying ass clear out of the state"—before realizing the caller hadn't hung up that time. Believing the caller might be legitimate—a friend or a business call—Terence quickly apologized and began to explain, but the caller, who never gave her name, said, "Then I guess you're not ready." When Terence asked

Of course I was scared. He knew my work schedule, and don't think he didn't know where I live. Knew my days off, when I'd be asleep, when I do my aerobic dance routine every day. I don't mind *who*ever wants to do aerobic dance with me—but it has to be at my place where I've got the proper flooring and music. It was just an idle, general invitation—an announcement—I wasn't *begging . . . any*one, him included, could come once or keep coming, that's all I meant, just harmless, healthy exercise. Does it mean I was looking to start my dancing career in that palace of high-class entertainment *he* frequents? Two pool tables, a juke box and big-screen TV. What a lousy front—looks exactly like what it really *is,* his lair, puts on his favorite funky music, her to clarify—ready for what?—she said, "To meet somewhere and work this out. To make my lawsuit obsolete garbage. To do what you really want to do to me. To finish all this."

Terence began refusing to answer the phone himself, relying on Maggie to screen calls, then purchasing an answering machine. As the caller left a message, Terence could hear who it was over a speaker, then he could decide whether or not to pick up the phone and speak to the party directly. He couldn't disconnect the phone completely because he had to stay in touch with his lawyer. The Imperial Penthouse was claiming Terence was not covered on their lawsuit insurance because he was on suspension at the time the suit was filed.

When he returned to work there was one more gift in Terence's locker: what looked like a small stiletto switchblade, but, when clicked open, turned out to be a comb. A note was attached, unsigned, which said, "I'd advise you to get a gun."

Terence purchased the miniature single-cartridge his undulating blue and green lights, snorts his coke, dazzles his partner—his doped-up victim—with his moves and gyrations, dances her into a corner and rapes her before the song's over, up against the wall—*that* song's in the juke box too. You think I don't *know?* I was having a hassle with a customer who ordered rare, complained it was overdone, wanted it *rare,* the cook was busy, so Terence grabs another steak and throws it on the grill— tsss on one side, flips it, tsss on the other—slams it on a plate. "Here, young lady, you just dance this raw meat right out to that john." I said I don't know how to dance. "My dear," he said, "*every*one knows how to dance, it's all a matter of moving your ass." Of course the gun was necessary! I tried to be reasonable. I tried everything!

hand gun the following day. After keeping it at work in his locker for a week, he kept it, unloaded, in a dresser drawer at home, unable to carry it to work every day, he said, because the outline of the gun was clearly recognizable in the pocket of his tux pants.

One Monday evening as Terence was leaving the sports bar—not drunk, but admittedly not with his sharpest wits either—three men stopped him. Terence was in a group with another man and three women, but, according to the others, the culprits ignored them, singling out Terence immediately. It was difficult for Terence to recall what happened that night. He believed the men might've asked him for his wallet, but two of the others with him say the men didn't ask for anything but were just belligerent drunks looking for a fight. Only one member of Terence's party remembered anything specific that was said, addressed to Terence:

Most people—you just don't know what goes on back there. You see this stylish, practically regal man in white tie and tails, like an old fashioned prince . . . or Vegas magician . . . but back there in the hot, steamy kitchen, what's *wrong* with him? Drunk? Drugs? He played sword fight with one of the undercooks, using the longest skewers, kept trying to jab each other in the crotch. The chef yelled at the undercook, but Terence didn't say a word, went to the freezer, got the meatballs out, thawed them halfway in the microwave, then started threading them onto the skewer. Said it was an ancient custom, like the Indians did with scalps, to keep

"Think you're special?" If the men had been attempting a robbery, Terence decided to refuse, he said, partly because he wasn't fully sober, and partly because it appeared the attackers had no weapons. In the ensuing fight—which, Terence said, happened as he was running down the street, but was unsure whether he was chasing or being chased—Terence was kicked several times in the groin area and sustained several broken ribs. He was hospitalized for two days.

Maggie Lovell visited Terence in the hospital once, informing him that she was asking her parents to stay with the kids until he was discharged because she was moving into a motel. She wouldn't tell Terence the name of the motel, insisting she didn't want anyone to know where she was, not even her parents, and besides, she informed him, there probably wouldn't even be a phone in her room. Terence, drowsy from pain killers, couldn't remember much about his wife's visit. He had vague recollections of her leaving through the window, or leaning out the window—

trophies from your victims on your weapon. He added vegetables in between the meatballs—whole bell peppers, whole onions, even whole eggplant, started dousing the whole thing with brandy. His private bottle? Maybe. He said we should put it on the menu, he wanted someone to order it, his delux kebab. He would turn off all the chandeliers and light the dining room with the burning food. Then he stopped. He and I were alone! He said, "The only thing my delux kebab needs is a fresh, ripe tomato." Isn't this incredible! He wanted to know how I would like to be the next juicy morsel to be poked onto the end of that thing. He was still pouring brandy all over it. Must've been a gallon bottle, still half full when he put it on the counter, twirled the huge shish-kebab again, struck his sword fighting pose and cut the bottle right in half. I can hardly believe it either. When the bottle cracked open, the force of the blow made the brandy shoot out, like the bottle had opened up and spit—it splattered the front of my skirt. In the next dow to pick flowers, or slamming the window shut, but when he woke the next day and checked, he saw that the window could not be opened. Terence never saw his wife again. Later he discovered that on the night of his accident there had been an incident at home. Although Terence had instructed his eight-year-old son not to answer the phone, the boy had forgotten, and, while his mother was giving a piano lesson, he picked up the receiver just after the machine had clicked on. The entire conversation was therefore recorded. The caller, a female, asked the boy who he was, so he replied that he was Andy Lovell. "The heir apparent," the voice said softly, to which Andy responded, "What? I mean, pardon?" There was a brief pause, then the caller said, "I'd really like to get rid of your mom so your dad could fuck me. If you're halfway like him, maybe I'll let you fuck me too." There is another pause on the tape. Investigators disagree as to whether it is the caller's breathing or the boy's that can be heard. The boy's voice,

second his kebab was in flames—maybe he'd passed it over a burner, I don't know, he was probably *breathing* flames by then—so naturally as soon as he pointed the thing at me again, my skirt ignited, scorched the hair off my legs before I managed to drop it around my feet and kick it away. What *wouldn't* he do? Looks like he'd finally gotten me undressed. It's ironic, isn't it, when you see that news article about him—I taped it to my mirror—and how about that headline, "Pomp and Circumstance Part of the Meal." There sure were some circumstances to consider, all right. Like he could rape me at gunpoint any time he wanted, using that cigarette lighter which looks like a fancy pistol. I wanted something to always remind me what to watch out for, but I didn't take the lighter. Why not? I'll kick myself forever for that. There was so much to choose from. Now one of his red satin cummerbunds hangs over my bed while he still has the lighter and can still use it!

obviously trembling, then said, "What?" The female caller snapped, "Tell your dad someone's going to be killed."

During Terence's convalescence, the Imperial Penthouse changed its format and operated without a floor captain, using the standard practice of a hostess who seated the guests and waitresses assigned to tables to take orders and serve meals. The restaurant's menu was also changed and now no longer offered flaming meals. When Terence returned to work he was given a position as a regular waiter, even though by this time most of the male food servers had left the restaurant and were replaced with women. Michelle Rae was given a lunch schedule, ten to three, Wednesday through Sunday. Terence would call the restaurant to make sure she'd clocked out before he arrived for the dinner shift.

During the first week he was back at work, Terence came home and found that

When he said "staff meeting," he didn't mean what he was supposed to mean by it. You know, there was a cartoon on the bulletin board, *staff meeting,* two sticks shaking hands, very funny, right? But long ago someone had changed the drawing, made the two sticks flaming shish-kebabs on skewers. So the announcement of the big meeting was a xerox of that cartoon, but enlarged, tacked to the women's restroom door. *Be There Or Be Square! Yes, You'll Be Paid For Attending!* You bet! It was held at that tavern. Everyone may've been invited, but I'm the one he wanted there. There's no doubt in my mind. What good was I to him merely as an employee? I had to see the real Terence Lovell, had to join the inner-most core of his life. Know what? It was a biker hangout, that bar, a his wife had returned to get the children. In a few days she sent a truck for the furniture, and the next communication he had with her was the divorce suit—on grounds of cruel and unusual adultery.

biker gang's headquarters. One or two of them were always there with their leather jackets, chains, black grease under their fingernails (or dried blood), knives eight inches long. They took so many drugs you could get high just lying on the reeking urine-soaked mattress in the back. That's where the initiations were. No one just *lets* you in. Know what he said the first day we started working, the first day of the women food servers, he said, "You don't just work here to earn a salary, you have to *earn* the right to work here!" So maybe I was naive to trust him. To ever set one foot in that bar without a suspicion of what could happen to me. That same ordinary old beer party going on in front— same music, same dancing, same clack of pool balls and whooping laughter—you'd never believe the scene in the back room. It may've looked like a typical orgy at first— sweating bodies moving in rhythm, groaning, changing to new contorted positions, shouts of encouragement, music blaring in the background. But wait, nothing ordinary or healthy like that for the girl who was chosen to be the center of his dark side—she'll have to be both the cause and cure for his violent ache, that's why he's been so relentless, so obsessed, so insane . . . he was driven to it, to the point where he had to paint the tip of his hard-on with 150 proof whiskey then use the fancy revolver to ignite it, screaming—not like any sound he ever made before—until he extinguished it in the girl of his unrequited dreams. *Tssss.*

The only thing left in Terence's living room was the telephone and answering machine. When the phone rang one Monday afternoon, Terence answered and, as instructed by his attorney, turned on the tape recorder:

caller: It's me, baby.
Lovell: Okay . . . .
caller: You've been ignoring me lately.
Lovell: What do you want now?
caller: Come on, now, Terry!
Lovell: Look, let's level with each other. How can we

end this? What do I have
to do?

caller: If it's going to end, the
ending has to be *better*
than if it continued.

Lovell: Pardon?

caller: A bigger deal. A big
bang. You ever heard of
the big bang theory?

Lovell: The beginning of the
universe?

caller: Yeah, but the big
bang, if it started the
whole universe, it also
ended something. It
may've started the uni-
verse, but what did it
end? What did it *obliter-
ate?*

Lovell: I still don't know
what you want.

caller: What do *you* want,
Terry?

Lovell: I just want my life to
get back to normal.

caller: Too late. I've changed
your life, haven't I? Good.

Lovell: Let's get to the point.

caller: You sound anxious. I
love it. You ready?

Lovell: Ready for what?

caller: To see me. To end it.
That's what you wanted,
wasn't it? Let's create the
rest of your life out of our
final meeting.

Lovell: If I agree to meet, it's
to talk, not get married.

caller: Once is all it takes, baby. *Bang.* The rest of your life will start. But guess who'll still be there at the center of everything you do. Weren't you going to hang out at the bar tonight?

Lovell: Is that where you want to meet?

caller: Yeah, your turf.

Terence estimated he sat in his empty living room another hour or so, as twilight darkened the windows, holding the elegant cigarette-lighter look-alike gun; and when he tested the trigger once, he half expected to see a little flame pop from the end.

Lady the Brach

Gilbert Sorrentino

What if this young woman, who writes such bad poems, in
competition with her husband, whose poems are equally bad,
should stretch her remarkably long and well-made legs out
before you, so that her skirt slips up to the tops of her stock-
ings? It is an old story. Then she asks you what you think of
the trash you have just read—her latest effort. She is not un-
intelligent and she is—attractive. A use of the arts perhaps
more common than any other in this time. Aphrodisia. Powerful as Spanish fly or the scent of jasmine. The most delicate
equivocation about the poem, the most subtle relaxation of
critical acumen, will hasten you to bed with her. The poem is
about a dream she had. In it she is a little girl. Again. Most of
her poems are about dreams. In them she drowns in costume,
or finds herself flying naked. At the end of the dream she is
trapped. Well, critic, tell her the poem has the clear and unmistakable stink of decay to it. Tell her. Is seeing, finally, the
hair glossy between her thighs so important that you will lie?
About art? You shift your body and hold the poem out—judi-
ciously—before you, one eye half-closed. Reach for a cigarette. Well, you say. Well—this poem . . . Her eyes are shin-
ing, they are beautifully sculptured, and dark. She uncrosses
her legs, the nylon whispering, and recrosses them. The nylon whispering. Bends forward to accept a light, looking at
you, seriously, intently, waiting for your judgment. I have
nothing to say, the poem is unknown to me. Others, that I
have read, are watery and vulgar, but perhaps her craft has
somewhat improved. She's been reading Lawrence—a bad
sign, but . . . she understands him. As who does not? Well, you
say, again. Penis a bar of steel. We can have a large third-rate

abstract expressionist or hard-edge oil behind this scene, or a window with a view of a Gristede's. If in the country, a small grassy hill falls gently away from the picture window behind which the two figures are arranged, gently away to a lawn on which a group of young drunks is playing touch football in the darkening November afternoon.

Sept. 25, 1964

Dear Mama,

I just wanted to drop you a line to tell you that Lou and I are back here now in Berkeley, the honeymoon is over,* and I've settled down to becoming a pretty good housewife. Our honeymoon was really great and Laguna is too beautiful for words. Lou and I tried to learn how to surf there, and you would have laughed to see the spills we took. After a while, though, I must say, we got pretty profisient at it, especially me. You know I've never been modest!

The apartment we have here is a studio type with blonde furniture, matching drapes and rugs, everything is color-keyed. Looks like a Hollywood apartment—or should I say "flat"? Lou is going to school, and doing pretty well there, considering the fact that most of his instructors stopped thinking about ten years ago. I'm learning to cook and even bake, and Lou's not dead yet, so I suppose I'm not doing too badly. Lou has this job that I told you about in my last letter, driving a truck for the Examiner, so he has to leave the house about one every morning. But he's back at six, sleeps a few hours, then has breakfast and goes to school. It's hard on him with school, the job, and his writing, but we're very happy. I spend my free time reading, so that I can talk to Lou and his friends without being too hopeless. Berkeley is a lovely town, lots of trees, quiet, very collegiate. Our next-door neighbors are two grad students, a husband and wife, both anthropologists, and we've been over to see them twice since we got back, for drinks.

Well, I just wanted to let you know that we're safe and sound, and that married life agrees with me. I'm re-

---

*This phrase is used without irony.

ally sorry that you and Daddy couldn't come to our wedding, but I'm glad that you're happy for us. And Lou and I are *delighted* that you and Daddy have met Lou's mother and that you hit it off. I've got to go now and meet Lou. We're having our "traditional" Monday night Chinese dinner.

All love to you and Daddy, and xxxx
Sheila

December 27, 1963

Dear Fred,

I'm writing because I'm embarrassed to speak to you. Actually, I'm also embarrassed to write.

I won't be able to see you. I'll explain. Due to my "clear-eyedness" and not to my clear thinking, I've hurt someone very much. Next, you were going to be hurt.

Last night, my future husband made visible his jealousy and disproportionate dislike for you. I was unable to assure him of the innocence of our future meeting. Prehaps I wasn't convinced myself. You see, I find it difficult to understand why anyone would accept "one-time-only" circumstances without having some "designs." The more I tried to explain, last night, the weaker, I felt, my convictions were becomming. No, I don't understand at all.

I think you'll not be too angry with me, though. You may or may not know what it is to love someone and be hurt because you've hurt them.

Sheila

From intelligence to art. So Sheila Henry's progression. A learning of trigonometry, locked into a milieu which has as its mentors and guides the mediocre. This is not odd, nor out of the ordinary. On the contrary, the talented amateur is everywhere apparent. "If I could climb mountains or sky-dive, I wouldn't write poems." So Freud is "proved." In the case of Mrs. Henry, sex also operates as a factor. Her energies directed toward the poem, since to the uninformed, it takes little energy, and less time. Hacking out a novel, on the other hand, is sheer labor, no matter the ineptitude. We deal here with a specific young woman, one whose childhood is not germane to our desires. Art as mathematics. Good students and bad. It is a matter of how one's intelligence is fitted to the social possibilities of the environment, no? That is, the bright star of the cultural clique in Indianapolis, at his brightest, is less "interesting" than his brother star in San Francisco. That is why New York is filled with glittering people who play with vomit. To propose a clear situation: Sheila Henry is the wife of Louis Henry, a bad poet. Through him she meets other poets. She begins to write too. The only difference between her poems and his is the degree of surface ability achieved, i.e., his bag of tricks is fuller. You see, she wants to be some one. A laudable goal. The Dean's list, the whole name, in type, the precise letters of the true name. Out of the swamp of half-drunk wives of young executives and university instructors who discuss the Beatles and Stones and call policemen pigs. Revolutionaries of the elegant lofts. Supporters of the NLF in Great Neck. Sheila wants to be some one. The clear letters on the list, her name. Sweet erections a bonus. You will understand that they are not necessary, but a bonus. Is there a creative figure who has not had a desperately confused sex life? Perhaps even Lou is somewhat pleased by the confusion. Laboring over his formulated verse, proffering criticism to Sheila. She wants him to care. Who else on Ocean Parkway had read *Paterson?*

FANTASY
>   *for D.*
you said
they were holy elements
that comprised the earth

>   and i believed you
>   i believed you
meant it.
>   and is love a holy element? i asked
>   in your love-
lit eyes i see
the smart of lust

>   —Sheila Henry

These men—who did such marvelous things—*wanted* her. So what should she do but avail herself to them? What marvelous things? Well, they thought about things, they talked about things, some of them were doctors in residence at the most fashionably grim urban hospitals. There was experience etched into their faces, their young faces. One owned a share in a terrific bar to which the most brilliant young people crowded. Another pleasantly shocked her by knowing his Yeats as well as Lou did. And he wasn't, well, he wasn't *Lou*. He had a Corvette, smoked elegant, thin cigars. His teeth shone when he cracked an easy smile at her. They thought about things. They marched in the peace parades. The one with the interns from Bellevue. So moving, the wind snapping the American flag above the dazzling brightness of their whites.

She and Lou were drunk, the party had been a bore. Somewhere uptown, vaguely in Washington Heights. The girls had been single for the most part, and young, but Lou had danced only with her, excited. He had had only one extended conversation with an older man, about the verse of Samuel Greenberg. They weren't that drunk that they couldn't get home on the subway. Along the dark streets bordering Prospect Park he kissed her repeatedly, letting his hand move gently over her thighs and up between her buttocks. She remotely wanted him. She may have thought of her current lover, as perhaps Lou did, who knew him, and rather liked him. He was a lawyer with a special interest in the eighteenth-century novel. In the apartment, she pulled off her dress and sat on the couch while Lou went to mix them a nightcap.

It is pertinent that I say that Sheila was not a particularly lascivious woman. What she wanted was thorough and repeated orgasms. How they were achieved was of little moment to her, so that, while she was, in effect, a particular kind of modern-day whore, there was none of the whore's finesse about her; she had little sexual style. At this moment she relaxed on the couch, still open to the pleasure that she knew Lou would give her if she allowed it. Perhaps a sweet tinge of guilt at being unfaithful to her lover.

Lou came in to the living room with two Scotches. He was naked, his penis swollen and half-erected. On his face he had painted, with her mascara, a mustache and goatee.

There is no point in writing pornography here. To be clear, this: instead of mounting Sheila, he masturbated himself and her, while he worked a candle in and out of her anus with great skill, so that Sheila came almost at the moment that she became aware of what he was doing. A minute later she wanted this. She had always wanted this. It was part of the mental paraphernalia of the erotic that she had taken with her on their honeymoon. Not this specific act, but something weird, something thrilling. Lou was a decisively uninteresting man, most times preferred to make love in the dark. He would say, "O baby, O my dear baby" in orgasm. There were times when she ached to ask him for certain gratifications. Just to try them out. What was the use?

But here he was, with this painted face, the candle, he said nothing, but worked for her, she was aware of how she must look to him, her hips moving, straining to meet his silent lust. He was her lover. Not even—real, but a man from a dirty book, a blue-movie man, the salesman, the cop, the priest, the man with shoes and black socks on. She thought of him with these things on. No. Rather, she thought of Lou as her lover with these things on. She thought of Lou as Che Guevara with black socks and patent leather shoes, and Che was her lover. He was—let's call him Milt. His name doesn't matter, I don't recall her lover's name, but Milt will do. So she said, "Milt, O Milt, fuck me." She whispered then, "Fuck my asshole, Milt, fuck my asshole."

What she wanted was a mirror so that she could look swiftly and see what she knew was her face serene in her pleasure, its idiotic half-smile. "The lineaments of gratified desire," she said. "Fuck my ass." Lou reached his orgasm— this is heavily literary, but nonetheless true—precisely at the moment she quoted Blake.

When she next met her lover, who had, let's assume, a real

mustache and goatee, she wanted him to do what Lou had done, but of course, he didn't, and of course, she couldn't ask him to. All they went through was the usual cunnilingus, fellatio, and fornication. That sentence sounds like a fragment of a dirty joke. She was cold and aloof, and he was troubled. Women! he thought, and knew that their affair was about over. She was disappointed in him, because she wanted him to be Lou, who was not Lou, but her lover. So she sought, and found, a new lover soon after.

It is clear that Sheila's husband can only satisfy or at the least intrigue her by being someone else. If this is a common experience—which it may well be—among the married, shall we then select the "perverse" for our observation? We will select then, it would seem, much of our world. The most incredible fantasies hover behind the simplest kiss at a party. Sheila desires what only the man she lives with can give to her. But he cannot give this to her as the man he is. So does he seek his balm in art, thinking that it can establish his ego. Suicide is committed out of despair much less grievous than this. I cannot define the final configuration of their lives, except to guess that divorce will not remedy it.

But this story is invention only. Put yourself into it. Perhaps you are already in it, or something like it. Suppose that a lover had moved Sheila to Lou in this way? That the entire situation had swung in the opposite direction? In that case, this couple could have found perhaps, in their marriage—all the pleasure inherent in all the flesh of the world.

May 12, 1966

Dear Dick,

I think it's clear, after the other night, that we ought to stay away from each other. I don't want to hurt Lou any more than I've already hurt him.* He's put up with my "indiscretions" on more than, I'm afraid, one occasion, and I really am sure that his esteem and friendship for you would really affect him terribly, no matter how ephemeral an "affair" we might have. I'm also think-

---

*This sentence is an example of automatic writing.

ing of April, whom I have always had a really warm and marvelous relationship with. It would be almost nauseating, physically, to go to your apartment while she is at work.* I may be attracted to you, I think that it may even be a mutual attraction, but we have to consider Lou and April.

I've written half a dozen poems trying to crystalize what I feel after the other night, but I've thrown them all away, except for one. I'd like to show it to you—if you want to see it. But it's best if I mail it to you. Another meeting seems out of the question, at least until we've both got hold of ourselves and realized that we have a responsibility to other people who love us and whom we love.**

So, Dick, let's be good friends, as we have been, and try to forget the other night. It was just a kind of magic anyway, black magic. Something like poetry?†

> With devotion, and care,
> Sheila

Some Things Sheila Henry Grew to Care for: 1966–1967.
Larry Poons' work: Bart Kahane pointed out his excellence.
Larry Rivers: She met him at a party.
Pantyhose: SMOOTH UNBROKEN LEG LINE.
Madame Bovary: She understood her anguish.
Guy Lewis: Who even drunk yet hath his mind entire.
Bunny Lewis: Her gentle guidance of Guy's life and writing.
Samuel Greenberg: Probably the most underrated poet of his time.
Emanuel Carnevali: Probably the most underrated prose-writer of his time
Barbary Shore: It has Mailer's most brilliant flashes of pure prose.
Harry Langdon: Really the best of the Great Clowns.

---

*This may be taken to mean: Is there any chance she might return before six o'clock?

**"and whom we love" is an afterthought.

†The question mark is intended to make the remark profound. An error of youth.

Ricard: More subtle and somehow more—*exact*—than
Pernod.
Murray Mednick: Had claim to the top rung of the American
theater.
Frank O'Hara: He died.
Jack Spicer: He died.
Leo Kaufman: He was a sweet guy.
Che Guevara: He was a *man*.
Ho Chi Minh: He was a *great* old *man*.
Anal intercourse: She almost fainted with the pleasure.
Algernon Blackwood: As good as Poe in his way.
Lou: He loved her.

We discover the young woman on the beach at Laguna back
in 1964. It is dawn, actually just after. Glittering sea, etc.
Sun, the powdery sand, etc. Whatever Laguna is like, another California beach. Sheila is dressed in a black one-piece
swimsuit, a flowered blouse to keep the dawn's chill off. Ship
'n' Shore, part of her trousseau. A half-mile back at the beach
hotel, Lou is asleep, unaware that Sheila has left the marriage bed. He went to sleep thinking of their "first breakfast
together." Now, it seems clear that their first breakfast will
be somewhat strained, unless Sheila can get back to the room
and into bed again before Lou wakes. Let's say that she won't
be able to make it. Why is she walking on the beach, alone, on
this first morning of her wedded life? Now, we shall bring the
powers of the novelist to bear.*

    Sheila, tense and nervous after the disappointment of . . .
Sheila, disappointed after the nervous consummation of . . .
Sheila Henry, Lou's wife (I am Lou's wife, she thought) . . .
When she woke that morning she gazed at her husband's quietly sleeping face with enormous tenderness . . . Now she was
a woman, she thought, a true, complete woman . . . (Slight,
fleeting leer) . . . and so big it was, so big and hard . . .

    Now we have the idea. Television and the film are by
some thought to be more subtle and sophisticated than prose

---

*This is not a novel. More a collection of "bits and pieces."

because they can register this cliché in one swift image, that is, the cliché is somehow ameliorated because it passes swiftly. One bad still worth a bad short story.

Sheila wasn't disappointed, she was slightly stunned at Lou's lack of imagination. He was a remarkably virile man and had achieved (a good word) five orgasms by two in the morning. She had come herself "countless" times. (Years later, she was first to say, and then believe, that their wedding night had been a total disaster. That's because she retained of it this single cinematic image of herself walking on the beach in the early morning, alone, somehow forlorn, while her insensitive husband slept numbly on, oblivious to her needs.)

You have to understand that she and Lou had been lovers for a year before their marriage. They had made love in cars, in parks, at parties, in hotel rooms, on beaches, in hallways, on the street, on a roof, etc. That was perfectly fine with Sheila. But she had an idea that marriage would engender a spicy perversity, an elaboration of method, that would signal to her the fact that she was, indeed, married. She had come out of the bathroom the previous night wearing a short, transparent black negligee, under it matching bikini panties. Lou had said, Wow, and removed them, the way he had many times removed her panty girdle. Hands on, garment off. She had no idea what she wanted him to do, but it was off so fast, so—decisively. A dollop of honey on her vulva? Strawberry jam on her nipples? Trading food back and forth between their (eager, searching, straining) mouths. That was in Joyce somewhere.

Her problem was that she had married Lou. If she had married another young man, this would have been expected. But Sheila had never met a man who was going to be a poet. Who was a poet. That Lou was a rotten poet was beside the point. She didn't know he was a rotten poet. When she finally came to realize he was a rotten poet, she was a rotten poet too. Rotten poets who think of furthering their careers come to think of themselves as: (I) ahead of their time; (2) important minor figures; (3) part and parcel of the "exciting" art world. But in Sheila's mind at this time of her marriage, a poet was not a man who would remove one's Bonwit Teller negligee and panties as if they were weekday foundation garments. She didn't know, as noted, what a poet should do with them, but not that. So she was disappointed. Lou missed. Though she purred, in postcoital splendor, as he read to her from *Personae*, that was later on in the honeymoon. The wedding night had been lacking in brilliance for her. And because certain films had taught her to do this (certain books too), she put her Whispery Blush of Allure Bonwit ensemble away, never to wear it for Lou again. She wore it for other men, who also removed it peremptorily, but that was different.

Is it thoroughly foolish to think that if he had paid homage to her resplendently seductive figure in its carefully selected deshabille—and yet had been fumbling, perhaps even barely potent, in the act of love—she would have felt thoroughly tender toward him? I think it *is* foolish to think that. She may even have hated him. In that event, he might never have encouraged her literary efforts, and her remarkable future infidelities would have had to be unilaterally achieved.

Sheila missed Brooklyn. This may be thought to be a facetious remark, though I once said, in a poem, "there is absolutely nothing funny about Brooklyn." But it wasn't Brooklyn that she missed, it was proximity to the familiar. She wanted to play Lou off against the known. She was thoroughly tired of him by now, and thought there must be something wrong with her, since they had been married only six months. She didn't need Brooklyn, or any other place; what she needed was a divorce, or separation. But even those swinging, hip, groovy, rich, and intense people in Hollywood made marriages that lasted longer than six months. What could she tell her mother? She had married Lou against her advice. Her mother had been against it, because her mother had a picture of Sheila in her head: gangly limbs, hairless genitals, tiny breasts that needed no brassiere. Lou, on the other hand—whom she had spoken to twice—hairy hands, big feet, a five o'clock shadow, etc. It wasn't quite "my little daughter."

Mrs. Ravish* knew better than that. But the image of this hairy student covering her daughter set her against the marriage. Mr. Ravish, on the other hand, liked Lou because Lou liked football, and liked it the way Mr. Ravish did. It wasn't just a game to them. It was a calling, a combat, the Whole World Made Game. Nobility of Battle. They brought to football the mentality of the "intelligent columnist," i.e., the world is what you make it. When they weren't discussing the game, they watched it or played a table model that Y. A. Tittle himself thought was great. (Y. A. wouldn't say that if he didn't believe it.) The hulking linemen, the fleet backs, the serene quarterback, head filled with arcane codes. At all events, they liked each other, so Mr. Ravish was in favor of the marriage.

Her mother would say, "See?" Her father, "Why?" So Brooklyn and its familiar streets would substitute for separation. But how would she persuade Lou to go back? He had another year at Berkeley before his Masters. (American Literature, thesis on "The Geography of *Paterson*.") He wanted to finish there.

To get her back after a long talk with Lou would be boring to read as well as write. You have all this conversation. Editors can say, "He certainly has a fine ear," or "He certainly can write." We've had enough conversation to last us a thousand years. They imagine that dialogue is hard to compose. Confusion of mime with selection. I'll bet you five dollars that all novels written by editors (let's not forget journalists) are filled with pages of Incisive Dialogue. These are the wits who make fun of Henry James.** You know the type, they say: "Did you ever read James' dialogue?" (They just finished novels with catchy titles: *Rumble in Heaven. Pudding Junction. A See of Delight. New Haven for Lovers.*) Action! We need action! End of digression. I think we'll put her head in the oven one calm Sunday morning.

She did it when Lou went out for the Sunday papers and coffee cake. It was an act, and Lou, smelling gas when he got

*Not a bad maiden name for Sheila.
**They read *Daisy Miller* and *Washington Square*.

home, found her on the floor, the oven door open, the windows closed. She was groggy and tears rolled down her face as Lou kissed her in front of the door, open to their back yard. He knew that she had rigged this, but he also knew that if she were desperate enough to rig this, something was wrong. She wanted to go home, she said. Something was happening to them, to their marriage, out here. They went home to Brooklyn.

This is better than a long talk, right? Think of them as Steve McQueen and Jean Seberg. Coffee cake all over the floor. Then a few seconds of a Boeing 707.

Some Things Sheila Henry Liked about Lou Henry, 1963–1967.

Ears.

Desert boots.

He sniffled when he read *Nineteen Hundred and Nineteen.*

The way he tossed salad.

The way he wore his hat.

His poems.

Calling William Carlos Williams, "Doc" Williams.

His admiration for Dick Detective.*

His knowledge of football.

The way he held his knife.

His buttocks.

His understanding of D. H. Lawrence.

A crown of Petrarchan sonnets he wrote for her twentieth birthday.

The way he alternately washed and sucked her breasts when they showered together.

Old suede jacket.

The look of his genitals in jockey shorts.

His contempt for his instructors.

His acceptance of Milt, her first real lover.

The way he sang off-key.

---

*Who may figure large in our story.

Sheila's lovers were all unsatisfactory. Not true. What was true is the fact that Sheila's taking of lovers was unsatisfactory. She retained a strong affection for Lou. She loved him, even, and the love surfaced at times with fierce strength. This is a common occurrence. The mind will not let us rest. The most disastrous affair or marriage has moments of great serenity that assert themselves long after the couples have parted. We deny their truth to our grievous cost. The problem is . . . the problem is to comprehend the feeling of loss in the fall. I won't stand still for an instant about the death of the earth, coming of winter. Spring is more bitter than any smoky October. Take the fall, in relation to yourself. The blood stills. The problem is . . . to love, to love, but at the same time understand that we all ache for each other. The young wife whose thighs set your mouth tense with desire: her husband lusts to caress your own wife's breasts. Then why can't happiness spring clear from the adulterous affair? Why doesn't Don Juan grow strong in his rutting? The problem is . . . to realize that assuaged desire does not sate, or still, the mind's hilarious complexities. Those who do not understand this are at a loss to comprehend the true anguish of the flesh—that in imagination we die, and die, and die again. The careless and perennial adulterer is understandable only outside any moral framework: he is a man who lacks imagination. In his orgasms is centered the energy that can generate the subtle differences that drive the poet to his obsession. Out of this sort of spastic adultery come remarks like "they're all the same upside down," "they're all the same in the dark." If those things were true we might all be able to let rest our painful intercourse. The Devil walking to and fro upon the earth. For what? Cannot the Devil take any shape and possess any flesh he so desires? Incubus or succubus, animal or silent zephyr—they are his province and possession. But in his imagination he constructs the lambent chastity of paradise: which he has lost. Love is no comforter, the poet said. Rather a nail in the skull. However read, that sits true. It *is* a nail in the skull. Or: rather to *have* a nail in the skull. What anodyne to ease that agony? While the body heaves and shudders the imagination staggers through the sweet wind off the ocean, straining to recall the precise contours of the youthful face its earlier acrobatics played over.

In old New York, in old New York, etc., etc. Old Brooklyn. It was here that Sheila came to think of Lou as an unvarnished schmuck. Since she was Jewish, the word came naturally to her. She was once awed by him. Who else on Ocean Parkway had read *Paterson?* But she had begun to write poems herself. Why not? "I could write a book" is a timeworn phrase of the educated. To which there is no reply. Or a buck and wing, a fast smile, slow shuffle of the feet. Don't get me wrong—I like Sheila. She might as well write poems as Norman Mailer. Or Alan Dugan. (What of Hyam Plutzik? I hear you say.) Hyam Plutzik as well. But Sheila did not think of Lou as a schmuck *because* she had begun to write poems. It was because he helped her in her writing, became her reader, critic, and mentor. She was "influenced"* by him. If there is one thing that had become immutable in Sheila's beliefs, it was that the poet, the real poet, did not help his wife to become a poet too. The real poet was obsessed with his poems, his life, an egoist, selfish, boorish, rude, crazy. A great, romantic thing, into the breach, kill me tomorrow let me live tonight! and so on. Long hair and flowing lips, falling on the thorns of life, tortured to death in stifling university jobs, the Great Soul Writhing Underneath.** Swift, intense, and destructive affairs with female undergraduates, too many vodka martinis, Fuck the Dean! Fuck the Chairman! Casual quotations from Mao dropped into a discussion of Camus (bourgeois colonialist mentality). Anything. Everything. But not teaching one's wife to write poems. Let her cook food. (Ah, food! Chomp, slurp, good!) Arrange a single daisy in the slender and exquisite vase some literary friend brought from Japan. So that the poet might compose a verse or two about this daisy and his love: an occasional verse, a fragile thing that may grace the first page of the new campus mimeo magazine,

---

*"Influenced" is a mouthful, no?
**A snide reference to Theodore Roethke may be intended here.

Mu'fugga, of which he is faculty advisor. "Well, we can't really call it *Motherfucker,* boys," he laughs, the motherfucker,
"but there *are* ways around that!"

But not to teach her to write poems. In old New York, in
old New York, they lived in Lou's old house, with Lou's
mother, who acted as if they had just been married the day
before, sex jokes in the morning, grins, laughter. Ah well, she
was doing her best too. An old and dear friend of mine
stopped going to his analyst because he got tired of the analyst telling him about the disastrous effect his parents had
had on him: whereas he knew that he had been the major
reason for the destruction of his parents' marriage. As Dr.
Williams says: "But through art the psychologically maimed
may become the most distinguished man of his age. Take
Freud for instance."

We can then realize her misery and sadness when it became apparent to her that her poems were becoming as good
as, if not better, than Lou's. So that she begins to criticize his
work, self-effacing and diffident, but: "Well, Lou, don't you
think you've already *said* this . . . ? I mean this stanza is really all taken care of here at the beginning of the poem? I've
found, in my own work—" With the phrase, "in my own
work," she asserts her serious ambitions.

AN OLD PROVERB*

and in the dream lou
and i were going to skin a cat. our
cat.
          that's an old pro-
          verb
i thought i said. i said i
don't want to, lou.
but he was smi-
ling at my
                    terror holding the raw blood-
                    y carcass in red hands

---

*The first poem Sheila wished to preserve.

Feb. 14, 1967 (Valentine's Day)

My dearest Lou,

Everything is lovely here, but now that I've been here 3 days, more and more, I wish you had come. I'm grateful to you for letting me get off by myself like this, and I'm sure we both needed it to think things out, but I miss you terribly, and think of you all day long. I hope you're working on that long poem that's been giving you so much trouble. Although I've got my notebook here I haven't written anything—all I do is read (when I'm not skiing and gossiping with all the single girls). How old and wise and married I feel! I've read A Clockwork Orange, In Cold Blood, and am about into The Lady in the Lake, which is really a teriffic book! Why didn't you insist earlier that I read Chandler? He's so much more than just another detective story writer.*

Lou, my dear, I'm sure now that everything will be better when I get back home—it's just the effect of having lived with your mother for so long. It upset me terribly. I felt as if I was competing with her for your affection. But I miss you terribly and I've thought so much about all the ways I've hurt you and, I suppose, about all the ways we've hurt each other, that I think we have possibly been foolish.** I've been cruel to you Lou, but I *do* love you, and always shall.

I'm going to go and have a bite of lunch now with a *very* chic girl who works for a Mad Av ad agency as some sort of super girl Friday. She's quite shallow, but really very groovy, and sweet. A lot of fun. I think we'll go skating this afternoon and see a movie tonight. Help and Hard Day's Night are in town and you know how mad I am about the Beatles.

Thinking of you, always, my dear. And love and love and love on Valentine's Day—

Sheila

*A commonly held opinion.
**The meaning of this sentence is obscure.

*Some Things Sheila Henry Disliked about Lou Henry, 1963–
1967.*
Baggy pants.
His passion for football.*
The wispy mustache he tried growing on and off.
Ketchup on pork chops.
The way he sipped his tea.
Dislike of cats.
His lack of interest in her dreams.
His dislike of Guy Lewis.
Unshined shoes.
That he hated straight whiskey yet drank it consistently.
The way he undressed her.
Was absolutely lost on the IND and never admitted it.
Penchant for kasha knishes.

*Psychological Background to Assist the Reader in Under-
standing Sheila's Character Development and Motivations.*
When Sheila was ten she masturbated in her father's car
outside Nathan's Famous in Coney Island. Rhythmically
squeezing together and relaxing her thighs, she ate a hot dog
the while.
When Sheila was an innocent ten, she masturbated in
her father's sinister car outside Nathan's Famous in sordid
Coney Island. Rhythmically squeezing together and relaxing
her nervous thighs, she stealthily ate a hot dog the while.
The "hot dog" is a bona fide phallic symbol. Any book
dealing with Erotica worth its salt will have a picture or two
of some starlet (say Diana Dors or Mamie Van Doren), lips
wetly gleaming,** about to surround with eager mouth the
pedestrian wiener. These pictures are under the section
headed "Fellatio." The reader's response should run: "Looka
that, looks like she's suckin' a cock!" This is a subtle business.

A future of college towns, trees, frost on the lawns, alert faces
of Lou's adoring female students. Stretched before her. (No

---
*She suspected it was a false passion.
**He turns a nice phrase.

matter that Lou had left his job. She knew it was a temporary perversity.) Literary parties, weekends and holidays in New York. Intelligent people, terrific lovers with good manners and unflagging virility, muscular thighs and white teeth. Ah, God, what a bore. Ennui. She would become Madame Bovary. She thought. Lou's academic career solidly progressing, teaching courses in Contemporary American Literature, his work being published more and more widely, his criticism, and translations of Lorca (by "a poet in his own right"). She was twenty-five and this would take up perhaps forty-five more years. She could have staggered and fallen with the re-alization of it. Instead she slept. She seemed always to be asleep, and Lou wrote a series of poems (a cycle, he called it) entitled *Sheila Sleeping*. They were published here and there, and finally came out in a small portfolio, limited edi-tion, on rag paper, with linoleum cuts by Guy Lewis. A collector's item. Sheila slept on.

Give me something, she said. Make me happy. She was waiting for life to give her something, this was intolerable. Take me to the zoo. Fly me to the moon. A new blender to make a pineapple-spinach frappé. No cavities. An orgy at the home of John Lennon. She slept, lovely girl. There would be art, she would take new lovers and write more bad poems. New things. Maybe children. *The Collected Poems of W. B. Yeats*. A new restaurant. A new bar where Norman Mailer hangs out (with his boxer's walk, dear Jesus).

She will not allow her imagination to yield up the clear image that death is the reward and life no preparation for it. It's a pleasure to lose—like Frank Sinatra. She slept, she slept, through days and nights, laid Dick Detective with a kind of spectacular carelessness, which pleased her because it frightened him. I mean, she was game for anything. Stand-ing at a bar one night she masturbated him without opening his pants. Lou, "a poet in his own right," "also a poet, who has been widely published," at home (wherever that would be) battering Lorca's delicate measures to death. I would end this all tragically, but there is no tragedy here.

The roach is millions of years old. Tell the roach. Tell the exquisite ephemeroptera, that has no mouth parts. Tell the female mantis as she devours her mate. With perfect calm he continues fucking as she eats him.* Tell your mother and father. Tell a marriage counselor. Tell Lou. No need to tell Lou, he knows you want something. He'll take you to the country for a weekend. "A change of scene," he says, his heart dying in him. Tell George Plimpton, he'll turn into Lou for a month and write a book that will explain it to you. (Explain it to me! Sheila says. Explain it, Dick! She says to the Detective, sucking his anus. He groans in pleasure and later, over a nightcap, tells her how much he loves April.)

There was a boy of fifteen sent to a hospital for the criminally insane for a misdemeanor. Through a mixup of records, he was kept there for fifty years. Imagine his gentle, stunned face, his body flinching in the noise from the jukebox in her bar. He has never had a woman, nor man either. He has never heard a word of love. Sheila can tell him. He's standing by himself at the end of the bar. Somebody says he thinks he's an old surrealist painter who's lived in Paris since the twenties.

---

*The genitals are left till last.

A Little Novel

Gertrude Stein

Fourteen people have been known to come again. One came. They asked her name. One after one another. Fourteen is not very many and fourteen came. One after another. Six were known to be at once. Welcomed. How do you do. Who is pleasant. How often do they think kindly. May they be earnest.

What is the wish.

They have fourteen. One is in a way troubled may he succeed. They asked his name. It is very often a habit in mentioning a name to mention his name. He mentioned his name.

Earnest is partly their habit.

She is without doubt welcome.

Once or twice four or five there are many which is admirable.

May I ask politely that they are well and wishes.

Cleanly and orderly.

Benjamin Charles may amount to it he is wounded by their doubt.

Or for or fortunately.

No blame is a blemish.

Once upon a time a dog intended to be mended. He would be vainly thought to be pleasant. Or just or join or clearly. Or with or mind or flowery. Or should or be a value.

Benjamin James was troubled. He had been certain. He had perused. He had learned. To labor and to wait.

Or why should he be rich. He was. He was lamentable and discovered. He had tried to sin. Or with perplexity.

She may be judicious.

Many will be led in hope.

He was conveniently placed for observation. They will.

They may well
Be happy.
Any and every one is an authority.
Does it make any difference who comes first.

She neglected to ask it of him. Will he like gardening. She neglected to ask her to be very often. Made pleasantly happy. They were never strange. It is unnecessary never to know them.

And they

Little Expressionless Animals
David Foster Wallace

Julie
straight-edge

It's 1976. The sky is low and full of clouds. The gray clouds are bulbous and wrinkled and shiny. The sky looks cerebral. Under the sky is a field, in the wind. A pale highway runs beside the field. Lots of cars go by. One of the cars stops by the side of the highway. Two small children are brought out of the car by a young woman with a loose face. A man at the wheel of the car stares straight ahead. The children are silent and have very white skin. The woman carries a grocery bag full of something heavy. Her face hangs loose over the bag. She brings the bag and the white children to a wooden fencepost, by the field, by the highway. The children's hands, which are small, are placed on the wooden post. The woman tells the children to touch the post until the car returns. She gets in the car and the car leaves. There is a cow in the field near the fence. The children touch the post. The wind blows. Lots of cars go by. They stay that way all day.

moral
science?
Realism?

It's 1970. A woman with hair like fire sits several rows from a movie theater's screen. A child in a dress sits beside her. A cartoon has begun. The child's eyes enter the cartoon. Behind the woman is darkness. A man sits behind the woman. He leans forward. His hands enter the woman's hair. He plays with the woman's hair, in the darkness. The cartoon's reflected light makes faces in the audience flicker: the woman's eyes are bright with fear. She sits absolutely still. The man plays with her red hair. The child does not look over at the

woman. The theater's cartoons, previews of coming attrac-
tions, and feature presentation last almost three hours.

Alex Trebek goes around the "JEOPARDY!" studio wearing a
button that says PAT SAJAK LOOKS LIKE A BADGER. He and Sajak
play racquetball every Thursday.

It's 1986. California's night sky hangs bright and silent as an
empty palace. Little white sequins make slow lines on streets
far away under Faye's warm apartment.

Faye Goddard and Julie Smith lie in Faye's bed. They
take turns lying on each other. They have sex. Faye's cries
ring out like money against her penthouse apartment's walls
of glass.

Faye and Julie cool each other down with wet towels.
They stand naked at a glass wall and look at Los Angeles.
Little bits of Los Angeles wink on and off, as light gets in the
way of other light.

Julie and Faye lie in bed, as lovers. They compliment
each other's bodies. They complain against the brevity of the
night. They examine and reexamine, with a sort of unhappy
enthusiasm, the little ignorances that necessarily, Julie says,
line the path to any real connection between persons. Faye
says she had liked Julie long before she knew that Julie liked
her.

They go together to the *O.E.D.* to examine the entry for
the word "like."

They hold each other. Julie is very white, her hair prickly
short. The room's darkness is pocked with little bits of Los
Angeles, at night, through glass. The dark drifts down
around them and fits like a gardener's glove. It is incredibly
romantic.

On 12 March 1988 it rains. Faye Goddard watches the freeway outside her mother's office window first darken and then

shine with rain. Dee Goddard sits on the edge of her desk in stocking feet and looks out the window, too. "JEOPARDY!" 's director stands with the show's public relations coordinator. The key grip and cue-card lady huddle over some notes. Alex Trebek sits alone near the door in a canvas director's chair, drinking a can of soda. The room is reflected in the dark window.

"We need to know what you told her so we can know whether she'll come," Dee says.

"What we have here, Faye, is a twenty-minutes-tops type of thing," says the director, looking at the watch on the underside of her wrist. "Then we're going to be in for at least another hour's setup and studio time. Or we're short a slot, meaning satellite and mailing overruns."

"Not to mention a boy who's half catatonic with terror and general neurosis right this very minute," Muffy deMott, the P.R. coordinator, says softly. "Last I saw, he was fetal on the floor outside Makeup."

Faye closes her eyes.

"My husband is watching him," says the director.

"Thank you ever so much, Janet," Dee Goddard says to the director. She looks down at her clipboard. "All the others for the four slots are here?"

"Everybody who's signed up. Most we've ever had. Plus a rather scary retired WAC who's not even tentatively slotted till late April. Says she can't wait any longer to get at Julie."

"But no Julie," says Muffy deMott.

Dee squints at her clipboard. "So how many is that all together, then?"

"Nine," Faye says softly. She feels at the sides of her hair.

"We got nine," says the director; "enough for at least the full four slots with a turnaround of two per slot." The rain on the aluminum roof of the Merv Griffin Enterprises building makes a sound in this room, like the frying of distant meat.

"And I'm sure they're primed," Faye says. She looks at the backs of her hands, in her lap. "What with Janet assuming the poor kid will bump her. Your new mystery data guru."

"Don't confuse the difference between me, on one hand,

Realism

and what I'm told to do," says the director.

"He won't bump her," the key grip says, shaking her head. She's chewing gum, stimulating a little worm of muscle at her temple.

Alex Trebek, looking at his digital watch, begins his pre-slot throat-clearing, a ritual. Everyone in the room looks at him.

Dee says, "Alex, perhaps you'd put the new contestants in the booth for now, tell them we may or may not be experiencing a slight delay. Thank them for their patience."

Alex rises, straightens his tie. His soda can rings out against the metal bottom of a wastebasket. He clears his throat.

"A good host and all that." Dee smiles kindly.

"Gotcha."

Alex leaves the door open. The sun breaks through the clouds outside. Palm trees drip and concrete glistens. Cars sheen by, their wipers on Sporadic. Janet Goddard, the director, looks down, pretends to study whatever she's holding. Faye knows that sudden sunlight makes her feel unattractive.

In the window, Faye sees Dee's outline check its own watch with a tiny motion. "Questions all lined up?" the outline asks.

"Easily four slots' worth," says the key grip; "categories set, all monitors on the board check. Joan's nailing down the sequence now."

"That's my job," Faye says.

"Your job," the director hisses, "is to tell Mommy here where your spooky little girlfriend could possibly be."

"Alex'll need all the cards at the podium very soon," Dee tells the grip.

"Is what your job is today." Janet stares at Faye's back.

Faye Goddard gives her ex-stepfather's wife, Janet Goddard, the finger, in the window. "One of those for every animal question," she says.

The director rises, calls Faye a bitch who looks like a praying mantis, and leaves through the open door, closing it.

"Bitch," Faye says.

Dee complains with a weak smile that she seems simply to be surrounded by bitches. Muffy deMott laughs, takes a seat in Alex's chair. Dee eases off the desk. A splinter snags and snaps on a pantyho. She assumes a sort of crouch next to her daughter, who is in the desk chair, at the window, her bare feet resting on the sill. Dee's knees crackle.

"If she's not coming," Dee says softly, "just tell me. Just so I can get a jump on fixing it with Merv. Baby."

It is true that Faye can see her mother's bright-faint image in the window. Here is her mother's middle-aged face, the immaculately colored and styled red hair, the sore-looking wrinkles that triangulate around her mouth and nose, trap and accumulate base and makeup as the face moves through the day. Dee's eyes are smoke-red, supported by deep circles, pouches of dark blood. Dee is pretty, except for the circles. This year Faye has been able to see the dark bags just starting to budge out from beneath her own eyes, which are her father's, dark brown and slightly thyroidic. Faye can smell Dee's breath. She cannot tell whether her mother has had anything to drink.

Faye Goddard is twenty-six; her mother is fifty.

Julie Smith is twenty.

Dee squeezes Faye's arm with a thin hand that's cold from the office.

Faye rubs at her nose. "She's not going to come, she told me. You'll have to bag it."

The key grip leaps for a ringing phone.

"I lied," says Faye.

"My girl." Dee pats the arm she's squeezed.

"I sure didn't hear anything," says Muffy deMott.

"Good," the grip is saying. "Get her into Makeup." She looks over at Dee. "You want her in Makeup?"

"You did good," Dee tells Faye, indicating the closed door.

"I don't think Mr. Griffin is well," says the cue-card lady.

"He and the boy deserve each other. We can throw in the WAC. We can call *her* General Neurosis."

Dee uses a thin hand to bring Faye's face close to her

own. She kisses her gently. Their lips fit perfectly, Faye thinks suddenly. She shivers, in the air-conditioning.

"JEOPARDY!" QUEEN DETHRONED AFTER THREE-YEAR REIGN

—Headline, *Variety,* 13 March 1988.

unhappy
unaccomplished

"Let's all be there," says the television.

"Where else would I be?" asks Dee Goddard, in her chair, in her office, at night, in 1987.

"We bring good things to life," says the television.

"So did I," says Dee. "I did that. Just once."

Dee sits in her office at Merv Griffin Enterprises every weeknight and kills a tinkling pitcher of wet weak martinis. Her office walls are covered with store-bought aphorisms. Humpty Dumpty was pushed. When the going gets tough the tough go shopping. Also autographed photos. Dee and Bob Barker, when she wrote for "Truth or Consequences." Merv Griffin, giving her a plaque. Dee and Faye between Wink Martindale and Chuck Barris at a banquet.

Dee uses her remote matte-panel to switch from NBC to MTV, on cable. Consumptive-looking boys in makeup play guitars that look more like jets or weapons than guitars.

"Does your husband still look at you the way he used to?" asks the television.

"Safe to say not," Dee says drily, drinking.

"She drinks too much," Julie Smith says to Faye.

"It's for the pain," Faye says, watching.

Julie looks through the remote viewer in Faye's office.

"For killing the pain, or feeding it?"

Faye smiles.

Julie shakes her head. "It's mean to watch her like this."

"You deserve a break today," says the television. "Milk likes you. The more you hear, the better we sound. Aren't you

maybe these characters
force themselves to remain unhappy.

hungry for a flame-broiled Whopper?"

"No I am not hungry for a flame-broiled Whopper," says Dee, sitting up straight in her chair. "No I am not hungry for it." Her glass falls out of her hand.

"It was nice what she said about you, though." Julie is looking at the side of Faye's face. "About bringing one good thing to life."

Faye smiles as she watches the viewer. "Did you hear about what Alex did today? Sajak says he and Alex are now at war. Alex got in the engineer's booth and played with the Applause sign all through "The Wheel" 's third slot. The audience was like applauding when people lost turns and stuff. Sajak says he's going to get him." Alex

"So you don't forget," says the television. "Look at all you get."

"Wow," says Dee. She sleeps in her chair.

Faye and Julie sit on thin towels, in 1987, at the edge of the surf, nude, on a nude beach, south of Los Angeles, just past dawn. The sun is behind them. The early Pacific is lilac. The women's feet are washed and abandoned by a weak surf. The sky's color is kind of grotesque.

Julie has told Faye that she believes lovers go through three different stages in getting really to know one another. First they exchange anecdotes and inclinations. Then each tells the other what she believes. Then each observes the relation between what the other says she believes and what she in fact *does*.

Julie and Faye are exchanging anecdotes and inclinations for the twentieth straight month. Julie tells Faye that she, Julie, best likes: contemporary poetry, unkind women, words with univocal definitions, faces whose expressions change by the second, an obscure and limited-edition Canadian encyclopedia called *LaPlace's Guide to Total Data,* the gentle smell of powder that issues from the makeup compacts of older ladies, and the *O.E.D.*

"The encyclopedia turned out to be lucrative, I guess you'd have to say."

Julie sniffs air that smells yeasty. "It got to be just what the teachers tell you. The encyclopedia was my friend."

"As a child, you mean?" Faye touches Julie's arm.

"Men would just appear, one after the other. I felt so sorry for my mother. These blank, silent men, and she'd hook up with one after the other, and they'd move in. And not one single one could love my brother."

"Come here."

"Sometimes things would be ugly. I remember her leading a really ugly life. But she'd lock us in rooms when things got bad, to get us out of the way of it." Julie smiles to herself. "At first sometimes I remember she'd give me a straightedge and a pencil. To amuse myself. I could amuse myself with a straightedge for hours."

"I always liked straightedges, too."

"It makes worlds. I could make worlds out of lines. A sort of jagged magic. I'd spend all day. My brother watched."

There are no gulls on this beach at dawn. It's quiet. The tide is going out.

"But we had a set of these *LaPlace's Data Guides*. Her fourth husband sold them to salesmen who went door-to-door. I kept a few in every room she locked us in. They did, really and truly, become my friends. I got to be able to feel lines of consistency and inconsistency in them. I got to know them really well." Julie looks at Faye. "I won't apologize if that sounds stupid or dramatic."

"It doesn't sound stupid. It's no fun to be a kid with a damaged brother and a mother with an ugly life, and to be lonely. Not to mention locked up."

"See, though, it was *him* they were locking up. I was just there to watch him."

"An autistic brother simply cannot be decent company for somebody, no matter how much you loved him, is all I mean," Faye says, making an angle in the wet sand with her toe.

"Taking care of him took incredible amounts of time. He wasn't company, though; you're right. But I got so I wanted him with me. He got to be my job. I got so I associated him with my identity or something. My right to take up space. I wasn't even eight."

"I can't believe you don't hate her," Faye says.

"None of the men with her could stand to have him around. Even the ones who tried couldn't stand it after a while. He'd just stare and flap his arms. And they'd say sometimes when they looked in my mother's eyes they'd see him looking out." Julie shakes some sand out of her short hair. "Except he was bright. He was totally inside himself, but he was bright. He could stare at the same thing for hours and not be bored. And it turned out he could read. He read very slowly and never out loud. I don't know what the words seemed like to him." Julie looks at Faye. "I pretty much taught us both to read, with the encyclopedia. Early. The illustrations really helped."

"I can't believe you don't hate her."

Julie throws a pebble. "Except I don't, Faye."

"She abandoned you by a road because some guy told her to."

Julie looks at the divot where the pebble was. The divot melts. "She really loved this man who was with her." She shakes her head. "He made her leave *him*. I think she left me to look out for him. I'm thankful for that. If I'd been without him right then, I don't think there would have been any me left."

"Babe."

"*I'd* have been in hospitals all this time, instead of him."

"What, like he'd have been instantly unautistic if you weren't there to take care of him?"

Among things Julie Smith dislikes most are: greeting cards, adoptive parents who adopt without first looking inside themselves and evaluating their capacity for love, the smell of sulphur, John Updike, insects with antennae, and animals in general.

"What about kind women?"

"But insects are maybe the worst. Even if the insect stops moving, the antennae still wave around. The antennae never stop waving around. I can't stand that."

"I love you, Julie."

Saddened by Love

"I love you too, Faye."

"I couldn't believe I could ever love a woman like this."

Julie shakes her head at the Pacific. "Don't make me sad."

Faye watches a small antennaeless bug skate on legs thin as hairs across the glassy surface of a tidal pool. She clears her throat.

"OK," she says. "This is the only line on an American football field of which there is only one."

Julie laughs. "What is the fifty."

"This, the only month of the year without a national holiday, is named for the Roman emperor who . . ."

"What is August."

The sun gets higher; the blood goes out of the blue water. The women move down to stay in the waves' reach.

"The ocean looks like a big blue dog to me, sometimes," Faye says, looking. Julie puts an arm around Faye's bare shoulders.

> 'We loved her like a daughter,' said "JEOPARDY!" public relations coordinator Muffy deMott. 'We'll be sorry to see her go. Nobody's ever influenced a game show like Ms. Smith influenced "JEOPARDY!" '
>
> —Article, *Variety,* 13 March 1988.

Weak waves hang, snap, slide. White fingers spill onto the beach and melt into the sand. Faye can see dark sand lighten beneath them as the water inside gets tugged back out with the retreating tide.

The beach settles and hisses as it pales. Faye is looking at the side of Julie Smith's face. Julie has the best skin Faye's ever seen on anyone anywhere. It's not just that it's so clear it's flawed, or that here in low sun off water it's the color of a good blush wine; it has the texture of something truly alive, an elastic softness, like a ripe sheath, a pod. It is vulnerable and has depth. It's stretched shiny and tight only over Julie's high curved cheekbones; the bones make her cheeks hollow, her eyes deep-set. The outlines of her face are like clefs, almost Slavic. Everything about her is sort of permeable: even the slim dark gap between her two front teeth seems a kind of slot, some recessive invitation. Julie has used the teeth and their gap to stimulate Faye with a gentle deftness Faye would not have believed.

Julie has looked up. "Why, though?"

Faye looks blankly, shakes her head.

"Poetry, you were talking about." Julie smiles, touching Faye's cheek.

Faye lights a cigarette in the wind. "I've just never liked it. It beats around bushes. Even when I like it, it's nothing more than a really oblique way of saying the obvious, it seems like."

Julie grins. Her front teeth have a gap. "Olé," she says. "But consider how very, very few of us have the equipment to deal with the obvious."

Faye laughs. She wets a finger and makes a scoreboard mark in the air. They both laugh. An anomalous wave breaks big in the surf. Faye's finger tastes like smoke and salt.

Pat Sajak and Alex Trebek and Bert Convy sit around, in slacks and loosened neckties, in the Merv Griffin Entertainment executive lounge, in the morning, watching a tape of last year's World Series. On the lounge's giant screen a batter flails at a low pitch.

"That was low," Trebek says.

Bert Convy, who is soaking his contact lenses, squints at the replay.

Trebek sits up straight. "Name the best low-ball hitter of all time."

"Joe Pepitone," Sajak says without hesitation.

Trebek looks incredulous. "Joe Pepitone?"

"Willie Stargell was a great low-ball hitter," says Convy. The other two men ignore him.

"Reggie Jackson was great," Sajak muses.

"Still is," Trebek says, looking absently at his nails.

A game show host has a fairly easy professional life. All five of a week's slots can be shot in one long day. Usually one hard week a month is spent on performance work at the studio. The rest of the host's time is his own. Bert Convy makes the rounds of car shows and mall openings and "Love Boat" episodes and is a millionaire several times over. Pat Sajak plays phenomenal racquetball, and gardens, and is learning his third language by mail. Alex, known in the industry as the most dedicated host since Bill Cullen, is to be seen lurking almost daily in some area of the MGE facility, reading, throat-clearing, grooming, worrying.

There's a hit. Sajak throws a can of soda at the screen. Trebek and Convy laugh.

Sajak looks over at Bert Convy. "How's that tooth, Bert?"

Convy's hand strays to his mouth. "Still discolored," he says grimly.

Trebek looks up. "You've got a discolored tooth?"

Convy feels at a bared canine. "A temporary thing. Already clearing up." He narrows his eyes at Alex Trebek. "Just don't tell Merv about it."

Trebek looks around, as if to see who Convy is talking to. "Me? This guy right here? Do I look like that sort of person?"

"You look like a game show host."

Trebek smiles broadly. "Probably because of my perfect and beautiful and flawless teeth."

"Bastard," mutters Convy.   *all conscious*

Sajak tells them both to pipe down.   *of appearance*

watching a Re-run

The dynamics of the connection between Faye Goddard and Julie Smith tend, those around them find, to resist clear articulation. Faye is twenty-six and has worked Research on the "JEOPARDY!" staff for the past forty months. Julie is twenty, has foster parents in LaJolla, and has retained her "JEOPARDY!" championship through over seven hundred market-dominating slots.

Forty months ago, game-show production mogul Merv Griffin decided to bring the popular game "JEOPARDY!" back from syndicated oblivion, to retire Art Flemming in favor of the waxily handsome, fairly distinguished, and prenominately dedicated Alex Trebek, the former model who'd made his bones in the game show industry hosting the short-lived "High Rollers" for Barris/NBC. Dee Goddard, who'd written for shows as old as "Truth or Consequences" and "Name That Tune," had worked Promotion/Distribution on "The Joker's Wild," and had finally produced the commercially shaky but critically acclaimed "Gambit," was hired by MGE as the new "JEOPARDY!"'s production executive. A period of disordered tension followed Griffin's decision to name Janet Lerner Goddard—forty-eight, winner of two Clios, but also the wife of Dee's former husband—as director of the revised show; and in fact Dee is persuaded to stay only when Merv Griffin's executive assistant puts in a personal call to New York, where Faye Goddard, having left Bryn Mawr in 1982 with a degree in library science, is doing an editorial stint at *Puzzle* magazine. Merv's right-hand man offers to put Faye on staff at "JEOPARDY!" as Category-/Question-researcher.

Faye works for her mother.

Summer, 1985, Faye has been on the "JEOPARDY!" team maybe four months when a soft-spoken and weirdly pretty young woman comes in off the freeway with a dirty jeans jacket, a backpack, and a *Times* classified ad detailing an MGE contestant search. The girl says she wants "JEOPARDY!"; she's been told she has a head for data. Faye interviews her and is mildly intrigued. The girl gets a solid but by no means spectacular score on a CBE general knowledge quiz, this particular version of which turns out to feature an important zoology section. Julie Smith barely makes it into an audition round.

In a taped audition round, flanked by a swarthy Shriner from Encino and a twig-thin Redding librarian with a towering blond wig, Julie takes the game by a wide margin, but has trouble speaking clearly into her microphone, as well as difficulty with the quirky and distinctive "JEOPARDY!" inversion by which the host "asks" the answer and a contestant supplies the appropriate question. Faye gives Julie an audition score of three out of five. Usually only fives and fours are to be called back. But Alex Trebek, who spends at least part of his free time haunting audition rounds, likes the girl, even after she turns down his invitation for a cola at the MGE commissary; and Dee Goddard and Muffy deMott pick Julie out for special mention from among eighteen other prospectives on the audition tape; and no one on the staff of a program still in its stressful initial struggle to break back into a respectable market share has anything against hauntingly attractive young female contestants. Etc. Julie Smith is called back for insertion into the contestant rotation sometime in early September 1985.

"JEOPARDY!" slots forty-six through forty-nine are shot on 17 September. Ms. Julie Smith of Los Angeles first appears in the forty-sixth slot. No one can quite remember who the reigning champion was at that time.

Palindromes, Musical Astrology, The Eighteenth Century, Famous Edwards, The Bible, Fashion History, States of Mind, Sports Without Balls.

Julie runs the board in both rounds. Every question. Never been done before, even under Flemming. The other two contestants, slack and gray, have to be helped off-stage. Julie wins $22,500, every buck on the board, in half an hour. She earns no more in this first match only because a flustered Alex Trebek declares the Final Jeopardy wagering round moot, Julie Smith having no incentive to bet any of her winnings against opponents' scores of $0 and –$400, respectively. A wide-eyed and grinning Trebek doffs a pretend cap to a blank-faced Julie as electric bongos rattle to the running of the closing credits.

Ten minutes later Faye Goddard locates a missing Julie Smith in a remote section of the contestants' dressing area. (Returning contestants are required to change clothes between each slot, conducing to the illusion that they've "come back again tomorrow.") It's time for "JEOPARDY!" slot forty-seven. A crown to defend and all that. Julie sits staring at herself in a harsh makeup mirror framed with glowing bulbs, her face loose and expressionless. She has trouble reacting to

stimuli. Faye has to get her a wet cloth and talk her through
dressing and practically carry her upstairs to the set.

Faye is in the engineer's booth, trying to communicate to
her mother her doubts about whether the strange new champion can make it through another televised round, when
Janet Goddard calmly directs her attention to the monitor.
Julie is eating slot forty-seven and spitting it out in little
pieces. Lady Bird Johnson's real first name turns out to be
Claudia. The Florida city that produces more Havana cigars
than all of Cuba is revealed to be Tampa. Julie's finger
abuses the buzzer. She is on Alex's answers with the appropriate questions before he can even end-punctuate his clues.
The first-round board is taken. Janet cuts to commercial.
Julie sits at her little desk, staring out at a hushed studio
audience.

Faye and Dee watch Julie as the red lights light and
Trebek's face falls into the worn creases of a professional
smile. Something happens to Julie Smith when the red lights
light. Just a something. The girl who gets a three-score and
who stares with no expression is gone. Every concavity in
that person now looks to have come convex. The camera lin-
gers on her. It seems to ogle. Often Julie appears on-screen
while Trebek is still reading a clue. Her face, on-screen, gives
off an odd lambent UHF flicker; her expression, brightly serene, radiates a sort of oneness with the board's data.

Trebek manipulates the knot of his tie. Faye knows he
feels the something, the odd, focused flux in the game's flow.
The studio audience gasps and whispers as Julie supplies the
Latin name for the common radish.

"No one knows the Latin word for radish," Faye says to
Dee. "That's one of those deadly ones I put in on purpose in
every game."

The other two contestants' postures deteriorate. Someone
in the audience loudly calls Julie's name.

Trebek, who has never before had an audience get away
from him, gets more and more flustered. He uses forty expensive seconds relating a tired anecdote involving a Dodgers
game he saw with Tom Brokaw. The audience hoots impa-

tiently for the game to continue.

"Bad feeling, here," Faye whispers. Dee ignores her, bends to the monitor.

Janet signals Alex for a break. Moist and upstaged, Alex promises America that he'll be right back, that he's eager to inquire on-air about the tremendous Ms. Smith and the even more tremendous personal sacrifices she must have made to have absorbed so much data at such a tender age.

"JEOPARDY!" breaks for a Triscuit advertisement. Faye and Dee stare at the monitor in horror. The studio audience is transfixed as Julie Smith's face crumples like a Kleenex in a pocket. She begins silently to weep. Tears move down the clefs of her cheeks and drip into her mike, where for some reason they hiss faintly. Janet, in the booth, is at a loss. Faye is sent for a cold compress but can't make the set in time. The lights light. America watches Julie Smith murder every question on the Double Jeopardy board, her face and vinyl jacket slickered with tears. Trebek, suddenly and cucumbrously cool, pretends he notices nothing, though he never asks (and never in hundreds of slots does he ask) Julie Smith any of the promised personal questions.

The game unfolds. Faye watched a new, third Julie respond to answer after answer. Julie's face dries, hardens. She is looking at Trebek with eyes narrowed to the width of paper cuts.

In Final Jeopardy, her opponents again cashless, Julie coolly overrides Trebek's moot-motion and bets her entire twenty-two-five on the fact that the first part of Peking Man discovered was a parenthesis-shaped fragment of mandible. She ends with $45,000. Alex pretends to genuflect. The audience applauds. There are bongos. And in a closing moment that Faye Goddard owns, captured in a bright glossy that hangs over her iron desk, Julie Smith, on television, calmly and deliberately gives Alex Trebek the finger.

A nation goes wild. The switchboards at MGE and NBC begin jangled two-day symphonies. Pat Sajak sends three-dozen long-stemmed reds to Julie's dressing table. The market share for the last segment of "JEOPARDY!" slot forty-seven is a fifty—on a par with Super Bowls and assassinations. This is 17 September 1985.

"My favorite word," says Alex Trebek, "is *moist*. It is my favorite word, especially when used in combination with my second-favorite word, which is *induce*." He looks at the doctor. "I'm just associating. Is it OK If I just associate?"

Alex Trebek's psychiatrist says nothing.

"A dream," says Trebek. "I have this recurring dream where I'm standing outside the window of a restaurant, watching a chef flip pancakes. Except it turns out they're not pancakes—they're faces. I'm watching a guy in a chef's hat flip faces with a spatula."

The psychiatrist makes a church steeple with his fingers and contemplates the steeple.

"I think I'm just tired," says Trebek. "I think I'm just bone weary. I continue to worry about my smile. That it's starting to maybe be a tired smile. Which is *not* an inviting smile, which is professionally worrying." He clears his throat. "And it's the *worry* I think that's making me tired in the first place. It's like a vicious smiling-circle."

"This girl you work with," says the doctor.

"And Convy reveals today that he's getting a discolored tooth," Trebek says. "Tell me *that* augurs well, why don't you."

"This contestant you talk about all the time."

"She lost," Trebek says, rubbing the bridge of his nose. "She lost yesterday. Don't you read papers, ever? She lost to her own brother, after Janet and Merv's exec snuck the damaged little bastard in with a rigged five audition and a board just crawling with animal questions."

The psychiatrist hikes his eyebrows a little. They are black and angled, almost hinged.

"Queer story behind that," Trebek says, manipulating a broad bright cufflink to produce lines of reflected windowlight on the ceiling's tile. "I got it about fourth-hand, but still. Parents abandoned the children, as kids. There was the girl and her brother, Lunt. Can you imagine a champion named

Lunt? Lunt was autistic. Autistic to where this was like a mannequin of a kid instead of a kid. Muffy said Faye said the girl used to carry him around like a suitcase. Then finally he and the girl got abandoned out in the middle of nowhere somewhere. By the parents. Grisly. She got adopted and the brother was institutionalized. In a state institution. This hopelessly autistic kid, who it turns out he's got the whole *LaPlace's Data Guide* memorized. They were both forced to somehow memorize this thing, as kids. And I thought *I* had a rotten childhood, boy." Trebek shakes his head. "But he got put away, and the girl got adopted by some people in La Jolla who were not, from the sense I get, princes among men. She ran away. She got on the show. She kicked ass. She was fair and a good sport and took no crapola. She used her prize money to pay these staggering bills for Lunt's autism. Moved him to a private hospital in the desert that was supposed to specialize in sort of . . . *yanking* people outside themselves. Into the world." Trebek clears his throat.

"And I guess they yanked him OK," he says, "at least to where he could talk. Though he still hides his head under his arm whenever things get tense. Plus he's weird-looking. And but he comes and bumps her off with this torrent of zoology data." Trebek plays with the cufflink. "And she's gone."

"You said in our last hour together that you thought you loved her."

"She's a lesbian," Trebek says wearily. "She's a lesbian through and through. I think she's one of those political lesbians. You know the kind? The kind with the anger? She looks at men like they're unsightly stains on the air. Plus she's involved with our ditz of a head researcher, which if you don't think the F.C.C. took a dim view of *that* little liaison you've got another. . . ."

"Free-associate," orders the doctor.

"Image association?"

"I have no problem with that."

"I invited the girl for coffee, or a Tab, years ago, right at the start, in the commissary, and she gave me this haunting, moisture-inducing look. Then tells me she could never imbibe

people live through others

caffeine with a man who wore a digital watch. The hell she says. She gave me the finger on national television. She's practically got a crewcut. Sometimes she looks like a vampire. Once, in the contestant booth—the contestant booth is where we keep all the contestants for all the slots—once one of the lights in the booth was flickering, they're fluorescent lights—and she said to get her the hell out of that booth, that flickering fluorescence made her feel like she was in a nightmare. And there *was* a sort of nightmary quality to that light, I remember. It was like there was a pulse in the neon. Like blood. Everybody in the booth got nervous." Trebek strokes his mustache. "Odd girl. Something odd about her. When she smiled things got bright, too focused. It took the fun out of it, somehow.

"I love her, I think," Trebek says. "She has a way with a piece of data. To see her with an answer . . . Is there such a thing as an intellectual caress? I think of us together: seas part, stars shine spotlights. . . ."

"And this researcher she's involved with?"

"Nice enough girl. A thick, friendly girl. Not fantastically bright. A little emotional. Has this adoration-versus-loathing] ᶠᵃʸᵉ thing with her mother." Trebek ponders. "My opinion: Faye is the sort of girl who's constantly surfing on her emotions. You ¹⁶⁵ know? Not really in control of where they take her, but not quite ever wiping out, yet, either. A psychic surfer. But scary-looking, for so young. These black, bulging, buggy eyes. Perfectly round and black. Impressive breasts, though."

"Mother-conflicts?"

"Faye's mother is one very tense production exec. Spends far too much time obsessing about not obsessing about the fact that our director is her ex-husband's wife."

"A woman?"

"Janet Lerner Goddard. Worst director I've ever worked with. Dee hates her. Janet likes to play with Dee's head; it's a head that admittedly tends to be full of gin. Janet likes to put little trinkety reminders of Dee's ex in Dee's mailbox at the office. Old bills, tie clips. She plays with Dee's mind. Dee's obsessing herself into stasis. She's barely able to even func-

Trebek Knows the other char.

tion at work anymore."

"Image associated with this person?"

"You know those ultra-modern rifles, where the mechanisms of aiming far outnumber those of firing? Dee's like that. God am I worried about potentially ever being like that."

The psychiatrist thinks they have done all they can for today. He shows Trebek the door.

"I also really like the word *bedizen*," Trebek says.

In those first fall weeks of 1985, a public that grows with each Nielsen sweep discerns only two areas of even potential competitive vulnerability in Ms. Julie Smith of Los Angeles. One has to do with animals. Julie is simply unable to respond to clues about animals. In her fourth slot, categories in Double Jeopardy include Marsupials and Zoological Songs, and an eidetic pharmacist from Westwood pushes Julie all the way to Final Jeopardy before she crushes him with a bold bet on Eva Braun's shoe size.

In her fifth slot (and what is, according to the game's publicized rules, to be her last—if a winner, she'll be retired as a five-time champion), Julie goes up against a spectacularly fat Berkeley mailman who claims to be a co-founder of the California chapter of MENSA. The third contestant is a neurasthenic (but gorgeous—Alex keeps straightening his tie) Fullerton stenographer who wipes her lips compulsively on the sleeve of her blouse. The stenographer quickly accumulates a negative score, and becomes hysterically anxious during the second commercial break, convinced by the skunked, vengeful, and whispering mailman that she will have to pay "JEOPARDY!" the nine hundred dollars she's down before they will let her leave the set. Faye dashes out during Off-Air; the woman cannot seem to be reassured. She keeps looking wildly at the exits as Faye runs off-stage and the red lights light.

A bell initiates Double Jeopardy. Julie, refusing to meet the audience's eye, begins pausing a bit before she reponds to Alex. She leaves openings. Only the mailman capitalizes.

Julie stays ahead of him. Faye watches the stenographer, who is clearly keeping it together only through enormous exercise of will. The mailman closes on Julie. Julie assumes a look of distaste and runs the board for several minutes, down to the very last answer, Ancient Rome For A Thousand: author of *De Oratore* who was executed by Octavian in 43 B.C. Julie's finger hovers over the buzzer; she looks to the stenographer. The mailman's eyes are closed in data-search. The stenographer's head snaps up. She looks wildly at Julie and buzzes in with Who is Tully. There is a silence. Trebek looks at his index card. He shakes his head. The stenographer goes to –$1,900 and seems to suffer something resembling a petit mal seizure.

Faye watches Julie Smith buzz in now and whisper into her mike that, though Alex was doubtless looking for the question Who is Cicero, in point of fact one Marcus Tullius Cicero, 106–43 B.C., was known variously as both Cicero *and* Tully. Just as Augustus's less-common appellation is Octavian, she points out, indicating the card in the host's hand. Trebek looks at the card. Faye flies to the Resource Room. The verdict takes only seconds. The stenographer gets the credit and the cash. Out of the emotional red, she hugs Julie on-camera. The mailman fingers his lapels. Julie smiles a really magnificent smile. Alex, generally moved, declaims briefly on the spirit of good clean competition he's proud to have witnessed here today. Final Jeopardy sees Julie effect the utter annihilation of the mailman, who is under the impression that the first literature in India was written by Kipling. The slot pulls down a sixty-five share. Hardly anyone notices Julie's and the stenographer's exchange of phone numbers as the bongos play. Faye gets a tongue-lashing from Muffy deMott on the inestimable importance of researching all possible questions to a given answer. The shot of Julie buzzing in with the correction makes the "Newsmakers" column of *Newsweek*.

That night Merv Griffin's executive assistant calls an emergency policy meeting of the whole staff. MGE's best minds take counsel. Alex and Faye are invited to sit in. Faye calls downstairs for coffee and Cokes and Merv's special seltzer.

Griffin murmurs to his right-hand man. His man has a shiny face and a black toupee. The man nods, rises:

"Can't let her go. Too good. Too hot. She's become the whole show. Look at these figures." He brandishes figures.

"Rules, though," says the director. "Five slots, retire undefeated, come back for Champion's Tourney in April. Annual event. Tradition. Art Flemming. Fairness to whole contestant pool. An ethics type of thing."

Griffin whispers into his shiny man's ear. Again the man rises.

"Balls," the shiny man says to the director. "The girl's magic. Figures do not lie. The Triscuit people have offered to double the price on thirty-second spots, long as she stays." He smiles with his mouth but not his eyes, Faye sees. "Shoot, Janet, we could just call this the Julia Smith Show and still make mints."

"Julie," says Faye.

"Absolutely."

Griffin whispers up at his man.

"Need Merv mention we should all see substantial salary and benefit incentives at work here?" says the shiny man, flipping a watch fob. "A chance here to be industry heroes. Heroines. MGE a Camelot. You, all of you, knights." Looks around. "Scratch that. Queens. Entertainment Amazons."

"You don't get rid of a sixty share without a fight," says Dee, who's seated next to Faye, sipping at what looks to Faye a little too much like water. The director whispers something in Muffy deMott's ear.

There's a silence. Griffin rises to stand with his man. "I've seen the tapes, and I'm impressed as I've never been impressed before. She's like some lens, a filter for that great unorganized force that some in the industry have spent their whole lives trying to locate and focus." This is Merv Griffin saying this. Eyes around the table are lowered. "What is that force?" Merv asks quietly. Looks around. He and his man sit back down.

Alex goes to the door to relieve a winded gofer of refreshments.

Griffin whispers and the shiny man rises. "Merv posits that this force, ladies, gentleman, is the capacity of facts to transcend their internal factual limitations and become, in and of themselves, meaning, feeling. This girl not only kicks facts in the ass. This girl informs trivia with import. She makes it human, something with the power to emote, evoke, induce, cathart. She gives the game the simultaneous transparency and mystery all of us in the industry have groped for, for decades. A sort of union of contestantorial head, heart, gut, buzzer finger. She is, or can become, the game show incarnate. She is mystery."

"What, like a cult thing?" Alex Trebek asks, opening a can of soda at arm's length.

Merv Griffin gives Trebek a cold stare.

Merv's man's face gleams. "See that window?" he says. "That's where the rules go. Out the window." Feels at his nose. "Does your conscientious entertainer retain—and here I say think about all the implications of 'retention,' here"— looking at Janet—"I mean does he cling blindly to rules for their own sake when the very goal and purpose and *idea* of those rules walks right in off the street and into the hearts of every Triscuit consumer in the free world?"

"Safe to say not," Dee says drily.

The man: "So here's the scoop. She stays till she's bumped. We cannot and will not give her any help on-air. Off-air she gets anything within what Merv defines as reason. We get her to play a little ball, go easy on the board when strategy allows, give the other players a bit of a shot. We tell her we want to play ball. DeMott here is one of our carrots."

Muffy deMott wipes her mouth on a commissary napkin. "I'm a carrot?"

"If the girl plays ball, then you, deMott, you start in on helping the kid shelter her income. Tell her we'll give her shelter under MGE. Take her from the seventy bracket to something more like a twenty. Kapisch? She's got to play ball, with a carrot like that."

"She sends all her money to a hospital her brother's in,"

Julio

Faye says softly, next to her mother.

"Hospital?" Merv Griffin asks. "What hospital?"

Faye looks at Griffin. "All she told me was her brother was in Arizona in a hospital because he has trouble living in the world."

"The world?" Griffin asks. He looks at his man.

Griffin's man touches his wig carefully, looks at Muffy. "Get on that, deMott," he says. "This hospitalized brother thing. If it's good P.R., see that it's P.'d. Take the girl aside. Fill her in. Tell her about the rules and the window. Tell her she's here as long as she can hang." A significant pause. "Tell her Merv might want to do lunch, at some point."

Muffy looks at Faye. "All right."

Merv Griffin glances at his watch. Everyone is instantly up. Papers are shuffled.

"Dee," Merv says from his chair, absently fingering a canine tooth. "You and your daughter stay for a moment, please."

Idaho, Coins, Truffaut, Patron Saints, Historical Cocktails, Animals, Winter Sports, 1879, The French Revolution, Botanical Songs, The Talmud, 'Nuts to You.'

One contestant, slot two-eighty-seven, 4 December 1986, is a bespectacled teenage boy with a smear of acne and a shallow chest in a faded Mozart T-shirt; he claims on-air to have revised the Western solar calendar into complete isomorphism with the atomic clocks at the U.S. Bureau of Time Measurement in Washington. He eyes Julie beadily. Any and all of his winnings, he says, will go toward realizing his father's fantasy. His father's fantasy turns out to be a spa, in the back yard of the family's Orange County home, with an elephant on permanent duty at either side of the spa, spouting.

"God am I tired," Alex intones to Faye over a soda and handkerchief at the third commercial break. Past Alex, Faye sees Julie, at her little desk, looking out at the studio audience. People in the audience vie for her attention.

The boy's hopes for elephants are dashed in Final Jeopardy. He claims shrilly that the Islamic week specifies no particular sabbath.

"Friday," Julie whispers.

Alex cues bongos, asks the audience to consider the fact that Californians never (*"never,"* he emphasizes) seem to face east.

"Just the facts on the brother who can't live in the world is all I want," Merv Griffin says, pushing at his cuticles with a paper clip. Dee makes soft sounds of assent.

"The kid's autistic," Faye says. "I can't really see why you'd want data on a damaged person."

Merv continues to address himself to Dee. "What's wrong with him exactly. Are there different degrees of autisticness. Can he talk. What's his prognosis. Would he excite pathos. Does he look too much like the girl. And et cetera."

"We want total data on Smith's brother," iterates the gleaming face of Merv's man.

"Why?"

Dee looks at the empty glass in her hand.

"The potential point," Merv murmurs, "is can the brother do with a datum what she can do with a datum." He switches the paper clip to his left hand. "Does the fact that he has, as Faye here put it, trouble being in the world, together with what have to be impressive genetics, by association," he smiles, "add up to mystery status? Game-show incarnation?" He works a cuticle. "Can he do what she can do?"

"Imagine the possibilities," says the shiny man. "We're looking way down the road on this thing. A climax type of deal, right? Antigone-thing. If she's going to get bumped sometime, we obviously want a bumper with the same kind of draw. The brother's expensive hospitalization at the sister's selfless expense is already great P.R."

"Is he mystery, I want to know," says Merv.

"He's *autistic*," Faye says, staring bug-eyed. "Meaning

they're like trying to teach him just to talk coherently. How not to go into convulsions whenever somebody looks at him. You're thinking about maybe trying to put him on the air?"

Merv's man stands at the dark office window. "Imagine sustaining the mystery beyond the individual girl herself, is what Merv means. The mystery of total data, that mystery made a sort of antic, ontic self-perpetuation. We're talking fact sustaining feeling, right through the change that inevitably attends all feeling, Faye."

"We're thinking perpetuation, is what we're thinking," says Merv. "Every thumb over at Triscuit is up, on this one."

Dee's posture keeps deteriorating as they stand there.

"Remember, ladies," Merv's man says from the window. "You're either part of the solution, or you're part of the precipitate." He guffaws. Griffin slaps his knee.

Nine months later Faye is back in the office of Griffin's man. The man has different hair. He says:

"I say two words to you, Faye. I say F.C.C., and I say separate apartments. We do not I repeat not need even a whiff of scandal. We do not need a "Sixty-Four-Thousand-Dollar-Question"-type-scandal kind of deal. Am I right? So I say to you F.C.C., and separate pads.

"You do good research, Faye. We treasure you here. I've personally heard Merv use the word *treasure* in connection with your name."

"I don't give her any answers," Faye says. The man nods vigorously.

Faye looks at the man. "She doesn't need them."

"All I'm saying to you is let's make our dirty linen a private matter," says the shiny man. "Treasure or no. So I say keep your lovely glass apartment, that I hear so much about."

That first year, ratings slip a bit, as they always do. They level out at incredible. MGE stock splits three times in nine months. Alex buys a car so expensive he's worried about driving it. He takes the bus to work. Dee and the cue-card lady acquire property in the canyons. Faye explores IRAs with the help of Muffy deMott. Julie moves to a bungalow in Burbank, continues to live on fruit and seeds, and sends everything after her minimal, post-shelter taxes to the Palo Verde Psychiatric Hospital in Tucson. She turns down a *People* cover. Faye explains to the *People* people that Julie is basically a private person.

It quickly gets to the point where Julie can't go out anywhere without some sort of disguise. Faye helps her select a mustache and explains to her about not too much glue.

Extrapolation from LAX Airport flight-plan data yields a scenario in which Merv Griffin's shiny man, "JEOPARDY!" director Janet Goddard, and a Mr. Mel Goddard, who works subsidiary rights at Screen Gems, board the shiny man's new Piper Cub on the afternoon of 17 September 1987, fly nonstop to Tucson, Arizona, and enjoy a three-day stay among flying ants and black spiders and unimaginable traffic and several sizzling, carbonated summer monsoons.

> Dethroning Ms. Smith after 700 plus victories last night was one 'Mr. Lunt' of Arizona, a young man whose habit of hiding his head under his arm at crucial moments detracted not at all from the virtuosity with which he worked a buzzer and board that had, for years, been the champion's own.
> —Article, *Variety,* 13 March 1988.

> WHAT NEXT FOR SMITH?
> —Headline, *Variety,* 14 March 1988.

Los Angeles at noon today in 1987 is really hot. A mailman in mailman shorts and wool knee socks sits eating his lunch in the black guts of an open mailbox. Air shimmers over the concrete like fuel. Sunglasses ride every face in sight.

Faye and Julie are walking around west L.A. Faye wears a bathing suit and rubber thongs. Her thongs squeak and slap.

"You did *what?*" Faye says. "You did *what* for a living before you saw our ad?"

"A psychology professor at UCLA was doing tests on the output of human saliva in response to different stimuli. I was a professional subject."

"You were a professional salivator?"

"It paid me, Faye. I was seventeen. I'd had to hitch from La Jolla. I had no money, no place to stay. I ate seeds."

"What, he'd like ring bells or wave chocolate at you and see if you'd drool?"

Julie laughs, gap-toothed, in mustache and sunglasses, her short spiked hair hidden under a safari hat. "Not exactly."

"So what, then?"

Faye's thongs squeak and slap.

"Your shoes sound like sex," Julie says.

"Don't think even one day doesn't go by," says veteran reference-book sales representative P. Craig Lunt in the office of the game-show production mogul who's looking studiously down, manipulating a plastic disk, trying to get a BB in the mouth of a clown.

Dee Goddard and Muffy deMott sit in Dee's office, overlooking the freeway, today, at noon, in the air-conditioning, with a pitcher of martinis, watching the "All New Newlywed Game."

"It's the 'All New Newlywed Game'!" says the television.

"Weak show," says Dee. "All they do on this show is humiliate newlyweds. A series of low gags."

"I like this show," Muffy says, reaching for the pitcher that's refrigerating in front of the air-conditioner. "It's people's own fault if they're going to let Bob Eubanks embarrass them on national daytime just for a drier or a skimobile."

"Cheap show. Mel got a look at their books once. A really . . . a really chintzy operation." Dee jiggles a lemon twist.

Bob Eubanks' head fills the screen.

"Jesus will you look at the size of the head on that guy."

"Youthful-looking, though," Muffy muses. "He never seems to age. I wonder how he does it."

"He's traded his soul for his face. He worships bright knives. He makes sacrifices to dark masters on behalf of his face."

Muffy looks at Dee.

"A special grand prize chosen just for you," says the television.

Dee leans forward. "Will you just look at that head. His forehead simply *dominates* the whole shot. They must need a special lens."

"I sort of like him. He's sort of funny."

"I'm just glad he's on the inside of the set, and I'm on the outside, and I can turn him off whenever I want."

Muffy holds her drink up to the window's light and looks at it. "And of course you never lie there awake in the dark considering the possibility that it's the other way around."

Dee crosses her ankles under her chair. "Dear child, we are in this business precisely to make sure that that is *not* a possibility."

They both laugh.

"You hear stories, though," Muffy says. "About these lonely or somehow disturbed people who've had only the TV all their lives, their parents or whomever started them right off by plunking them down in front of the set, and as they get older the TV comes to be their whole emotional world, it's all they have, and it becomes in a way their whole way of defining themselves as existents, with a distinct identity, that they're outside the set, and everything else is inside the set." She sips.

"Stay right where you are," says the television.

"And then you hear about how every once in a while one of them gets on TV somehow. By accident," says Muffy. "There's a shot of them in the crowd at a ball game, or they're interviewed on the street about a referendum or something, and they go home and plunk right down in front of the set, and all of a sudden they look and they're *inside* the set." Muffy pushes her glasses up. "And sometimes you hear about how it drives them mad, sometimes."

"There ought to be special insurance for that or some-thing," Dee says, tinkling the ice in the pitcher.

"Maybe that's an idea."

Dee looks around. "You seen the vermouth around here anyplace?"

She drinks because she knows her life revolves around her exhusband.

Julie and Faye walk past a stucco house the color of Pepto-Bismol. A VW bus is backing out of the driveway. It sings the high sad song of the Volkswagen-in-reverse. Faye wipes her forehead with her arm. She feels moist and sticky, something hot in a Baggie.

"But so I don't know what to tell them," she says.

"Being involved with a woman doesn't automatically make you a lesbian," says Julie.

"It doesn't make me Marie Osmond, either, though."

Julie laughs. "A cross you'll have to bear." She takes Faye's hand.

Julie and Faye take walks a lot. Faye drives over to Julie's place and helps her into her disguise. Julie wears a mustache and hat, Bermuda shorts, a Hawaiian shirt, and a Nikon.

"Except what if I am a lesbian?" Faye asks. She looks at a small child methodically punching a mild-faced father in the back of the thigh while the father buys Häagen-Dazs from a vendor. "I mean, what if I am a lesbian, and people ask me why I'm a lesbian?" Faye releases Julie's hand to pinch sweat off her upper lip. "What do I say if they ask me why?"

"You anticipate a whole lot of people questioning you about your sexuality?" Julie asks. "Or are there particular people you're worried about?"

Faye doesn't say anything.

Julie looks at her. "I can't believe you really even care."

"Maybe I do. What questions I care about aren't really your business. You're why I might be a lesbian; I'm just ask-ing you to tell me what I can say."

faye does not know who she is.

Julie shrugs. "Say whatever you want." She has to keep straightening her mustache, from the heat. "Say lesbianism is simply one kind of response to Otherness. Say the whole point of love is to try to get your fingers through the holes in the lover's mask. To get some kind of hold on the mask, and who cares how you do it."

"I don't want to hear mask theories, Julie," Faye says. "I want to hear what I should really tell people."

"Why don't you just tell me which people you're so worried about."

Faye doesn't say anything. A very large man walks by, his face red as steak, his cowboy boots new, a huge tin star pinned to the lapel of his business suit.

Julie starts to smile.

"Don't smile," says Faye.

They walk in silence. The sky is clear and spread way out. It shines in its own sun, glassy as aftershave.

Julie smiles to herself, under her hat. The smile's cold. "You know what's fun, if you want to have fun," she says, "is to make up explanations. Give people reasons, if they want reasons. Anything you want. Make reasons up. It'll surprise you—the more improbable the reason, the more satisfied people will be."

"That's fun?"

"I guarantee you it's more fun than twirling with worry over the whole thing."

"Julie?" Faye says suddenly. "What about if you lose, sometime? Do we stay together? Or does our being together depend on the show?"

A woman in terry-cloth shorts is giving Julie a pretty brazen look.

Julie looks away, in her hat.

"Here's one," she says. "If people ask, you can give them this one. You fall totally in love with a man who tells you he's totally in love with you, too. He's older. He's important in terms of business. You give him all of yourself. He goes to France, on important business. He won't let you come. You wait for days and don't hear from him. You call him in France, and a woman's voice says a French hello on the phone, and you hear the man's electric shaver in the background. A couple days later you get a hasty French postcard he'd mailed on his first day there. It says: 'Scenery is here. Wish you were beautiful.' You reel into lesbianism, from the pain."

Faye looks at the curved side of Julie's face, deep skin of a perfect white grape.

Julie says: "Tell them this man who broke your heart quickly assumed in your memory the aspects of a political cartoon: enormous head, tiny body, all unflattering features exaggerated."

"I can tell them all men everywhere look that way to me now."

"Give them this one. You meet a boy, at your East Coast college. A popular and beautiful and above all—and this is what attracts you most—a terribly *serious* boy. A boy who goes to the library and gets out a copy of *Gray's Anatomy,* researches the precise location and neurology of the female clitoris—simply, you're convinced, to allow him to give you pleasure. He plays your clitoris, your whole body, like a fine instrument. You fall for the boy completely. The intensity of your love creates what you could call an organic situation: a body can't walk without legs; legs can't walk without a body. He becomes your body."

"But pretty soon he gets tired of my body."

"No, he gets obsessed with your body. He establishes control over your own perception of your body. He makes you diet, or gain weight. He makes you exercise. He supervises your haircuts, your make-overs. Your body can't make a move without him. You get muscular, from the exercise. Your clothes get tighter and tighter. He traces your changing outline on huge sheets of butcher's paper and hangs them in his room in a sort of evolutionary progression. Your friends think you're nuts. You lose all your friends. He's introduced you to all his friends. He made you turn slowly around while he introduced you, so they could see you from every conceivable angle."

"I'm miserable with him."

"No, you're deliriously happy. But there's not much you, at the precise moment you're feeling most complete."

"He makes me lift weights while he watches. He has barbells in his room."

"Your love," says Julie, "springs from your incompleteness, but also reduces you to another's prosthetic attachment, calcified by the Medusa's gaze of his need."

"I told you I didn't want abstractions about this stuff," Faye says impatiently.

Julie walks, silent, with a distant frown of concentration. Faye sees a big butterfly beat incongruously at the smoke-black window of a long limousine. The limousine is at a red light. Now the butterfly falls away from the window. It drifts aimlessly to the pavement and lies there, bright.

"He makes you lift weights, in his room, at night, while he sits and watches," Julie says quietly. "Pretty soon you're lifting weights nude while he watches from his chair. You begin to be uneasy. For the first time you taste something like degradation in your mouth. The degradation tastes like tea. Night after night it goes. Your mouth tastes like tea when he eventually starts going outside, to the window, to the outside of the window at night, to watch you lift weights nude."

"I feel horrible when he watches through the window."

"Plus, eventually, his friends. It turns out he starts inviting all his friends over at night to watch through the window with him as you lift weights. You're able to make out the outlines of all the faces of his friends. You can see them through your own reflection in the black glass. The faces are rigid with fascination. The faces remind you of the carved faces of pumpkins. As you look you see a tongue come out of one of the faces and touch the window. You can't tell whether it's the beautiful serious boy's tongue or not."

"I reel into lesbianism, from the pain."

"You still love him, though."

Faye's thongs slap. She wipes her forehead and considers.

"I'm in love with a guy and we get engaged and I start going over to his parents' house with him for dinner. One night I'm setting the table and I hear his father in the living room laughingly tell the guy that the penalty for bigamy is two wives. And the guy laughs too."

An electronics shop pulls up alongside them. Faye sees a commercial behind the big window, reflected in the fly's-eye prism of about thirty televisions. Alan Alda holds up a product between his thumb and forefinger. Smiles at it.

"You're in love with a man," says Julie, "who insists that he can love you only when you're standing in the exact center of whatever room you're in."

Pat Sajak plants lettuce in the garden of his Bel Air home. Bert Convy boards his Lear, bound for an Indianapolis Motor Home Expo.

"A dream," says Alex Trebek to the doctor with circumflex brows. "I have this dream where I'm standing smiling over a lectern on a little hill in the middle of a field. The field, which is verdant and clovered, is covered with rabbits. They sit and look at me. There must be several million rabbits in that field. They all sit and look at me. Some of them lower their little heads to eat clover. But their eyes never leave me. They sit there and look at me, a million bunny rabbits, and I look back."

"Uncle," says Patricia ("Patty-Jo") Smith-Tilley-Lunt, stout and loose-faced behind the cash register of the Holiday Inn Restaurant at the Holiday Inn, Interstate 70, Ashtabula, Ohio:

"Uncle uncle uncle uncle."

"No," says Faye. "I meet a man in the park. We're both walking. The man's got a tiny puppy, the cutest and most beautiful puppy I've ever seen. The puppy's on a little leash. When I meet the man, the puppy wags its tail so hard that it loses its little balance. The man lets me play with the puppy. I scratch its stomach and it licks my hand. The man has a picnic lunch in a hamper. We spend all day in the park, with the puppy. By sundown I'm totally in love with the man with the puppy. I stay the night with him. I let him inside me. I'm in love. I start to see the man and the puppy whenever I close my eyes.

"I have a date with the man in the park a couple days later. This time he's got a different puppy with him, another beautiful puppy that wags its tail and licks my hand, and the man's hand. The man says it's the first puppy's brother."

"Oh Faye."

"And but this goes on, me meeting with the man in the park, him having a different puppy every time, and the man is so warm and loving and attentive toward both me and the puppies that soon I'm totally in love. I'm totally in love on the morning I follow the man to work, just to surprise him, like with a juice and Danish, and I follow him and discover that he's actually a professional cosmetics researcher, who performs product experiments on puppies, and kills them, and dissects them, and that before he experiments on each puppy he takes it to the park, and walks it, and uses the beautiful puppies to attract women, who he seduces."

"You're so crushed and revolted you become a lesbian," says Julie.

Pat Sajak comes close to skunking Alex Trebek in three straight games of racquetball. In the health club's locker room Trebek experiments with a half-Windsor and congratulates Sajak on the contract renewal and iterates hopes for no hard feeling re that Applause-sign gag, still. Sajak says he's forgotten all about it, and calls Trebek big fella; and there's some towel-snapping and general camaraderie.

"I need you to articulate for me the dynamics of this connection between Faye Goddard and Julie Smith," Merv Griffin tells his shiny executive. His man stands at the office window, watching cars move by on the Hollywood Freeway, in the sun. The cars glitter.

"You and your mother happen to go to the movies," Faye says. She and Julie stand wiping themselves in the shade of a leather shop's awning. "You're a child. The movie is *Son of*

Flubber, from Disney. It lasts pretty much the whole afternoon." She gathers her hair at the back of her neck and lifts it. "After the movie's over and you and your mother are outside, on the sidewalk, in the light, your mother breaks down. She has to be restrained by the ticket man, she's so hysterical. She tears at her beautiful hair that you've always admired and wished you could have had too. She's totally hysterical. It turns out a man in the theater behind you was playing with your mother's hair all through the movie. He was touching her hair in a sexual way. She was horrified and repulsed, but didn't make a sound, the whole time, I guess for fear that you, the child, would discover that a strange man in the dark was touching your mother in a sexual way. She breaks down on the sidewalk. Her husband has to come. She spends a year on antidepressants. Then she drinks.

"Years later her husband, your stepfather, leaves her for a woman. The woman has the same background, career interests, and general sort of appearance as your mother. Your mother gets obsessed with whatever slight differences between herself and the woman caused your stepfather to leave her for the woman. She drinks. The woman plays off her emotions, like the insecure and basically shitty human being she is, by dressing as much like your mother as possible, putting little mementos of your stepfather in your mother's In-box, coloring her hair the same shade of red as your mother does. You all work together in the same tiny but terrifyingly powerful industry. It's a tiny and sordid and claustrophobic little community, where no one can get away from the nests they've fouled. You reel into confusion. You meet this very unique and funny and sad and one-of-a-kind person."

"The rain in Spain," director Janet Goddard says to a huge adolescent boy so plump and pale and vacant he looks like a snowman. "I need you to say 'The rain in Spain' without having your head under your arm.

"Pretend it's a game," she says.

It's true that, the evening before Julie Smith's brother will beat Julie Smith on her seven-hundred-and-forty-first "JEOPARDY!" slot, Faye tells Julie about what Merv Griffin's man and the director have done. The two women stand clothed at Faye's glass wall and watch distant mountains become Hershey kisses in an expanding system of shadow.

Faye tells Julie that it's because the folks over at MGE have such respect and admiration for Julie that they want to exercise careful control over the choice of who replaces her. That to MGE Julie is the mystery of the game show incarnate, and that the staff is understandably willing to do pretty much anything at all in the hopes of hanging on to that power of mystery and incarnation through the inevitability of change, loss. Then she says that that was all just the shiny executive's bullshit, what she just said.

Julie asks Faye why Faye has not told her before now what is going to happen.

Faye asks Julie why Julie sends all her sheltered winnings to her brother's doctors, but will not talk to her brother.

Julie isn't the one who cries.

Julie asks whether there will be animal questions tomorrow.

There will be lots and lots of animal questions tomorrow. The director has personally compiled tomorrow's categories and answers. Faye's been temporarily assigned to help the key grip try to repair a defectively lit E in the set's giant "JEOPARDY!" logo.

Faye asks why Julie likes to make up pretend reasons for being a lesbian. She thinks Julie is really a lesbian because she hates animals, somehow. Faye says she does not understand this. She cries, at the glass wall.

Julie lays her hands flat on the clean glass.

Faye asks Julie whether Julie's brother can beat her.

Julie says that there is no way her brother can beat her, and that deep down in the silence of himself her brother knows it. Julie says that she will always know every fact her brother knows, plus one.

Through the window of the Makeup Room Faye can see a
gray paste of clouds moving back over the sun. There are tiny
flecks of rain on the little window.

Faye tells the makeup lady she'll take over. Julie's in the
makeup chair, in a spring blouse and faded cotton skirt, and
sandals. Her legs are crossed, her hair spiked with mousse.
Her eyes, calm and bright and not at all bored, are fixed on a
point just below her own chin in the lit mirror. A very small
kind smile for Faye.

"You're late I love you," Faye whispers.

She applies base.

"Here's one," Julie says.

Faye blends the border of the base into the soft hollows
under Julie's jaw.

"Here's one," says Julie. "To hold in reserve. For when
you're really on the spot. They'll eat it up."

"You're not going to get bumped. He's too terrified to
stand up, even. I had to step over him on the way down here."

Julie shakes her head. "Tell them you were eight. Your
brother was silent and five. Tell them your mother's face
hung tired from her head, that first men and then she herself
made her ugly. That her face just hung there with love for a
blank silent man who left you touching wood forever by the
side of the road. Tell them how you were left by your mother
by a field of dry grass. Tell them the field and the sky and the
highway were the color of old laundry. Tell them you touched
a post all day, your hand and a broken baby's bright-white
hand, waiting for what had always come back, every single
time, before."

Faye applies powder.

"Tell them there was a cow." Julie swallows. "It was in the
field, near where you held the fence. Tell them the cow stood
there all day, chewing at something it had swallowed long

ago, and looking at you. Tell them how the cow's face had no expression on it. How it stood there all day, looking at you with a big face that had no expression." Julie breathes. "How it almost made you need to scream. The wind sounds like screams. Stand there touching wood all day with a baby who is silence embodied. Who can, you know, stand there forever, waiting for the only car it knows, and not once have to understand. A cow watches you, standing, the same way it watches anything."

A towelette takes the excess powder. Julie blots her lipstick on the blotter Faye holds out.

"Tell them that, even now, you cannot stand animals, because animals' faces have no expression. Not even the possibility of it. Tell them to look, really to look, into the face of an animal, sometime."

Faye runs a gentle pick through Julie's moist spiked hair.

Julie looks at Faye in a mirror bordered with bulbs. "Then tell them to look closely at men's faces. Tell them to stand perfectly still, for time, and to look into the face of a man. A man's face has nothing on it. Look closely. Tell them to look. And not at what the faces do—men's faces never stop moving—they're like antennae. But all the faces do is move through different configurations of blankness."

Faye looks for Julie's eyes in the mirror.

Julie says, "Tell them there are no holes for your fingers in the masks of men. Tell them how could you ever even hope to love what you can't grab onto."

Julie does not love her brother.

Julie turns her makeup chair and looks up at Faye. "That's when I love you, if I love you," she whispers, running a finger down her white powdered cheek, reaching to trace an angled line of white onto Faye's own face. "Is when your face moves into expression. Try to look out from yourself, different, all the time. Tell people that you know your face is least pretty at rest."

She keeps her fingers on Faye's face. Faye closes her eyes against tears. When she opens them Julie is still looking at her. She's smiling a wonderful smile. Way past twenty. She takes Faye's hands.

"You asked me once how poems informed me," she says. Almost a whisper—her microphone voice. "And you asked whether we, us, depended on the game, to even be. Baby?"— lifting Faye's face with one finger under the chin—"Remember? Remember the ocean? Our dawn ocean, that we loved? We loved it because it was like us, Faye. That ocean was *obvious*. We were looking at something obvious, the whole time." She pinches a nipple, too softly for Faye even to feel. "Oceans are only oceans when they move," Julie whispers. "Waves are what keep oceans from just being very big puddles. Oceans are just their waves. And every wave in the ocean is finally going to meet what it moves toward, and break. The whole thing we looked at, the whole time you asked, was obvious. It was obvious and a poem because it was us. See things like that, Faye. Your own face, moving into expression. A wave, breaking on a rock, giving up its shape in a gesture that *expresses* that shape. See?"

It wasn't at the beach that Faye had asked about the future. It was in Los Angeles. And what about the anomalous wave that came out of nowhere and broke on itself?

Julie is looking at Faye. "See?"

Faye's eyes are open. They get wide. "You don't like my face at rest?"

The set is powder-blue. The giant "JEOPARDY!" logo is lowered. Its *E* flickers a palsied fluorescent flicker. Julie turns her head from the sick letter. Alex has a flower in his lapel. The three contestants' names appear in projected cursive before their desks. Alex blows Julie the traditional kiss. Pat Sajak gives Faye a thumbs-up from stage-opposite. He gestures. Faye looks around the curtain and sees a banana peel on the pale blue carpet, carefully placed in the tape-marked path Alex takes every day from his lectern to the board full of answers. Dee Goddard and Muffy deMott and Merv Griffin's shiny man hunch over monitors in the director's booth. Janet Goddard arranges a shot of a pale round boy who dwarfs his little desk. The third contestant, in the middle, feels at his makeup a little. Faye smells powder. She watches Sajak rub his hands together. The red lights light. Alex raises his arms in greeting. There is no digital watch on his wrist.

The director, in her booth, with her headset, says something to camera two.

Julie and the audience look at each other.

Bonanza

Curtis White

woaoaoaoaoaoaoaoaoaiiiiiiiiiiiiiNNNNNNNNNGGGGGGGG
dum da da dum dada duddle duddle dum da da DUM DUM
dum da da dum dada duddle duddle dum dum dada dum dum dum
dum da da dum dada duddle duddle dum dada DUM DUM
dum da da dum dada duddle duddle dum dum dada dum dum dum
dum dum dum
dum dum dum
da da da da dum
dum da da dum dada duddle duddle dum dada DUM DUM
dum da da dum dada duddle duddle dum dum dada dum dum dum

DA DUM DUM

DA

DUM!

The
Ponderosa
is burning.
It started with
a little discoloration,
a darkening, then red hot,
like someone lighting parchment
from the backside with the glowing
tip of a cigarette. Within moments
it had spread thousands of acres, miles,
flattened Virginia City, reduced the fabled
ponderosa pines to twigs, black and dead.
Miraculously riding out of the very center of this
apocalypse are the Cartwrights.
Little Joe, Ben and Hoss. They're all smiles.
We'll need men like this after the apocalypse.
Ben looks about him: beautiful!
I'll give this to my boys someday.
Little Joe and Hoss smile too
'cause their Pa is going to
give them the Ponderosa.
Hope
it's not
too
Hot.

The Cartwrights ride off and the commercial break is about to begin, but if you rewind to just the last moment before the break, freeze frame, now enlarge, you see that there is someone running, trying to catch up to the Cartwrights. He is naked and matted with hair and his penis is cheesy and he babbles loudly. He is Wild Father. He will tell this story titled "The Bridegroom."

"God, *Bonanza*. This show makes me sick. I thought it was dead. I thought I killed them all myself. I thought it was all burnt up."

"I taped it off the Family Channel, Wild Father. It plays reruns twice every day. The Family Channel is owned by Christian corporate interests. They believe that *Bonanza*, the saga of the admirable Cartwrights, fosters family values in America."

"So it's not dead yet? Hoss is dead, I know that. Dan Blocker died of his own girth in 1972. And Little Joe is dead of cancer caused by constant exposure to radioactive tabloids. Ben lives in dog food commercials. That's hell, ain't it?"

"Peace, Old Man of the Earth. Why don't you just tell us this story of 'The Bridegroom'?"

The Wild Father Tells All

"I never really met the Cartwrights, you understand. I lived on the Ponderosa in a gully full of sticks. The producer hired crews of derelicts left over from mining days in the Comstock to clean up. Every one of them looked like Gabby Hayes. They were men like me with hair on their bodies. Ben Cartwright told these men to pick up anything that wasn't a big ass pine tree and put it in my gully.

"Before every episode, the Cartwrights would ride by,

fearlessly, joyfully, riding straight into the heart of this forest
fire that had consumed the entire region. Well, every single
time I'd come up out of my gully yelling and waving my hands
trying to catch their attention. I wanted to say, 'Hey, who the
fuck do you think you pretty boys are dumping all these twigs
and sticks in my gulley? Just cut that shit.' And ol' Ben he'd
just sit so stiff and proud in his saddle and say, 'Ignore him,
boys. That's the Wild Father.' 'Just ignore him,' he says. Oh
that makes me so durned mad! Why couldn't they take me
with them? Every stinkin' week they'd find some galoot
camping out on their spread, a wounded Indian or a runaway
or a tragic Johnny Reb or some other dumb fuck with trouble
but a heart that only the Cartwrights could demonstrate
pure. What was wrong with me? Sure I was covered with hair
and some of it was crusty with my own smelly shit and my
dick was a bit cheesy like you said earlier, still is if you've got
any sense of smell left to you by the government agencies
regulating the use of your nose, but I would have liked being
saved. I would have liked being put in the guest room and
Hop Sing could make me some nice food and Ben would tell
Little Joe he 'better go get Doc' just to be on the safe side. And
Doc would say, 'Well he's undernourished and dirty and his
private parts are thick with an interesting scum, kinda like a
Ricotta cheese product, but I think all he really needs is a hot
bath and a haircut and some of Hop Sing's good food.'

"And Hop Sing would smile and move from toe to toe and
squint in his glee, and say, 'Oh Hop Sing can makee vely fine
food for Wide Fatha.' And then everyone would laugh because
Chinese is some funny little shits. Later in the show, of
course, I would test my benefactor's patience by doing something savage. I'd steal something. A gravy boat would be
found under my pillow. Or, or I'd be caught in the barn playing with the horses' doodads. Then Ben would have to sit me
down and say, 'Now, Wild Father, we're your friends. You
know that. And we're just trying to help you. Don't you want
to be like us? Even the ferocious Indians, who leave their own
kind for dead served up in the grasses for wolves, even they
want to be like us. To wear our hats. To eat our potatoes when

they are mashed. But we can't have this . . . whatever you'd call it. White people don't play with horses' doodads.'

"But this is just idle fantasy, boy. The Cartwrights never took me to their house. I guess I just wasn't good enough for the likes of them or I was so bad that they saw no hope of making me an American. Bloody hell, I AM AMERICA. I take out America's garbage every Tuesday night. Don't that make me America? I scarf up ozone. Hell, I am the damned ozone hole. I fart plutonium out of a sense of national responsibility. I keep toxic waste incinerators burning round the clock with my nose pickings."

"I don't doubt a word of it, Wild Father. Why don't you just tell this story?"

"Sure. I have no choice but to take my revenge any way I can. I'll tell each and every one of their weekly episodes going all the way back to 1963, only I'll tell it my way. To hell with the consequences! I don't give a damn if they lose their corporate sponsors! I don't care if the people at Ralston Purina say, 'You know this Wild Father character is making it difficult to promote our delightful Chex party mixes.' Those ad execs can go chase the colorful banners that flutter from my asshole.

"What it comes to is this: the Cartwrights wouldn't be my family, my father and brothers. Little Joe wouldn't let me ride behind him on his painted palomino. So what are family values to a poor fuck that no family will have?"

Wild Father was working up a sweat. Some of the excremental matter about him was getting humid and starting to stink.

"So, Son, pay attention to what your Wild Father says. This episode is called 'The Bridegroom.' The first scene is coffee time at the Ponderosa. Ben sits at a coffee table in the living room (really it's just like your house in the burbs except they've got the television console covered up with a saddle blanket for historical authenticity's sake). Sitting with him are Tuck (a local rancher) and Tuck's only daughter, Maggie. Ben is sipping his coffee from a delicate china teacup. This signifies that he is an atypical cowboy hero. He will shoot you dead with his gun, but he would rather represent the virtues of the landed gentry. Tuck, on the other hand, pours his coffee from the cup into the saucer, hence to his thirsty lips.

"Maggie says, 'Pa, that's not very polite.'

"Tuck replies, 'Maggie, when a man's been saucerin' for forty years it's too late to make him change his ways.'

"What in the funny heck is *saucerin'*, son? Do you know? Do you believe this prime-time crapola? Saucerin'! [sings] *I'm a saucerin' man, done a lot of saucerin'* . . . hee hee. Why doesn't he just slice his belly open and pour it right in there? Then he could say, 'Maggie, when a man's been caesarian his coffee for forty years it's too late to change his ways.' " Wild Father throws his hands up in his riotous laughter and strings of a pudding-like substance fly off his fingers up toward the ceiling leaving little greasy tapioca marks.

" 'Now, now, Maggie, don't worry about that,' says Ben, 'I guess everyone's got their bad habits.'

" 'You're darned right about that, Ben. Maggie here, she's got her habit too. The spinster habit.'

"Ouch. You could have heard a pin drop. You could have heard Hoss falling in the distant woods. It was time for fathers to bruise their children again.

" 'Pa!' says Maggie, a hurt look on her plain face. Well, she wasn't so stinkin' plain. Anyone could see that she was a Hollywood actress with her hair tied back in matching buns over each ear like stereo headphones. *Hair buns=homely* in T.V. sign language. Soon as she lets her hair down, you watch, wham, she'll be a beauty.

"Ben saves the day: 'Maggie, I seem to have forgotten the cream. Would you be a good girl and get it?'

"Well, Maggie, there's your moral universe. You can be a spinster or a good girl. It's your choice. Lots of luck.

" 'Tuck,' says wise, kind ol' Ben, 'what's the matter with you? If brains were dynamite, you couldn't blow your nose.'

"Oh a fine line," croons the Wild Father, his eyes turned heavenward, hopping now from side to side, his legs spread and bent like a Sumo wrestler, complicated debris shaking from his furry haunches with each bounce. "Truly, sirrah, a most comely, melodious, and memorable line. Oh you rare hearts, you brave and inspired hearts that do pen the noble poetry of television drama. Or try this on, 'I wouldn't cross the street to spit on you, even if you were on fire.' A pearl! A ruby! Little oysters of moist adulation come to my lips and launch themselves into your perfumed beards. I grovel at your Florsheimed feet and pass mustard on your argyles. You geniuses! You billfolded muses! I flay the fox on the path on which you tread.

"But Father Tuck knows his mind and his daughter. 'Ben, you don't know how lucky you are to have sons. The plain truth is my Maggie is a homely woman.'

"Little Joe comes into the house just then, the soles of his boots smoldering, little flames licking up from the hot leather. He overhears Tuck with a frown. 'That ain't so, Tuck.'

"Frown or no frown, there's no question that Little Joe's a cutie. Eh? Little silk kerchief around his neck, tiny Paul McCartney pretty face, and curly hair comin' down like he half-admired hippies." Wild Father leers and teases out his own wiry hair in imitation. It seems to have clumps of oatmeal in it.

" 'Oh, is that right, Little Joe? Then how come you never once asked my Maggie to go to a social?'

"He's got you there, Little Joe, you masterpiece. He knows like you know that every week brings its episode and every episode brings new butt, creamy wanna-be-a-T.V.-starlet butt for you to stroke between takes. You don't fool nobody, buster. And why didn't you take Maggie to a social or somethin'?

" 'It just never worked out that way is all.'

"LAME! Lame, Brother Joe. Don't cut it. You'll have to do better than that.

"A few days later, Ben, Little Joe, Tuck and Maggie visit Jarrod, a widower now living alone on his ranch. They're looking at horses that Jarrod has for sale.

"Tuck pulls Jarrod over confidentially and they have the following conversation.

" 'Just touch that.'

" 'That's a good lookin' animal.'
" 'You better believe it.'
" 'That's a fine lookin' animal.'
" 'Now touch this part.'
" 'That's mighty soft there.'
" 'And here.'
" 'I can't touch there. It wouldn't bo right.'
" 'It's even softci.'
" 'Well I know that but . . . '
" 'Okay, never mind, but why don't you just come over to the house tonight and we can talk it over?'
"God I love Christian Broadcasting, son!"

Women and Horses:
The Secret Connection

By Dr. James Wildfather
University of Twigs at Gully

Consider the following scene from an episode of *Bonanza* titled "The Bridegroom." Jarrod has come over to the home of Tuck and Maggie one evening in order to discuss a livestock deal.

"Well, well, Jarrod. Come on in."

"Good evening, Tuck, Miss Maggie."

[Maggie smiles stiffly, a look of dread in her eyes. For months now she's been feeling this creeping sense of unreality and dread. She feels that people want to hurt her. Even people she knows to love her. Her psychiatrist has suggested tricyclic antidepressants, but the mood of doom has not begun to lift. In particular, she thinks her father is trying to sell her like a horse. This neurotic delusion causes Maggie to experience a sudden onset of raw fear as Jarrod enters her father's house. In quick order she feels shortages of breath, palpitations, chest pain, a choking feeling, dizziness, hot flashes, faintness, nausea, trembling, fear of dying, and fear of losing control. All of this gives a little flush to her cheek which Jarrod finds charming.]

"Jarrod," says Tuck, "You notice anything different about Maggie tonight?"

"Well, she looks very pretty."

"Oh, come on now, son. You don't have to say what's not true. She's a homely thing that no self-respectin' man would pay court to. No, it's something else."

"Well, I give up. What is it?"

[Maggie squirms. Her eyes mist. She'd like to run from the room. She'd like to be dead. She imagines herself capable of running through a wall.]

Tuck walks straight over to the hearth. He lifts Maggie's arms. She is manacled to the hearth.

"Chains, Jarrod. It's chains. I've got Maggie chained to the hearth!"

[Jarrod approaches uncertainly. He's amazed.]

"What do you think about that?" asks Tuck.

"I don't know what to think," replies Jarrod, a little sheepish.

"I'll tell you somethin' else you might not know about. Now, Maggie looks very proper tonight, don't she? Hair in that tight spinster's bun. Nice long calico dress that she sewed herself—she's fine with a needle, Jarrod. But guess what? Turn around, Maggie honey, that's a good girl. Look she ain't got no underthings on. Put your hand there on her shank, son. That's good, ain't it? Soft and warm."

"Do you really like this, Miss Maggie?"

"Sure she does, don't you girl?"

"Yes. I like it Pa."

"Now, how many women you know, pretty or plain, that really like this kinda thing? Tell me that."

"Not many that I know of," replies Jarrod. [He takes a step away, pushes his rancher's hat back on his forehead. Eyes linger on the fine marble turn of Maggie's hip.] "This does put things in a brand new light."

Tuck laughs outloud. "That's it! I knew you'd come

around. Let's sit over here and talk this out over a glass of Maggie's fine plum wine."

Wild Father, you too much, babes.

Huh?

You a funky-ass motherfucker.

What?

You solid, man. You stoned. You gone.

Is that you, boy?

You a gangsta of funky-ass love.

Why you talkin' like a nigger? Niggers don't count here. This world is all Christian T.V.

You gone. You way gone. You my cheesy hambone man.

You think it's fun bein' the Wild Father? You think it's all runnin' round and chaining your daughter to household appliances and lettin' your business associates play with her butt? You think that's what Wild Fatherin' is all about? Well, come on sit yourself down here, even if you are a nigger or maybe my son talkin' funny, and I'll give you the Wild Father rant.

The Wild Father's Rant

First, you gotta have this hair all over your body. You ever try to grow the hair real long and thick on the underside of your arms? You know, the part of your arm where it's soft and pink even when you're sixty-five and hair's growing out of your nose like pampas grass? Well, it's all in the diet. You must eat: canned beef tamales, Dintymoore beef stew, sardines in mustard sauce, potted meat, lots and lots of non-dairy cheese products like Velveeta and Cheeze Whiz (eat the Cheeze Whiz right straight from the aerosol container, boy), SPAM (don't cook it), Vienna wienies right from the can, season all your foods with the cheapest off-brand of liverwurst you can find (liverwurst made from the things that even Oscar Mayer won't put in their liverwurst; I'm not talkin' snout or entrails; that's clean and invigorating; I'm talkin' stuff that's barely associated with the livestock industry like squirrels that happened to die in the vicinity of the slaughterhouse). For a vegetable you eat Pillsbury Mashed Potato Flakes.

"And this effort just gets you the hair. We're not even talkin' attitude yet! To get the Wild Father attitude you get up real early because your brain chemistry is so fucked up you can't sleep through the night. So you get up at five. Don't eat anything yet, that's for later. Do all your eatin' at one time. Now drink a pot of coffee to scour the GI track, read the newspaper and get a good coughin' jag going. Don't be shy about it. Rattle the damned walls. If you do it right, your children will think they woke up in a tuberculosis ward. Soon as you feel that last cough gone, light up. You've got three, four packs of cigarettes to do today so you've got to get started early. (Note: when coughing, try to drag that phlegm way up, all the way up, and spit it into a cheap paper napkin. Let the fatty stain leak through. Leave the napkin on the kitchen table next to your cigarette butts and coffee dregs. When your wife and children get up, they'll see the wads and any ideas of shredded wheat and OJ, health and happiness will go right out the window, if this kitchen nook had a window.) And remember, it's up to every Wild Father to reproduce his kind. In particular, when your son gets up, let off a good audible fart. Don't apologize. In general, say nothing to nobody. It's your house and you can fill it with farts if you like. Let it float foully up like a helium balloon. Fuck everybody else. Someday your sons will have their own houses to fart in. Next, a real Wild Father retreats to the throne and shits out all the wild canned animal products he consumed the previous day. Check it out. Be proud.

"Now you're ready to start your day. Put on your plastic windbreaker that you won at the Brutal Inn and Out Pro-Am, 'cause that's your hang out. 'The Brute' it's known as. And that's where you're going. At the Brute reinforce your neighbor's bigotry. Drink nine vodkas and accept the warm comradery of the other Wild Fathers. Talk about life on T.V. Now go home for lunch. (Pause only if some bitch has parked too close in the parking lot. She's in buying groceries, so give her a little bang in the passenger side door. Bitches is the Wild Father's big enemy.)

"When you get home in the afternoon everyone will have fled your odor, aura, mean drunk temper. Make some lunch in the lovely quiet you have achieved with your own rare works. Canned oysters in skim milk heated to near boiling. Break a handful of soda crackers on top and mix well. A lunch fit for a Wild Father. Now sit in front of the T.V. and watch re-runs of *Perry Mason*. Doze. *Streets of San Francisco*. Doze. *Hawaii Five-O*. Doze. *Mannix*. Doze. *Kojak*. Doze. *Cannon*. Doze. *Rockford Files*. Doze. *The Untouchables*. It's midnight. Your long meditation has achieved Wild Father nirvana. If Robert Stack sat on your face you couldn't be happier.

"At two in the morning get out of the recliner, turn off the T.V. and go to bed. The Wild Father's wife smells funny. She's too clean. He sleeps anyway. Three hours is all he gets. Then it's up and the regimen begins again."

Oh, Wild Father, babes, you a motherfuckin' dead man.

Maggie: He tried to sell me like a cow, Joe. I wish I were dead, I'm so homely.

Joe: Maggie, you're not homely.

M: Joe, I am, everyone says I am.

J: Who says you are?

M: Pa. Pa says so. All the kids I went to school with. Don't tease me Joe, you're the only friend I have in the world.

J [grabbing her by the arms]: Now you listen to me, Maggie. I'm just trying to make you see the truth.

M: I do see it. That's the trouble. I'm so homely my father would pay a man to get me off his hands. Nobody wants me, Joe. I know that. I'm not blind.

J: I think you're blind. I think your father's blind, I think everybody in this town is blind. Maggie, you can be pretty, but you just have to try.

M: Oh Joe. Maybe tomorrow I'll wake up and I'll be pretty.

J: There are lots of other men, other than Jarrod.

M: Oh no there are not. Not for me. And I can't just spend my life waiting around for something to happen.

J: Maggie, will you stop feeling sorry for yourself? You don't have a man because you don't want one. Stop playing the wilting violet. Go out and find the man you want and let him know it. Go after him, Maggie.

Ben Cartwright sits in his armchair, bent forward, his head in his hands. Hop Sing bounces about him chanting a sing-song homeopathic mantra. Something is wrong with Ben, Our Father. When he woke, his head was larger than usual. It was about the size of a large world globe. Because of its new size, Ben's hairs were spaced further apart making it easy for Hop Sing to find evidence. He felt about Ben's head like a boy looking for a lost marble in the grass. Up near the hairline on his forehead Hop Sing found what appeared to be a large bug shell, brown and long like the egg sack on a cockroach. This caused a more intensive search for intruders. Ben himself found a large inflamed area. He pressed it from both sides which easily and smoothly began to force out the hind end of the cockroach creature. But it wasn't a cockroach, it was a long worm-like thing, about the size of a child's index finger and similarly jointed. When at last it was out, Ben and Hop Sing could see that it had a tiny human face that was busy contorting. Probably wasn't used to the bright lights. It was clearly not happy being out in the clear air.

Hop Sing says, "Oh my! This no hut you, Missah Caltwight?"

"No, Hop Sing. I hadn't noticed it," says Ben. Then he remembered the voices. The intrusive thoughts. They weren't thoughts after all. It was this worm singing in him, saying, "Excuse me, I must die now. Excuse me, I must die now. Excuse me, I must die now."

"Oh let's all feel sorry for Mistah Cahtlight. Fuck him and his wormy head. He don't know pain. I'm the one with the pain. Having to tell these dumb *Bonanza* stories. Just to get even. This revenge is worse than the original grievance, for Christ sake.

"The end of 'The Bridegroom'? Why you care? You so dumb you can't figure it out? Okay, listen: Maggie and Little Joe pretend to be courting in order to make Jarrod jealous which he is and he punches Little Joe and runs off with Maggie. Tuck is pleased that men would fight over his Maggie and goes off to tell the boys at the Brutal Inn and Out.

"Now that's it, story's over. Get the fuck out of my face."

As the concluding credits roll, Wild Father thrusts himself before them, like the bad kids at the Saturday matinee mugging before the movie screen. He's playing air guitar. Actually, he has pulled his weirdly plastic penis out to an amusing length with his left hand and pretends to do windmilling Peter Townsend guitar strokes with his right. It's a good imitation. The audience is all little boys and they're howling with approval. He sings:

Wild Dad,
You make my heart sad,
You make life seem cheesy,
Wild Dad.

C'mon Wild Dad,
You make the world bad,
You're hooked by satellite
To everyone's favorite station.
Yea badass Wild Dad.

Surfiction

John Edgar Wideman

Among my notes on the first section of Charles Chesnutt's
Deep Sleeper there are these remarks:

> Not reality but a culturally learned code—that is, out of
> the infinite number of ways one might apprehend, be
> conscious, be aware, a certain arbitrary pattern or finite
> set of indicators is sanctioned and over time becomes
> identical with reality. The signifier becomes the signi-
> fied. For Chesnutt's contemporaries reality was *I* (eye)
> centered, the relationship between man and nature dis-
> junctive rather than organic, time was chronological, lin-
> ear, measured by man-made units—minutes, hours, days,
> months, etc. To capture this reality was then a rather
> mechanical procedure—a voice at the center of the story
> would begin to unravel reality: a catalog of sensuous de-
> tail, with the visual dominant, to indicate nature, *out
> there* in the form of clouds, birdsong, etc. A classical
> painting rendered according to the laws of perspective,
> the convention of the window frame through which the
> passive spectator observes. The voice gains its authority
> because it is literate, educated, perceptive, because it has
> aligned itself correctly with the frame, because it drops
> the cues, or elements of the code, methodically. The voice
> is reductive, as any code ultimately is; an implicit rein-
> forcement occurs as the text elaborates itself through the
> voice: the voice gains authority because things are in or-
> der, the order gains authority because it is established by
> a voice we trust. For example the opening lines of *Deep
> Sleeper* . . .
>
> It was four o'clock on Sunday afternoon, in the
> month of July. The air had been hot and sultry, but a

light, cool breeze had sprung up; and occasional cirrus
clouds overspread the sun, and for a while subdued his
fierceness. We were all out on the piazza—as the coolest
place we could find—my wife, my sister-in-law and I. The
only sounds that broke the Sabbath stillness were the
hum of an occasional vagrant bumblebee, or the fragmentary song of a mockingbird in a neighboring elm . . .

Rereading, I realize my *remarks* are a pastiche of received opinions from Barthes, certain cultural anthropologists and linguistically oriented critics and Russian formal-
ists, and if I am beginning a story rather than an essay, the
whole stew suggests the preoccupations of Borges or perhaps
a footnote in Barthelme. Already I have managed to embed
several texts within other texts, already a rather unstable
mix of genres and disciplines and literary allusion. Perhaps
for all of this, already a grim exhaustion of energy and possibility, readers fall away as if each word is a well-aimed bullet.

More Chesnutt. This time from the text of the story, a
passage unremarked upon except that in the margin of the
Xeroxed copy of the story I am copying this passage from,
several penciled comments appear. I'll reproduce the entire
discussion.

Latin: secundus-tertius-
quartus-quintus.

"Tom's gran'daddy wuz
name' Skundus," he be-
gan. "He had a brudder
name' Tushus en' ernudder
name' Squinchus." The old
man paused a moment
and gave his leg another
hitch.

"drawing out Negroes"—
custom in old south, new
north, a constant in
America. Ignorance of one
kind delighting ignorance
of another. Mask to mask.

My sister-in-law was
shaking with laughter.
"What remarkable names!"
she exclaimed. "Where in
the world did they get
them?"

The real joke.

Naming: plantation owner usurps privilege of family. Logos. Word made flesh. Power. Slaves named in order of appearance. Language masks joke. Latin opaque to blacks.	"Dem names wuz gun ter 'em by ole Marse Dugal' McAdoo, w'at I use' ter b'long ter, en' dey use' ter b'long ter. Marse Dugal' named all de babies w'at wuz bawn on de plantation. Dese young un's mammy wanted ter call 'em sump'n plain en' simple, like *Rastus* er *Caesar* er *George Wash'n'ton*, but ole Marse say no, he want all de niggers on his place ter hab diffe'nt names, so he kin tell 'em apart. He'd done use' up all de common names, so he had ter take sump'n else. Dem names he gun Skundus en' his brudders is Hebrew names en' wuz tuk out'n de Bible."
Note: last laugh. Blacks (mis)pronounce secundus. *Secundus = Skundus. Black speech takes over — opaque to white — subverts original purpose of name. Language (black) makes joke. Skundus has new identity.*	

I distinguish remarks from footnotes. Footnotes clarify specifics; they answer simple questions. You can always tell from a good footnote the question which it is answering. For instance: *The Short Fiction of Charles W. Chesnutt*, edited by Sylvia Lyons Render (Washington, D.C.: Howard University Press, 1974), 47. Clearly someone wants to know, Where did this come from? How might I find it? Tell me where to look. OK. Whereas remarks, at least my remarks, the ones I take the trouble to write out in my journal,* which is where the first long cogitation appears/appeared [the ambiguity here is not intentional but situational, not imposed for irony's sake but necessary because the first long cogitation—*my remark*—

Journal unpaginated. In progress. Unpublished. Many hands.

being referred to both *appears* in the sense that every time I
open my journal, as I did a few moments ago, as I am doing
NOW to check for myself and to exemplify for you the accu-
racy of my statement—the remark *appears* as it does/did just
now. (Now?) But the remark (original), if we switch to a different order of time, creating the text diachronically rather
than paradigmatically, the remark *appeared;* which poses
another paradox. How language or words are both themselves and *Others,* but not always. Because the negation implied by *appearance,* the so-called "shadow within the rock,"
is *disappearance.* The reader correctly anticipates such an
antiphony or absence suggesting presence (shadow play) between the text as realized and the text as shadow of its act.
The dark side paradoxically is the absence, the nullity, the
white space on the white page between the white words not
stated but implied. Forever], are more complicated.

The story, then, having escaped the brackets, can proceed. In this story, *Mine,* in which Chesnutt replies to
Chesnutt, remarks, comments, asides, allusions, footnotes,
quotes from Chesnutt have so far played a disproportionate
role, and if this sentence is any indication, continue to play a
grotesquely unbalanced role, will roll on.

It is four o'clock on Sunday afternoon, in the month of
July. The air has been hot and sultry, but a light, cool breeze
has sprung up; and occasional cirrus clouds (?) overspread
the sun, and for a while subdue his fierceness. We were all
out on the piazza (stoop?)—as the coolest place we could
find—my wife, my sister-in-law and I. The only sounds that
break the Sabbath stillness are the hum of an occasional
bumblebee, or the fragmentary song of a mockingbird in a
neighboring elm . . .

The reader should know now by certain unmistakable
signs (codes) that a story is beginning. The stillness, the
quiet of the afternoon tells us something is going to happen,
that an event more dramatic than birdsong will rupture the
static tableau. We expect, we know a payoff is forthcoming.
We know this because we are put into the passive posture of
readers or listeners (consumers) by the narrative unraveling

of a reality which, because it is unfolding in time, slowly begins to take up our time and thus is obliged to give us something in return; the story enacts word by word, sentence by sentence in *real* time. Its moments will pass and our moments will pass simultaneously, hand in glove if you will. The literary, storytelling convention exacts this kind of relaxation or compliance or collaboration (conspiracy). Sentences slowly fade in, substituting fictive sensations for those which normally constitute our awareness. The shift into the fictional world is made easier because the conventions by which we identify the real world are conventions shared with and often learned from our experience with fictive reality. What we are accustomed to acknowledging as awareness is actually a culturally learned, contingent condensation of many potential awarenesses. In this culture—American, Western, twentieth-century—an awareness that is eye centered, disjunctive as opposed to organic, that responds to clock time, calendar time more than biological cycles or seasons, that assumes nature is external, acting on us rather than through us, that tames space by manmade structures and with the *I* as center defines other people and other things by the nature of their relationship to the *I* rather than by the independent integrity of the order they may represent.

An immanent experience is being prepared for, is being framed. The experience will be real because the narrator produces his narration from the same set of conventions by which we commonly detect reality—dates, buildings, relatives, the noises of nature.

All goes swimmingly until a voice from the watermelon patch intrudes. Recall the dialect reproduced above. Recall Kilroy's phallic nose. Recall Earl and Cornbread, graffiti artists, their spray-paint cans notorious from one end of the metropolis to the other—from Society Hill to the Jungle, nothing safe from them and the artists uncatchable until hubris leads them to attempt the gleaming virgin flanks of a 747 parked on runway N-16 at the Philadelphia International Airport. Recall your own reflection in the fun house mirror and the moment of doubt when you turn away and it turns away and you lose sight of it and it naturally enough loses sight of you and you wonder where it's going and where you're going and the wrinkly reflecting plate still is laughing behind your back at someone.

The reader here pauses | Picks up in mid-

stream a totally irrelevant conversation:
. . . by accident twenty-seven double-columned pages by accident?

I mean it started that way

started yeah I can see starting curiosity whatever staring over somebody's shoulder or a letter maybe you think yours till you see not meant for you at all

I'm not trying to excuse just understand it was not premeditated your journal is your journal that's not why I mean I didn't forget your privacy or lose respect on purpose
    it was just there and, well we seldom talk and I was desperate we haven't been going too well for a long time

and getting worse getting finished when shit like this comes down

I wanted to stop but I needed something from you more than you've been giving so when I saw it there I picked it up you understand not to read

but because it was you you
and holding it was all a
part of you

you're breaking my heart

please don't dismiss

dismiss dismiss what I
won't dismiss your prying
how you defiled how you
took advantage

don't try to make me a
criminal the guilt I feel it
I know right from wrong
and accept whatever you
need to lay on me but I
had to do it I was desperate for something, any-
thing, even if the cost

was rifling my personal
life searching through my
guts for ammunition and
did you get any did you
learn anything you can
use on me Shit I can't even
remember the whole thing
is a jumble I'm blocking it
all out my own journal
and I can't remember a
word because it's not mine
anymore

I'm sorry I knew I shouldn't
as soon as I opened it I
flashed on the Bergman
movie the one where she
reads his diary I flashed
on how underhanded how
evil a thing she was doing
but I couldn't stop

A melodrama a god damned
Swedish subtitled melo-
drama you're going to
turn it around aren't you
make it into

The reader can replay the tape at leisure. Can amplify or expand. There is plenty of blank space on the pages. A sin really given the scarcity of trees, the rapaciousness of paper companies in the forests which remain. The canny reader will not trouble him/herself trying to splice the tape to what came before or after. Although the canny reader would also be suspicious of the straightforward, absolute denial of relevance dismissing the tape.

Here is the main narrative again. In embryo. A professor of literature at a university in Wyoming (the only university in Wyoming) by coincidence is teaching two courses in which are enrolled two students (one in each of the professor's seminars) who are husband and wife. They both have red hair. The male of the couple aspires to write novels and is writing fast and furious a chapter a week his first novel in the professor's creative writing seminar. The other redhead, there are only two redheads in the two classes, is taking the professor's seminar in Afro-American literature, one of whose stars is Charlie W. Chesnutt. It has come to the professor's attention that both husband and wife are inveterate diary keepers, a trait which like their red hair distinguishes them from the professor's other eighteen students. Something old-fashioned, charming about diaries, about this pair of hip graduate students keeping them. A desire to keep up with his contemporaries (almost wrote *peers* but that gets complicated real quick) leads the professor, who is also a novelist, or as he prefers novelist who is also a professor, occasionally to assemble large piles of novels which he reads with bated breath. The novelist/professor/reader bates his breath because he has never grown out of the awful habit of feeling praise bestowed on someone else lessens the praise which may find its way to him (he was eldest of five children in a very poor family—not an excuse—perhaps an extenuation—never enough to go around breeds a fierce competitiveness and being for four years an only child breeds a selfishness and ego-centeredness that is only exacerbated by the shocking arrival of contenders, rivals, lower than dogshit pretenders to what is by divine right his). So he reads the bait and nearly swoons when the genuinely good appears. The relevance of this to the story is that occasionally the professor reads systematically and because on this occasion he is soon to appear on a panel at a neighboring university (Colorado) discussing *Surfiction* his stack of novels was culled from the latest, most hip, most avant-garde, new *Tel Quel* chic, anti, non-novel bibliographies he could locate. He has determined at least three qualities of these novels. *One* — you can stack ten in the space required for two traditional novels. *Two* — they are *au rebours* the present concern for ecology since they sometimes include as few as no words at all on a page and often no more than seven. *Three* — without authors whose last names begin with *B*, surfiction might not exist. *B* for Beckett, Barth, Burroughs, Barthes, Borges, Brautigan, Barthelme . . . (Which list further discloses a startling coincidence or perhaps the making of a scandal — one man working both sides of the Atlantic as a writer and critic explaining and praising his fiction as he creates it: *Barth Barthes Barthelme.*)

The professor's reading of these thin (not necessarily a dig — thin pancakes, watches, women for instance are *à la mode*) novels suggests to him that there may be something to what they think they have their finger on. All he needs then is a local habitation and some names. Hence the redheaded couple. Hence their diaries. Hence the infinite layering of the fiction he will never write (which is the subject of the fiction which he will never write). Boy meets Prof. Prof reads boy's novel. Girl meets Prof. Prof meets girl in boy's novel. Learns her pubic hair is as fiery red as what she wears short and stylish, flouncing just above her shoulders. (Of course it's all fiction. The fiction. The encounters.) What's real is how quickly the layers build, how like a spring snow in Laramie the drifts cover and obscure silently.

Boy keeps diary. Girl meets diary. Girl falls out of love with diary (his), retreats to hers. The suspense builds. Chesnutt is read. A conference with Prof in which she begins analyzing the multilayered short story *Deep Sleeper* but ends in tears reading from a diary (his? hers?). The professor recognizes her sincere compassion for the downtrodden (of which in one of his fictions he is one). He also recognizes a fiction in her husband's fiction (when he undresses her) and reads her diary. Which she has done previously (read her husband's). Forever.

The plot breaks down. It was supposed to break down. The characters disintegrate. Whoever claimed they were whole in the first place? The stability of the narrative voice is displaced into a thousand distracted madmen screaming in the dim corridors of literary history. Whoever insisted it should be more ambitious? The train doesn't stop here. Mistah Kurtz he dead. Godot ain't coming. Ecce Homo. Dat's all, folks. Sadness.

And so it goes.

A Highly Eccentric List of 101 Books for Further Reading

The stories in this anthology offer only the slightest sample of the contemporary representatives of the tradition of innovation. I recommend the following books for the interested reader. Most, but not all, of these books were published in the second half of the twentieth century. The author's national origin and year of publication are indicated (for translations, the year of publication and the year of the translation into English).

Kathy Acker, *Empire of the Senseless* (U.S., 1988).
Felipe Alfau, *Chromos* (Spain, 1990).
Paul Auster, *The New York Trilogy* (U.S., 1987).
John Barth, *The Sot-Weed Factor* (U.S., 1960, rev. 1967).
Donald Barthelme, *Snow White* (U.S., 1967).
Samuel Beckett, *Murphy* (Ireland, 1938).
Thomas Bernhard, *Concrete* (Austria, 1982/1984).
Jorge Luis Borges, *Labyrinths* (Argentina, 1956-60/1964).
Richard Brautigan, *A Confederate General from Big Sur* (U.S., 1964).
Christine Brooke-Rose, *Thru* (U.K., 1975).
Brigid Brophy, *In Transit* (U.K., 1969).
Alan Burns, *Dreamerika!* (U.K., 1972).
William S. Burroughs, *Naked Lunch* (U.S., 1959).
Gabrielle Burton, *Heartbreak Hotel* (U.S., 1986).
Michel Butor, *Mobile, Study for a Representation of the United States* (France, 1962/1963).
Guillermo Cabrera Infante, *Three Trapped Tigers* (Cuba, 1965/1971).

Italo Calvino, *If on a Winter's Night a Traveler* (Italy, 1979/1981).

Julieta Campos, *The Fear of Losing Eurydice* (Cuba, 1979/1993).

Angela Carter, *Nights at the Circus* (U.K., 1984).

Louis-Ferdinand Céline, *Journey to the End of Night* (France, 1932/1934).

Robert Coover, *The Public Burning* (U.S., 1977).

Julio Cortázar, *Hopscotch* (Argentina, 1963/1966).

Ralph Cusack, *Cadenza* (Ireland, 1958).

Susan Daitch, *L. C.* (U.S., 1986).

Samuel R. Delany, *Dhalgren* (U.S., 1975).

Don DeLillo, *White Noise* (U.S., 1985).

Fernando Del Paso, *Palinuro of Mexico* (Mexico, 1977/1989).

William Demby, *The Catacombs* (U.S., 1965).

José Donoso, *The Obscene Bird of Night* (Chile, 1970/1973).

Coleman Dowell, *Island People* (U.S., 1976).

Rikki Ducornet, *Phosphor in Dreamland* (U.S., 1995).

Margaret Mitchell Dukore, *A Novel Called Heritage* (U.S., 1982).

William Eastlake, *Castle Keep* (U.S., 1965).

Umberto Eco, *The Name of the Rose* (Italy, 1980/1983).

Stanley Elkin, *The Living End* (U.S., 1979).

Eva Figes, *Ghosts* (Germany, 1988).

Carlos Fuentes, *Terra Nostra* (Mexico, 1975/1976).

William Gaddis, *The Recognitions* (U.S., 1955).

Janice Galloway, *The Trick Is to Keep Breathing* (Scotland, 1989).

Gabriel García Márquez, *One Hundred Years of Solitude* (Colombia, 1967/1970).

William H. Gass, *The Tunnel* (U.S., 1995).

Karen Elizabeth Gordon, *The Red Shoes and Other Tattered Tales* (U.S., 1996).

Juan Goytisolo, *Makbara* (Spain, 1980/1981).

Günter Grass, *The Tin Drum* (Germany, 1959/1962).

Alasdair Gray, *Lanark* (Scotland, 1981).

Henry Green, *Back* (U.K., 1946).

John Hawkes, *Second Skin* (U.S., 1964).

Joseph Heller, *Catch-22* (U.S., 1961).

Carol De Chellis Hill, *Henry James' Midnight Song* (U.S., 1993).

B. S. Johnson, *House Mother Normal* (U.K., 1971).

LeRoi Jones (Imamu Amiri Baraka), *Tales* (U.S., 1967).

Gert Jonke, *Geometric Regional Novel* (Austria, 1969/1994).

Danilo Kiš, *Hourglass* (Serbia, 1972/1990).

Tadeusz Konwicki, *A Minor Apocalypse* (Poland, 1979/1983).

José Lezama Lima, *Paradiso* (Cuba, 1966/1968).

Osman Lins, *The Queen of the Prisons of Greece* (Brazil, 1976/1995).

Alf MacLochlainn, *Out of Focus* (Ireland, 1977).

D. Keith Mano, *Take Five* (U.S., 1982).

Wallace Markfield, *Teitlebaum's Window* (U.S., 1970).

David Markson, *Wittgenstein's Mistress* (U.S., 1988).

Carole Maso, *AVA* (U.S., 1993).

Harry Mathews, *Cigarettes* (U.S., 1987).

Joseph McElroy, *Women and Men* (U.S., 1986).

Paul Metcalf, *Genoa* (U.S., 1965).

Steven Millhauser, *Edwin Mullhouse* (U.S., 1972).

Nicholas Mosley, *Impossible Object* (U.K., 1968)

Vladimir Nabokov, *Lolita* (Russia, 1955).

Charles Newman, *A Child's History of America* (U.S., 1973).

Flann O'Brien, *At Swim-Two-Birds* (Ireland, 1939).

Claude Ollier, *Mise-en-Scène* (France, 1958/1988).

Milorad Pavić, *Dictionary of the Khazars* (Serbia, 1984/1988).

Georges Perec, *Life A User's Manual* (France, 1978/1987).

Robert Pinget, *The Inquisitory* (France, 1962/1966).

Richard Powers, *The Gold Bug Variations* (U.S., 1991).

Manuel Puig, *Kiss of the Spider Woman* (Argentina, 1976/1979).

Thomas Pynchon, *Gravity's Rainbow* (U.S., 1973).

Raymond Queneau, *Exercises in Style* (France, 1947/1958).

Ann Quin, *Tripticks* (U.K., 1972).

Ishmael Reed, *Mumbo Jumbo* (U.S., 1972).

REYoung, *Unbabbling* (U.S., 1997).

Julián Ríos, *Larva* (Spain, 1983/1990).

Alain Robbe-Grillet, *Jealousy* (France, 1957/1959).

Jacques Roubaud, *The Great Fire of London* (France, 1989/1991).

Salman Rushdie, *The Satanic Verses* (India, 1988).

Severo Sarduy, *Cobra & Maitreya* (Cuba, *Cobra* 1972/1975, *Maitreya* 1978/1987, published together 1995).

Nathalie Sarraute, *Do You Hear Them?* (France, 1972/1973).

Claude Simon, *The Grass* (France, 1958/1960).

Josef Skvorecky, *The Engineer of Human Souls* (Czechoslovakia, 1977/1984).

Gilbert Sorrentino, *Imaginative Qualities of Actual Things* (U.S., 1971).

Piotr Szewc, *Annihilation* (Poland, 1987/1993).

Alexander Theroux, *Darconville's Cat* (U.S., 1981).

Luisa Valenzuela, *He Who Searches* (Argentina, 1969/1975).

Mario Vargas Llosa, *Conversation in The Cathedral* (Peru, 1969/1975).

William T. Vollmann, *The Ice Shirt* (U.S., 1990).

Kurt Vonnegut, *Slaughterhouse-Five* (U.S., 1969).

David Foster Wallace, *Infinite Jest* (U.S., 1996).

Curtis White, *Memories of My Father Watching TV* (U.S., 1998).

Edmund White, *Forgetting Elena* (U.S., 1973).

John Edgar Wideman, *Philadelphia Fire* (U.S., 1990).

William Carlos Williams, *Imaginations* (U.S., 1960).

Marguerite Young, *Miss MacIntosh, My Darling* (U.S., 1965).

The Authors

Felipe Alfau (b. 1902) was born in Barcelona and emigrated to the United States at the age of fourteen. His first novel, *Locos: A Comedy of Gestures*, was published in 1936 to little notice and quickly disappeared. It was reissued in 1988, and his long-unpublished second novel, *Chromos: A Parody*, was finally brought out in 1990. It was a finalist for the National Book Award.

Djuna Barnes (1892-1982) was one of the community of American writers who lived and wrote abroad in the 1920s and 1930s. After 1940 she lived, increasingly reclusively, in Greenwich Village. Her books include *Ladies Almanack* and *Ryder* (both 1928), *Nightwood* (1936), and *The Antiphon* (a play, 1958). Her many stories are gathered in *The Collected Stories of Djuna Barnes*.

John Barth (b. 1930) is the author of *The Floating Opera* (1956, revised 1967), *The End of the Road* (1958, revised 1967), *The Sot-Weed Factor* (1961, revised 1967), *Giles Goat-Boy* (1966), *Lost in the Funhouse* (1968), *Chimera* (1972, National Book Award), *LETTERS* (1979), *Sabbatical* (1982), *The Tidewater Tales* (1987), *The Last Voyage of Somebody the Sailor* (1991), *Once upon a Time* (1994), and *On with the Story* (1996).

Donald Barthelme (1931-1989) is most well-known for his short fiction, collected in *Sixty Stories* (1981) and *Forty Stories* (1987). His novels are *Snow White* (1967), *City Life* (1970), and *The Dead Father* (1975).

Robert Coover (b. 1932) is the author of *The Origin of the*

Brunists (1966), *The Universal Baseball Association, Inc., J. Henry Waugh, Prop.* (1968), *Pricksongs & Descants* (stories, 1969), *The Public Burning* (1977), *Spanking the Maid* (1981), *Gerald's Party* (1986), *A Night at the Movies* (1987), *Whatever Happened to Gloomy Gus of the Chicago Bears?* (1987), *Pinocchio in Venice* (1991), *John's Wife* (1996), and *Briar Rose* (1996).

William Gaddis (b. 1922) has published four important and influential novels in his long career: *The Recognitions* (1955), *JR* (1975, National Book Award), *Carpenter's Gothic* (1985), and *A Frolic of His Own* (1994, National Book Award). In 1982 he was awarded a MacArthur Foundation Fellowship, and in 1993 he received the Lifetime Achievement Award from the Lannan Foundation.

Cris Mazza (b. 1956) is the author of the story collections *Animal Acts* (1989), *Is It Sexual Harassment Yet?* (1991), *Revelation Countdown* (1993), and *Former Virgin* (1997) and the novels *Your Name Here:____* (1995) and *Dog People* (1997).

Gilbert Sorrentino (b. 1929) has published thirteen novels: *The Sky Changes* (1966), *Steelwork* (1970), *Imaginative Qualities of Actual Things* (1971), *Splendide-Hôtel* (1973), *Mulligan Stew* (1979), *Aberration of Starlight* (1980), *Crystal Vision* (1981), *Blue Pastoral* (1983), *Odd Number* (1985), *Rose Theatre* (1987), *Misterioso* (1989)—these last three collected as *Pack of Lies* (1997)—*Under the Shadow* (1991), and *Red the Fiend* (1996). In 1992 he received the Fiction Award from the Lannan Foundation.

Gertrude Stein (1874-1946) was one of the most important and influential of the expatriate writers of the 1920s and 1930s. Her books include *Three Lives* (1909), *Tender Buttons* (1914), *The Making of Americans* (1925), *Useful Knowledge* (1928), *How to Write* (1931), *The Autobiography of Alice B. Toklas* (1933), *Portraits and Prayers* (1934), *The Geographical History of America* (1936), *Everybody's Autobi-*

ography (1937), *Ida, A Novel* (1941), and *Wars I Have Seen* (1945).

David Foster Wallace (b. 1962) is the author of *The Broom of the System* (1987), *Girl with Curious Hair* (stories, 1989), *Infinite Jest* (1996), *A Supposedly Fun Thing I'll Never Do Again* (essays, 1997). In 1996 he received a Lannan Foundation Fiction Fellowship, and in 1997 he was awarded a MacArthur Foundation Fellowship.

Curtis White (b. 1951) has published two collections of short fiction, *Heretical Songs* (1980) and *Metaphysics in the Midwest* (1988), and three novels, *The Idea of Home* (1992), *Anarcho-Hindu* (1995), and *Memories of My Father Watching TV* (1998).

John Edgar Wideman (b. 1941) is the author of *A Glance Away* (1967), *Hurry Home* (1970), *The Lynchers* (1973), *Damballah* (1981), *Hiding Place* (1981), *Sent for You Yesterday* (1983)—these last three were collected as *The Homewood Trilogy* (1985)—*Brothers and Keepers* (1984), *Reuben* (1987), *Fever* (1989), *Philadelphia Fire* (1990), and *The Cattle Killing* (1996). In 1991 he received a Lannan Foundation Fiction Fellowship.

Robert L. McLaughlin, Assistant Professor of English at Illinois State University, received his Ph.D. from Fordham University with a dissertation on Thomas Pynchon's *Gravity's Rainbow*. He is Senior Editor of the *Review of Contemporary Fiction*.

DALKEY ARCHIVE PAPERBACKS

DALKEY ARCHIVE PAPERBACKS

Dalkey Archive Press
ISU Box 4241, Normal, IL 61790–4241
fax (309) 438–7422
Visit our website at www.cas.ilstu.edu/english/dalkey/dalkey.html